Murky Waters

By Robin Alexander

MURKY WATERS

ISBN 1-933113-33-2

THIS TRADE PAPERBACK ORIGINAL IS PUBLISHED BY **INTAGLIO PUBLICATIONS**, GAINESVILLE, FL USA

CREDITS

EXECUTIVE EDITOR: TARA YOUNG

COVER DESIGN BY SHERI (GRAPHICARTIST2020@HOTMAIL.COM)

DEDICATION

To Taylor and Phil, who I love with all my heart.

To Amy, because without her belief in me, I would have never written a word.

To my friends Kathy and Denise, who I have come to love dearly.

ACKNOWLEDEMENTS

The three Ds who spent countless hours beta reading for me: Denise Winthrop, D.E. King, and Donna Lorson. Their contributions made this story a much better read. And also E.C. Marks, who made some suggestions that really brought the characters to life.

Sheri, the graphic artist who graced this book with another of her wonderful creations. Her work pales in comparison to the beautiful person she is.

Michaela Krichbaum and again D.E. King, their support and encouragement have been unwavering.

Tara, my editor, who makes writing a joy for me. I hope I will always have the pleasure and honor of working with this beloved friend. Should anyone find errors in this book, please don't tell Tara, she'll never sleep again.

All of these ladies are dear friends of mine and hold a special place in my heart.

PROLOGUE

A small shaft of sunlight found its way through the blinds, inflicting pain on a pair of bloodshot eyes. Snapping her eyes shut, she rubbed her forehead and groaned. Her mouth was dry, and she felt like she had chewed on the pillow in her sleep. The overindulgence in alcohol the night before made itself known as she turned her head to take in her surroundings.

She fingered the blonde locks splayed across her chest before untangling herself from arms and legs. Standing slowly, her head began to pound. She picked up her clothes from the floor and dressed, hoping not to disturb the girl whose name she could not remember.

Without moving, the blonde spoke softly. "I suppose you don't want to stay for breakfast. I know we agreed that this was only for one night, but I could at least make you a cup of coffee." The blonde was also regretting the copious consumption of alcohol the previous night and whimpered when she opened her eyes to the morning light.

Running long fingers through her dark wavy hair, she sighed. "That's really not necessary. I don't think I could handle it right now." She pulled her shirt over her head, bent down and kissed the blonde on the cheek, and without saying a word, she left.

Suddenly feeling claustrophobic, she opened the sunroof and all the car windows. Rubbing the sleep from her eyes, she started toward home. A feeling of melancholy settled over her as it always did after such nights. She remembered the girl with whom she had spent the evening. The companionship was a welcome respite from the loneliness she felt deep inside. Most would see her actions as promiscuous, but what she had done the night before was not about sex. It was her desire to be surrounded by the warmth and affection of another human being. Sex was for the pleasure of her partner alone.

As always, she made it clear up front that there would be no strings attached. She didn't want any unpleasant misunderstandings when morning came. She did not want to get attached to anyone, nor did she want anyone attached to her. She viewed love as just a fleeting emotion. She'd never been in love and doubted that it really existed. She had come to the conclusion that she was incapable of loving anyone; therefore, no one could really be capable of loving her.

The morning was sunny and bright, and she wasn't ready to return to a silent house. Instead, she stopped at a convenience store and bought a soda and a pack of cigarettes and drove around the lakes of the university. Still too early for the sunbathing and volleyball crowd, the small beach area was empty, and parking places were in abundance. Choosing a spot near a picnic area, she parked and sat alone at one of the tables, staring out at the lake.

Enjoying the warm summer breeze blowing through her hair and across her skin, she rolled up her sleeves and basked in the simple pleasure. She could still smell the slight scent of the blonde's perfume and smoke intermingled on her clothes. It reminded her of how they had danced together the night before. She remembered how good it felt to hold her close and feel the warmth of her body pressed to hers. As she lit a cigarette, she wondered if her partner for the evening had sensed her desperate need for someone just to be close to.

Mentally, she acknowledged to herself that she had what most only dreamed of, an excellent job, a beautiful home, and a nice car, all the material things that one wanted in life. Still, the feeling of loneliness gnawed at her soul like a disease. She was torn, one side of her desiring to have someone in her life to share these things with and the other side believing that would always be unattainable.

Not one to have acquaintances, she only had a few close friends who had wormed their way into her heart. She did not share her feelings with them. Although she sensed they knew by some of the comments made in the past, still she would not allow anyone to know what she had kept held beneath the surface. She always made it a point to lie about how happy she was. Keeping her darkest secrets well hidden had taken its toll over the years, and she was exhausted mentally, as well as emotionally, from the constant battle of maintaining a normal and happy façade. Her inner demons clawed at her soul and haunted her dreams at night, and her days were filled with guilt and remorse for the things she harbored inside.

To express her feelings would give voice to them. Once she opened the floodgate, it would all spill out, leaving her vulnerable and feeling exposed. She was unsure if it were her pride or her self-preservation mechanism that prevented her from doing so. She had spent a lifetime carefully constructing the barriers that kept everyone at a safe distance.

Not a naïve person, she knew that life was not like the movies. Two people meet, fall in love, and that love would carry them through all difficulties in life. Eventually, they would ride off into the sunset together. Such romantic notions made many a movie popular, but in reality, it always took a lot more than a simple emotion such as love.

In her cocoon, she was safe from such difficulties; nevertheless, the emptiness at times was unbearable. During such periods, she would go out to one of the bars, searching for a companion for the evening, as she had done the previous night. For a few hours, she would comfort herself by pretending that she was with the love of her life, and all her emotion and desire would be poured into that person. As always, the stark morning light would bring her back to reality, and the dark feelings would return.

Her silent ponderings were interrupted by the sound of a car pulling in next to hers. She watched as a young woman and a little girl emerged from the parking lot. They both smiled and bid her good morning. She watched with interest as the small child, clutching a bag of bread, ran toward the water's edge, ignoring her mother's pleas to wait for her. The woman caught up with her daughter quickly and opened the bag. They tossed the pieces of bread into the water, drawing the ducks closer for their morning meal. The little girl squealed and laughed as the hungry ducks swam nearer. Her mother knelt by her side with her arm lovingly and protectively around the girl's waist. Neither noticed the dark-

Murky Waters

haired woman wiping the tears from her eyes as she got into her car.

CHAPTER ONE

At 7:30, the morning heat was already sweltering in Baton Rouge. Claire Murray fumbled nervously with the knobs of her air conditioner. Being a Houston native, she was accustomed to the heat. Sweat still poured down her spine and beaded on her top lip, threatening to wash away the makeup she had carefully applied.

She was surprised, however, that the rush-hour traffic was equally as bad in Baton Rouge as it had been in Houston. Inching along on I-10, she was relieved that she had given herself plenty of time to get to her new job. Being late was not the first impression she wanted to make.

Maneuvering her Jeep Cherokee into the already crowded parking lot with thirty minutes to spare, she took time to study the exterior of the new office building in which she would be working. It was four stories high, mostly glass, overlooking the Mississippi River.

This was the home office of Valor Marine. Claire had done her homework on her new employer and was impressed by her findings. Valor was well established in the marine industry. The company specialized in river transportation of petrochemicals. A large percentage of the nation's gasoline and chemical supplies were transported via barge and towboat. Many gas and oil manufacturers utilized Valor boats and barges to transport their products on the inland waterways throughout the country.

She lit up a cigarette and sipped her coffee. Claire had been a travel agent with the same agency for ten years. Suarez Travel specialized in dedicated corporate accounts. She was accustomed to working on site for many of them. Her willingness to relocate was always a feather in her cap. Finally, her diligence had paid off, and she was awarded the coveted position of travel manager for Valor Marine.

In addition to it being her first day, Claire had been invited to sit in on the managers' meeting. This made her especially nervous; she would meet the entire managerial staff at one time. She extinguished her cigarette, took the last sip of her coffee, and took a deep breath to calm herself before making the trek through the intense heat.

Upon entering the building, she was immediately impressed with the décor. The lobby was all brass and glass, just like a cruise ship. After being greeted by the receptionist, she sat down on one of the stylish leather couches to wait. The glass table in front of her held several marine industry magazines, which Claire only halfheartedly paid attention to, as she stole glances at the people who entered the building.

"Ms. Murray?" Claire looked up to find a woman who appeared to be in her mid-forties peering down at her. She recognized the voice instantly; the woman standing before her looked exactly like she sounded on the phone. She wasn't as tall as Claire and had salt and pepper-colored hair that looked like someone put a bowl on her head and cut the hair from around it. Claire stood and accepted the hand extended to her. "I'm Ellen Comeaux. We spoke on the phone. It's a pleasure to finally meet you in person. Welcome to Valor."

Claire liked Ellen immediately. She had a firm handshake, and she looked her directly in the eyes as she spoke. Being a good judge of character, Claire deemed Ellen to be a sincere person. Her relaxed demeanor helped to make Claire feel more at ease.

Claire followed Ellen through a maze of hallways decorated with pictures of towboats and nautical emblems to a room referred to as the galley. Ellen opened a few of the cabinets. "Since most of us spend more time here than at our own homes, we try to make this place as homey as possible. Our galley, or kitchen, as most call it, has everything you need to cook or warm meals. We keep snacks on hand if you are unable to get out for lunch. A lot of us cook gumbo or red beans and rice, and all are welcome to the meal. Don't be shy, or you'll miss out."

"I'm never shy when it comes to food," Claire responded politely as she eyed the doughnuts and pastries lying on the table

"I have to warn you about the coffee; we make it strong here, so you may want to cut it with some water," Ellen said as she filled a cup for Claire.

"I need all the help I can get this morning. A lot of caffeine is just the trick." Claire took a sip of the hot brew, and her eyes nearly bugged. "On second thought, I think I may add just a little water."

Alone on the elevator, Ellen tried to help an obviously nervous Claire relax a little. "After the morning meeting, I'll take you to your new office. That is ..." Ellen paused for effect, "if you survive." She laughed out loud at the horrified expression on Claire's face. "Honey, you have nothing to fear but boredom. Should you be talented enough to sleep with your eyes open, try not to drool on the conference table. It gives me away every time."

The elevator doors opened to reveal a large conference room that nearly dominated the entire fourth floor. The back wall of the spacious room was made of glass and overlooked the Mississippi River. In the center of the room was a huge conference table surrounded by high-backed leather chairs. Pictures of the Valor vessels hung framed and matted on the two opposing walls.

Happy with the fact that she and Ellen were first to arrive for the meeting, Claire made her way over to the glass. As the early morning sun shone from the eastern sky making the murky Mississippi River shimmer like diamonds, she watched with interest as boats of all types made their way up and down the river and as the turbulent water churned in their wake.

Ellen joined her at the window. "Looks peaceful and serene, doesn't it? Looks can be deceiving, though. That murky water has claimed many lives, not just within our company, but just about every company that operates on the river." She paused, wanting to make sure that Claire paid her full attention.

"The Mississippi is known for its strong current. Should a person fall off a barge or boat, the current usually pushes him under the vessel or barge tow. Many have drowned that way. A competitor of ours lost a man last week when he fell overboard and was crushed between two barges. We have to take safety very seriously here." Ellen looked at Claire, hoping she understood her point.

Murky Waters

"That's one of our boats making its way up river now. They've just finished loading the barges at the refinery and are headed north to discharge the product at another facility. I imagine all this sounds very foreign to you, so I have arranged for one of our managers to take you on a tour tomorrow. We'll have to get you some steel-toed boots and safety gear today after lunch."

Claire looked frightened. "I'm not sure I want to go on a tour after the lecture you just gave me." Looking down at the brown swirling water and hearing of the associated dangers made Claire apprehensive about being close and personal with the river.

Ellen laughed. "My husband works for the local electric company. When he went for his initial job training, they didn't tell him that the electricity would only give him a little nip. They explained in graphic detail what could happen should he become careless. That is exactly what I'm trying to do for you. I don't have to worry, though; the person taking you on the tour takes safety very seriously.

"The river can get very high. The huge tankers that are going to the oil docks are sometimes level with this window. I can look out my window and see the bridge of the ship at eye level. When the water is high like that, it makes it very difficult to manage the vessels making their way through here due to the strong current," Ellen said, turning to look at Claire.

"Why do the boats still try to navigate the river in such treacherous conditions?" Claire asked as she watched the Valor boat push its three-barge tow against the current.

"The boats and ships never stop. The Coast Guard will shut down the river at times when conditions are bad enough to warrant it. If a hurricane threatens the mouth of the Mississippi or if there has been some sort of accident, the river is closed to boat traffic. Otherwise, the boats stay in motion. Millions of dollars of gasoline and chemicals are shipped up and down this river daily, and if a boat is stopped or delayed, money is lost. The only exceptions are heavy fog or lock delays.

"Captains in this industry are specially trained to handle all sorts of emergencies. They encounter hazardous situations on a daily basis out there, more than anyone really knows. They have rescued stranded boaters and recovered people whose watercrafts have capsized. Unfortunately, the public only realizes they are out there when something bad happens. I'm sure the captain of the vessel you will board tomorrow will tell you all sorts of stories."

Claire grinned. "You mean I'll be able to take a ride on one of the boats? Can I drive?"

Ellen laughed at Claire's enthusiasm as she watched her co-workers enter the room. "It looks like everyone is filing in. Let's go get a good seat. I don't want you to miss anything." Ellen chuckled at her own sarcasm.

The last person to enter the room was a distinguished-looking man who Claire figured to be in his mid-sixties. "Father figure" popped into her mind as she observed him. It was obvious he was highly respected by the people gathered in the room, and there was warmth in his eyes when he regarded his employees, like a proud parent.

He moved to the head of the table and addressed the group. "Ladies and gentlemen, we have someone new with us today. Please allow me to first introduce myself. I am Cameron Hughes, the general manager of Valor Marine. It pleases me to welcome you aboard, Miss Murray."

Claire nodded and thanked him. "Claire Murray will be the new travel manager for Suarez Travel. She will replace Rhonda Hudson, who we all know is resigning to begin a family. Claire comes to us highly recommended, and I am happy to have her.

"Starting with Scott here on my right, I would like each manager to introduce him or herself and give a quick synopsis of what you do here. I hope that each one of you will take the time to make Claire feel welcome and help her with anything she needs."

Claire paid close attention to each name, hoping to at least commit a few to memory. One name stood out in her mind — Tristan Delacroix. Claire noticed her the minute she walked into the room. Tall and immaculately dressed with long brown hair beautifully cascading down her shoulders, Tristan exuded a confidence that Claire had always found irresistible in women. Claire smiled when she detected a slight Cajun accent as she listened to Tristan's low smooth voice.

"My name is Tristan Delacroix. I am the manager of the Valor personnel department. My co-workers and I crew our vessels with the appropriate staff trained in managing whatever product their vessel is assigned to carry. Our main task is getting the crew by plane or rental car to wherever the boat is they are assigned to at the time of crew change."

Claire listened intently. Feeling a twinge of excitement, she realized that she would be working very closely with the lovely woman who sat across from her. She was intrigued to say the least. Looking more like an attorney with her manicured nails and business suit, Tristan did not seem like the type to be working for a towboat company.

Occasionally, Tristan would run her fingers through her long dark hair, and it would fall in waves around her tanned face. Her brown eyes were big and expressive underneath a perfectly sculpted pair of eyebrows. Her makeup only enhanced her beautiful features. For the remainder of the meeting, Claire took every opportunity to study the intriguing woman. Only when she found Tristan's dark eyes on her did she make a point not to stare.

At the conclusion of the meeting, each member of the staff came by to greet Claire personally. When Tristan approached, Claire felt her pulse quicken. She was actually nervous about shaking the beautiful woman's hand.

"Miss Murray, it's a pleasure to meet you." Tristan stared into her eyes as she spoke and took her hand. The simple gesture of a handshake sent chills up Claire's spine. "You have your work cut out for you. I have not been pleased with the performance of Suarez Travel. I hope you will be an improvement, or your employment here may not be very enjoyable."

With that, Tristan excused herself and left the room, leaving a stunned and speechless Claire in her wake. Attempting to keep her cool and regain her composure, Claire stared at the door Tristan had just passed through. "That is the most beautiful woman I have ever met, and she's a complete asshole," Claire mumbled under her breath.

Ellen patted her on the back supportively. "Claire, we have to chat. I feel the need to explain what just happened. How about you and I take a ride down to the boot store and get some acceptable footwear for your tour tomorrow?"

Ellen led her down to the employee parking area and hissed when her hand came in contact with the hot door handle of her car. After settling inside, she avoided touching the steering wheel and quickly adjusted the air conditioner while glancing over at Claire with a wicked gleam in her eye. "Do you smoke?"

"Yes, I do," Claire replied with a grin. "Great! Because if you didn't, I was going to suggest you start. This business will make you do something unhealthy, and since we can't drink on the job, I decided to smoke. Good Lord knows I don't need to eat any more than I do." Ellen laughed as she lit her cigarette, exhaling the smoke. A look of pure pleasure washed over her face.

"Ellen, can I ask you something?" Ellen nodded at Claire, keeping her eyes on the road. "May I be very frank?"

This time, Ellen glanced from the road to her passenger. "Of course."

Claire lit her own cigarette and blew out the smoke slowly, debating how she should pose the question. "Why on earth does Tristan act like she has a hot pepper up her ass? I've only just met her, and she acted as though she wanted to take my head off. Is she always like that, or did she wake up on the wrong side of bed this morning?"

Ellen burst out laughing at Claire's candor. "I am truly sorry for her behavior, Claire. Knowing Tristan, once she gets to know you, she will apologize herself. She and Rhonda have gone head to head more than once. Rhonda has never really been dedicated to our account. She sees her department as simply a travel agency within our office.

"The whole reason we have a travel department in house is so you can become intimately involved with what we do. The more you know about us, the more you can do for us. Rhonda has gotten even worse since she became pregnant. Her head has simply not been in the game.

"Tristan's department is responsible for crewing all our vessels. Unless business is slow or they have mechanical failure, our boats are in constant movement. Therefore, in order to swap out crews, they have to hit a moving target. That's where you come in. Valor spends a large amount of money each year to make this happen. We need someone who can work closely with her and keep the travel costs down.

"Tristan is really a great person to work with. She is very dedicated and will work all the hours it takes to assure the job is done. As a manager, she is very well respected because she stands behind her people. She does not expect perfection, but she does expect those who work with her to strive for it. You will work more closely with her than you do your own people."

Claire didn't know whether to be excited about the prospect of working with Miss Pepper Ass or not. However, she did enjoy her shopping trip with Ellen and lunch at a Mexican restaurant not far from the office. While eating chips and salsa, Ellen decided to warn Claire that Tristan was an out and out lesbian. After the short choking spell, Claire recovered nicely.

"Don't get me wrong, Claire, I have no problem with that. Whatever floats your boat, but I thought I would give you a little heads up since you'll be working so closely with her."

Claire debated telling Ellen right then that she and Tristan had that in common, but at the last minute, she chickened out. She felt deep inside that she had started her new life out with a big fat lie hanging over her head. "It's no big deal to me, Ellen. I have worked with gays and lesbians before." She tried to look Ellen in the eye as she chatted on about it nonchalantly.

Two enchiladas and a half a pack of cigarettes later, they made their way back to Valor. Ellen took Claire to the third floor to her new office. They entered a large room with waist-high cubicles dividing it down the middle. The rear of the room was made up of three glass offices, affording its occupants a full view of the room that housed the cubicles, as well as the adjoining offices.

There were four people occupying the cubicles. Two were on the phone; the other two were diligently working at their computers. Each one glanced up at Claire and Ellen as they made their way to the glass offices. The largest of the three belonged to Tristan. The one next to hers was to be Claire's, and the one on the other side of Claire's housed the travel agents.

"As you can see, you will be right next to your staff and of course Tristan, who is probably still in meetings. This way, you will be accessible to your people and Tristan's staff, as well."

As Ellen chatted with one of the coordinators, Claire took a moment to peek into Tristan's office. Obviously, Tristan appreciated order; not one thing could be found out of place. The oak bookshelves were neatly kept and adorned with breathtaking undersea photos. A fish tank occupied one corner, and a replica of a towboat, complete with functioning running lights, that sat in a glass case, took up the remaining free wall of the office.

Claire excused herself from Ellen for a moment and went to visit the travel agents. It was a relief to see Mike and Lauren's familiar faces; she had worked with them before. Both greeted her with warm hugs.

"We've been looking forward to working with you again," Lauren said with a smile. "I'm sorry, but Rhonda decided to let Friday be her last day. I think she was avoiding Tristan. The two of them have been at each other's throats. She did leave you a detailed report of her daily duties. I don't think you will have any problems picking up where she left off."

"Tristan did tell me this morning that she was disappointed in Rhonda's performance and basically tore me a new one." Claire winced as she remembered the encounter. "I hope you both will work with me to improve our working relations. I'd like to meet with you later if time permits. This is something I want to tackle as soon as possible."

After Ellen helped familiarize Claire with her new office, she left her alone to get started. Claire made it a point first to look over Rhonda's filing system. Satisfied that everything was in order, she began customizing her computer to fit her work habits.

Glancing up from her project, she watched as Tristan entered the work area and spoke with the crew coordinators before heading to her office. Tristan acknowledged Claire with a slight nod and went on seemingly oblivious to her presence. Claire had hoped that they could start off on better footing, but Tristan made it obvious that she wasn't interested in chatting.

Claire silently thanked whomever designed their offices to include glass walls. She stole a few glances as Tristan entered her office and took off her jacket. She hung it neatly over the back of her chair as she checked her voice mail. Claire noticed that the silk shirt fit Tristan as though it was tailored just for her, displaying her well-developed figure. She grinned, thinking this would be a very pleasant distraction.

An hour had passed when Claire heard a soft knock on her already open door. Looking up, Claire noticed Tristan standing in the doorway. Claire silently appreciated her manners and invited her in. Tristan remained standing until Claire offered her a seat in one of the high-backed leather chairs.

"I only need a moment of your time. I've been designated as your tour guide for tomorrow." If Tristan took any pleasure in this task, her face did not show it. "Ellen tells me you already have your boots. I will have the rest of your safety gear by tomorrow morning. You'll need to wear a pair of jeans, and I brought you this." She handed Claire a denim shirt with the Valor logo on the breast pocket. "You don't have to wear it if you don't want to, but I thought it would make a nice welcome-aboard gift," Tristan went on nervously, hoping to avoid any awkward silence. "You will need to be here at 7 a.m. I would like to start out at our fleet; one of our boats is there having some repairs done."

Claire put on her best smile and tried to take advantage of the opportunity. "I really do want things to work out here. I'm hoping while we're out tomorrow that you and I can discuss candidly the issues you had with Rhonda. I don't want to make the same mistakes. Valor is our customer, and it is in our best interest to make sure you get the work you expect."

Tristan looked at her thoughtfully before she spoke. "I appreciate that, Claire. We have a lot to talk about." Saying nothing more, she politely excused herself and returned to her office. Claire sat back and expelled the breath that she had been holding the moment she stopped speaking. She was unsure of what the response would be after her little speech. As far as she could tell, she had scored a point for the travel team.

For the remainder of the afternoon, Claire met with Mike and Lauren. She nearly filled an entire notebook with the information she gleaned from the two agents. For the most part, they felt that Rhonda had brought the problems on herself. She was not very dedicated, and her attendance was poor, as well as her attitude. Claire felt confident that she could improve on those problems quickly.

She would do whatever was within her power to satisfy Tristan. Not merely because her job depended on it, but there was something within her that wanted to please the dark-haired woman whom she could not shake from her thoughts. It had been a long time since she had met anyone who excited her this way. Had anyone else treated her the way Tristan had the first day, Claire may have very well been on her way back to Houston.

CHAPTER TWO

The drive home that afternoon was the same as the drive in. Claire merged onto the interstate and came to a complete stop. Fortunately, she had been wise in choosing her apartment. She was only on the busy interstate for a few miles. Upon reaching her exit, she would go one mile before arriving at her complex.

She smiled and leaned back in her seat. The day had gone well, despite the rocky start with Tristan. With the exception of the tall, dark, and lovely woman, everyone had been kind and made her feel welcome. And it was a bonus to work with Mike and Lauren again; they were good agents, and she knew she could depend on them.

The terrain was not all that different from Houston, just on a much smaller scale. Baton Rouge seemed like a quaint sleepy little town and was just what she needed at this point in her life. She looked forward to having time to explore the new area in which she now lived. Perhaps if Tristan would get her underwear out of a wad, she might make a decent tour guide.

Claire parked in her designated spot, gathered her things, and made her way up the stairs to her second-story apartment. She was reluctant to leave Houston, but the cost of living was significantly cheaper in Baton Rouge, which had afforded her one of the nicest places she had ever lived. Walking into her two-bedroom apartment, she breathed a sigh of relief. She was home.

Dinner consisted of a pork chop, salad, and a huge glass of white wine. After which, Claire started her laundry and took the bottle of wine into the bath with her. She was bent on relaxing and forgetting the stresses of her first day on the job. She sank down in the warm water and read the latest edition of her favorite magazine. Two glasses of wine later, Claire emerged, feeling relaxed and refreshed.

One of the things Claire loved most about her new abode was the spiral staircase in the corner of the living room that led to a small loft. With its skylight, the loft would be the perfect place to put her potted plants. Ivy would be placed close to the ornate wrought iron railing, so the long vines could hang down over the living room.

Had her mother still been alive, she would have loved Claire's apartment. Claire sighed and wondered if things would have been different for her if her mom were still around. She missed having her to console her when life got tough. Mom always made everything right, but now, she was on her own and had to stand on her own two feet.

"First things first," she muttered and went into the spare room that would become her office. This was the last of her things to be sorted and put away. She took a healthy gulp of wine and began to tackle the piles of papers and folders occupying her desk.

Claire had positioned the desk to face the big bay window that graced her makeshift office. She sat briefly in her chair and stared out the large window at the oaks that the apartments had been built around. She appreciated that the builders had the forethought to leave the majestic trees.

After her home computer was set up, she went about arranging things in her little sanctuary. This would be the only room in which she would smoke. She tried to avoid having the rest of her home smelling like cigarettes, and this room would accommodate her vice.

She opened her window a bit and turned on the overhead fan. Leaning back in her chair, she propped up her feet, lit her cig, and basked in the fact that she had finally gotten the room the way she wanted it. With everything squared away in here, she could put her mind on other things. She opened the right-hand drawer and took out a large brown envelope. Claire took another sip of wine and stared at the package. This was one thing that she hoped stayed back in Houston and would not come to haunt her here.

She sat for a long time contemplating opening the envelope. After putting out her cigarette, she lit another and refilled her wine glass. She took a stress-relieving breath and opened the envelope. Slowly, she withdrew the pictures inside. The first few were of her getting out of her Cherokee and going into her old office in Houston. Others were of her and friends having dinner in a restaurant. There were even a few of her doing such mundane things as grocery shopping and picking out a movie at the video store.

Claire felt cold chills run up her spine, making her shiver. She never knew who the person was who took such an interest in her life. It was extremely unsettling to know that someone made it a point to follow her around capturing her on film. What she found even more disturbing were the intimate photos taken of her through her open windows while she was at home. For the first six months, she received only photos. But when one was taken of her kissing a date good night, the letters began, each one accusing her of being a slut. It made Claire ill to look at them.

She had suspected her ex-girlfriend Lisa of sending them at first. The breakup between the two had been tumultuous. When Claire confronted Lisa with the pictures and letters, Lisa begged her to take them to the police. She still remembered the shocked look on Lisa's face and her trembling hands as she looked at each photo and letter. Her persistent pleas for her to go to the police made Claire strike her from the list of possible suspects.

She never did involve the police, leery of the scandal it would cause to have them question everyone she came in contact with. She had reasoned that the letters were really not threatening, and by moving away, she might escape her stalker. It was a decision she hoped was right.

With all the lights on in the room where Claire worked, she was unable to see the dark figure who stood across the parking lot hidden in a cluster of oak trees. The stranger watched Claire's every move with interest through the telephoto lens of the camera, randomly clicking the shutter. Only when Claire turned off the lights and left the room did the stranger lower the camera and leave the safety of the well-chosen hiding place.

Later, as Claire lay in bed waiting for sleep to claim her, she found herself wondering about Tristan. She had no problem admitting to herself that she found the dark-haired woman attractive, even though she was an asshole. Unfortunately, she couldn't resign herself to simply enjoying the visual attributes of the obnoxious woman she wanted to know more of. "Maybe I'm just a glutton for punishment," she muttered to herself.

She wondered if Tristan were taken. She was one of the prettiest women Claire had ever laid eyes on. "She's probably got a girlfriend who looks like a supermodel, or worse, one who could beat me to a pulp," Claire mused. Tristan's hand in hers earlier that day was her last fleeting memory as she drifted off to sleep.

The alarm went off much too early for Claire's liking. She slapped the snooze button a few times before she finally crawled out of bed. As she showered, she wondered what the day might hold for her. She was actually looking forward to going on a tour with Tristan.

After getting dressed, Claire looked at her reflection in the full-length bedroom mirror. She was pleased with the hair and makeup, but she thought the steel-toed boots were a little butch. At least they were brown and matched her purse. She tucked her new Valor shirt into her jeans and was off to face the day.

Once Claire was on the road, she relaxed and sipped her coffee while enjoying the first cigarette of the day. She merged into traffic on I-10 and came to a complete stop. Normally, traffic pissed her off and reduced her to a blithering idiot by the time she reached her destination. This morning, however, the traffic allowed her to relax and mentally prepare herself for what lay ahead. She was undeniably nervous about spending an entire day with Tristan alone, unsure if she were simply anxious about making a good impression on a new client or if it were her attraction to the striking woman. She checked her makeup in the rearview mirror, knowing it was the latter.

After arriving at the office, she made a pit stop at the galley and got herself another coffee and made her way to Tristan's office. The crew coordinators were already there when Claire arrived. She took the time to chat with them and did her best to remember their names. Claire noticed that Tristan had her back to the room while she worked on her computer.

Claire poked her head in the office to let Tristan know she had arrived. "Good morning, Tristan. I just wanted to let you know that I'm ready when you are."

Tristan turned to look at her and stared for a moment before saying, "Good morning, *couillon*." All four of the crew coordinators burst into a fit of laughter.

"What is so funny, and what does *couillon* mean?" Claire could feel anger creeping up the back of her neck, sensing she had been made the butt of a joke. The raucous laughter dropped to snickers. All the crew coordinators looked to Tristan to explain. Claire stepped through the doorway and stared daggers at Tristan. "What does it mean, Miss Delacroix?" Claire demanded angrily.

"It's a Cajun French word that means foolish or funny person," Tristan replied with a smirk.

Claire slammed the door to Tristan's office hard enough to make the walls shake. "I may not know a thing about the Cajun language, but I assure you I am not a fool! I'm not so sure you can say the same."

Tristan's face turned cold, but her voice remained low. "Let me remind you, Miss Murray, I am still the customer, and you work for me. Furthermore, there was nothing degrading or malicious meant by what I said."

"Well, Ms. Delacroix, although I do work at the company that provides a service for yours, that does not mean I am any less human than you are. I would appreciate it if you would lay off busting my chops every time I come in contact with you. And furthermore ..." Claire fought the urge to grin as she threw the word back at Tristan, "if you think being referred to as a foolish or funny person in front of a roomful of people is not degrading, you have a really warped sense of humor."

Tristan stood slowly and walked around her desk to stand face-to-face with Claire. "I have to go to the warehouse and get our hardhats." She handed Claire two life jackets. "Meet me in the back of the building; my truck is the red Ford F-150."

Tristan had switched gears, knocking Claire off kilter. Claire stood there blinking for a moment before she took the life jackets from her. Tristan turned and walked out of the office, leaving Claire to stare at her, once again dumbfounded. To top it off, Claire could not help but notice how nice Tristan's butt looked in her jeans, and that pissed her off even more.

Claire found Tristan's truck unlocked. Even better, she had left her keys in the ignition. Claire reached over and started the engine and cranked the air up as high as it would go. The oppressive summer heat was already making its presence known. In addition, she had been drinking hot coffee all morning, which made her sweat, adding to her ire. Truth be known, her blood pressure was up a few notches, as well, and she had an overwhelming desire to slap the shit out of the condescending Ms. Delacroix.

Claire stood just outside the open door of the truck to smoke and take advantage of the cool air coming from the cab. "Get in; you can smoke in the truck." Startled, Claire gave Tristan a quick look and flicked out the cigarette, determined not to follow any orders she didn't have to. She got in, put on her seat belt, and waited for Tristan to pull out of the parking lot before beginning her verbal assault.

"What the hell is your problem with me, Tristan? We've only known each other one day, and you have managed to insult me twice. I understand you and Rhonda had some problems in your working relationship, but that's no reason to take it out on me! You haven't even given me a chance!"

Tristan glanced from the road to Claire. "You're right."

Again, Tristan had thrown Claire off with her unexpected response. For a moment, Claire was left speechless, and when it looked as though Tristan wasn't going to say anything more, Claire's anger ignited again. Claire played the card she thought would get a response out of Tristan, hoping to really piss her off.

"You can turn this truck around now, Tristan Delacroix, and take me back to the office. I plan to go to Mr. Hughes and tell him no one in my position will be able to work for his company effectively because you, Tristan, are not willing to work with us!"

Claire internally debated if it were a wise move to play that card when Tristan pulled the truck safely off the road, took off her seat belt, and turned to face her. "Yesterday, when I brought you the shirt, I was trying to make peace. My behavior has been very unprofessional. I was frustrated with Rhonda, and you bore the brunt of that. Actually, I'm very happy that she has been replaced and am looking forward to working with you. I am truly sorry we started out this way, and I know it's my fault. Incidentally, my dad used to call me *couillon* when I was a kid. It was a nickname. I didn't mean anything by it."

Claire sat and stared dumbfounded at Tristan for a long time. She was still angry and wanted the difficult woman to rant and scream at her. What she got was an obvious heartfelt apology, and that made her even more angry. "Apology accepted" was all she could muster as she chewed her lip, trying to quell the tirade that had been building since she laid eyes on Tristan that morning.

Tristan pulled the truck back onto the road, and after a mile or two, she lit up a cigarette. "You're welcome to smoke in my truck. All I ask is that you flick the ashes out the window. I don't like to use the ashtray."

Claire pulled out a cigarette, but before she could locate her lighter, Tristan reached over and lit the cigarette for her. They rode in silence all the way to the fleet, neither knowing what to say. By the time they had made it to their destination, all the anger had dissipated, making things between them seem even more awkward.

Tristan navigated the truck up the steep levee, and when it crested the hill, Claire got her first glimpse of the Valor fleet. Not knowing what to expect, she was a little surprised when the landing barge came into view and she noticed an entire office complex had been erected on top of it. She spied the familiar Valor logo on the smokestack of the vessel tied off to the landing barge.

"The office on the very top with all the windows is the fleet dispatcher's office. They dispatch the fleet vessels that build together barge tows that go out with our vessels," Tristan explained in detail, hating the idea of leaving the cool truck and venturing out into the heat. "We have a crew stationed here that strips and cleans the barges before they are taken to the refineries or chemical plants to be loaded. Mail and supplies are kept on the bottom floor to be picked up by the boats when they pass through here."

Tristan was the first out of the truck. She walked around to the passenger side and handed Claire a life vest. She put on her own jacket first, hoping Claire would mimic her actions. Claire wrestled with the straps and, within minutes, had the life jacket looking like a bear had mauled it.

Tristan fought the urge to snicker as she stood watching in amusement. "Would you like some help with that?"

Claire surrendered the mess she had made, looking a little sheepish. It took Tristan a few minutes to unscramble the straps, after which, she held up the jacket and had Claire slip her arms through it. When Claire turned around to face her, Tristan hesitated a moment, reluctant to fasten the closure over Claire's well-defined breasts. From her vantage point, Tristan could see Claire's cleavage, and the sight made her hands shake as she fastened the closure.

"Now, Claire, I am not trying to scare you when I tell you this. Should you go overboard, there are some things you should remember, the first of which is not to panic. Blow the whistle attached to the vest and try to avoid getting between the barges."

Claire stood wide-eyed and speechless as she stared down at the churning water below the catwalk and wondered why she had agreed to this. "Tristan, I'm having second thoughts about this."

"You have nothing to worry about, Claire. I'll be by your side. I just thought it was necessary to explain this to you. I've been going out on these boats for years and have never fallen over. I just want you to know what to do should anything happen."

Claire swallowed hard and nodded her head. Tristan presented her with a hardhat containing a mass of straps even more confusing than the life vest. "We are supposed to wear these when we are on the landing barge and also when we are on the barges that the boat pushes. I kind of fudge on the landing barge rule because I hate to get hat hair. So if you agree to keep my secret, I won't make you wear yours. Do we have a deal?" Claire quickly agreed.

They began to descend the levee toward the catwalk that would take them across a small portion of the turbulent Mississippi River to the landing barge. Before they could make it across the walk, Tristan stopped dead in her tracks. She turned with an embarrassed smile, finding Claire taking baby steps and looking down at the water. "Do you see that guy taking a piss off the side of the boat over there?"

"Oh, Dear Lord in Heaven, yes! Aggghh, that's just plain nasty! Don't they have toilets on the boats?"

Tristan laughed for a long time before she could respond. "Yes, they do, but some guys just don't want to take the time. It's easier to go off the side of the boat. The reason I brought your attention to his raunchy little display is because he is the engineer for that boat. The engineers do most of the cooking, so when they invite us to lunch, be sure to lie and say you're not hungry."

They continued down the catwalk to the landing barge and went directly to the fleet office. Slightly winded from climbing the stairs, Claire entered the fleet office behind Tristan, blinking her eyes to adjust to the darker room.

She heard a deep voice call out to Tristan in a heavy Cajun accent. "Del a crow! Where you been, girl? I've been down here for two days, and you just now come to see me. I cooked your favorite food yesterday, hoping you would smell it and show up."

"Hey, Sam, it's good to see you. I'm sorry I missed you yesterday. Hughes had me attending meetings with a bunch of suit types. I would have much rather been down here, trust me." Tristan hugged him as she spoke.

Sam wiggled his eyebrows. "Did you wear a dress? Was it sexy? Indulge an old man who spends far too much time on an old towboat."

"No, you little pervert." Tristan laughed. "I wore that same old suit I always wear to bullshit like that. Now behave, I have someone I want you to meet."

Witnessing yet another side of Tristan's personality, Claire watched with interest as her tour guide interacted with a fellow employee and friend. The bright smile that spread across her was warm and genuine. Claire silently hoped that she would be the cause of such a smile one day.

Claire took full advantage of the moment and studied Tristan from head to toe. The long dark ponytail protruding from the baseball cap beckoned Claire to run her fingers through its silkiness. Her tour guide was indeed a sight to behold standing before her in a snug pair of jeans accompanied by a pair of work boots. The short-sleeved denim shirt revealed a pair of tanned muscular arms. She marveled at how different Tristan looked from the day before in the office dressed in her business attire. She was not sure which look was sexier.

Tristan stepped aside and let Sam get a view of Claire, clearing her throat when she noticed Claire seemed to be in another world. He wiped his calloused hands off on his pants and held one out for

Claire to shake. He looked at her like she was a lamb chop until Tristan gave him a small slap to the back of the head.

Claire studied him, as well, and wondered if all Cajuns were short but changed her mind when she glanced at Tristan. The captain stood a little over five feet tall. Aside from his hair that was in serious need of a barber, he looked professional in his khaki uniform.

"Claire, this is Sam. He is the captain of the *Sarah Ann*, which is the boat tied off to the landing barge. He started out as a deckhand before I was born and now is one of our senior captains." The old man puffed out his chest with pride as Tristan described his accomplishments.

After the introductions were made, Sam offered to show Claire around his boat. The captain was genuinely delighted to be the one to escort the pretty blonde. Typical of the Louisiana summer, the heat was already becoming intense. Tristan watched intently as sweat beads broke out on Claire's lip as she was led from bow to stern. Tristan shook her head to clear the carnal thoughts that crept into her mind as she watched Claire's body react to the heat.

Sam took pleasure in showing Claire the outer decks of the vessel, seemingly unaffected by the rising temperature. It wasn't until he glanced at the now profusely sweating blonde that he realized he should continue the remainder of the tour below deck.

Another set of eyes watched both of them as they descended the stairs. He waited for the pair to get out of earshot before he keyed his hand-held radio and spoke.

"Here's the stats. She's about five-foot-seven. I figure she weighs about a hundred and thirty pounds. She's built like a brick shithouse! Tits and ass for days! Blonde hair, and I think the eyes are brown."

"Actually, they're hazel," Tristan interrupted.

The informer turned slowly to face Tristan. His eyes opened wide, mouth agape. He began to stutter an explanation as Tristan's dark eyes bore into him. At five-foot-eight, she towered over the short man.

Tristan's voice was low and calm as she spoke. "Do you think it's appropriate to announce the physical characteristics of a vessel visitor over the radio to the entire crew? Furthermore, do you think it's wise to tell a group of men who have been on a boat for thirty days that they have a woman built like a brick shithouse wandering the boat?"

He began to stammer. Tristan raised her hand to stop his babbling. "Don't try to explain yourself. However, while our visitor remains on board, I expect you and the rest of the crew to be gentlemen. Now, get back on that radio and tell them what I have just told you."

She watched as the crewman delivered her message. When she was satisfied they all understood, she went below deck to find Claire and Sam. Occasionally, she would glance over her shoulder to see a deckhand pretend to be hard at work. She could not help but giggle as she mentally agreed with the crewman. Claire was indeed built like a brick shithouse.

As Tristan descended the stairs, she decided that she would not allow Claire to get out of her sight again while touring the boat. The men had always paid her respect because of her position, and more importantly, they had known her father. She was a little concerned that Claire might not get the same treatment.

As she expected, Sam was showing off the captain's quarters to his captive audience. He was proudly pointing out all the state-of-the-art equipment that his wife had gotten him for Christmas, which included a DVD player, a seventeen-inch TV, and a stereo, complete with a CD player. Tristan smirked as she thought his wife had no idea how many hours Sam would spend watching porn on her gifts.

When Claire looked as though she would pass out from sheer boredom, Tristan interrupted. "Sam, Claire and I have to get back on the road. We have a schedule to keep today."

Sam looked disappointed. "Come on, Tris, you have to have lunch with us."

Claire shot a nervous glance Tristan's way. The memory of the man doing the cooking and relieving himself off the side of the boat was still fresh in her mind. Tristan smiled and gave her a small nod.

"All right, Tris, I will let you off the hook for lunch, but y'all have to come see the wheelhouse."

"The wheelhouse?" Claire asked curiously.

"Yeah, that's where I drive the boat from. It's the best place on the boat besides my quarters. Hey! I learned a new song on the old guitar; you gotta hear it. We can run up there now, and I can play it for you."

Tristan spoke up. "I'll make a deal with you, Sam. We will go see the wheelhouse, but you have to promise not to play the guitar, or worse, sing."

Sam pretended to be heartbroken. "Oh, Tris, you cut me deep on that one."

"You little liar," Tristan snorted.

Claire watched in fascination and amusement as Tristan bantered back and forth with the old captain. Tristan was so unlike the woman Claire met the previous day; her behavior was the complete opposite.

Sam took the long way to the wheelhouse. He took them through the huge engine room, where the sound was nearly deafening. All the while, he pointed out things and gave explanations of what they were and their purpose. Claire watched his mouth move but did not have a clue what he was saying. To her relief, they left the noisy room and went through a maze of hallways. She looked into the open bunkrooms as she passed. They reminded her of tiny dorm rooms.

Claire glared over her shoulder at Tristan as she was made to climb another two flights of stairs. Tristan simply smiled and shrugged. They passed through another door, and Claire found herself in a room resembling a miniature airport control tower.

The wheelhouse was on the very top deck, and surrounded by glass, it afforded the wheelman a bird's-eye view of the barge tow before him. Claire marveled at the bank of electronic equipment and fought the urge to push every button she could get her hands on. Sam insisted that Claire sit in the captain's chair while he showed off his gadgets.

Tristan made herself comfortable on a small bench and watched Claire with great interest as Sam allowed her to push a few buttons. Claire resembled a child on Christmas morning, grinning from ear to ear, waiting for Sam to let her play with all the toys. Claire was obviously enjoying herself and was not satisfied until she had explored every corner of the wheelhouse.

Tristan remembered the first time her dad took her out to one of the boats. For a ten-year-old, it was an adventure in Wonderland. Her dad stayed close to her side, knowing the dangers surrounding such vessels. Her fondest memory of that trip was the tour of the wheelhouse. At thirty-eight years old, she could still remember clearly the face of the old silver-haired captain who hoisted her up into the captain's chair. Time spent with her dad on the boats was the most peaceful and happy time of her childhood. Watching Claire's enthusiasm for something that had always been so special made her feel that same peaceful feeling that died with her dad.

Claire and Sam had become fast friends. She sat patiently as he played his guitar and sang a couple of his own songs. She even managed to keep a straight face when Tristan pretended to jump overboard behind his back. It took a little work, but Tristan finally managed to drag Claire from the wheelhouse and back on dry ground.

Tristan listened amused at Claire's excited chatter. She had many questions about life on the river that Tristan answered patiently. "Life on the river is similar to being on land. The boat stores function as little post offices. Boat personnel can pick up and send mail there. They shop at some of them for personal items. Their groceries and fuel are delivered by fleet boats that also pick up their trash. It's a world unto itself out here."

After climbing back up the levee, both women were relieved when they made it to the truck. Fortunately, the A/C cooled the cab shortly after they had gotten back on the road. Claire blotted her face with a tissue, trying to retain some of the makeup she had put on that morning, but the heat and humidity had done a number on her hair. No two hairs pointed in the same direction.

"How do you feel about pizza for lunch?" Tristan asked as she sped down River Road.

"Sounds heavenly to me. An iced tea would hit the spot, too." Claire was parched from being out in the heat. The diesel fumes on the boat were overwhelming and nauseated her a bit, and iced tea was exactly what she needed.

"Great, I will take you to my most favorite pizza place in the whole world. You have to understand, though. I only take my friends to this place, so we will have to get to know each other first. I will tell you about myself, then I will tell you what I know about you already. What do ya say?"

"Umm ... okay, I guess," Claire answered a little perplexed.

"I'm thirty-eight years old, not married, and no children, except for an orange tabby cat known as Ralph. My hobbies are anything to do with the water, camping, and believe it or not, gardening. I'm a neat freak, which is probably why I'm still single. My favorite food is pizza. So there, now you know me.

"Now, let me tell you what I know about you. You are also a neat freak. You're not married and have no children. Your hobby is shopping. I suppose you're around thirty-five, and you're a lesbian."

Claire sat listening to what Tristan had to say with a smirk on her face until she got to the lesbian part. Her smirk disappeared, and her jaw gaped open.

"Why on earth would you assume that about me?"

Tristan laughed. "What?"

"That I'm gay."

"I saw the gay pride flag on your sunglass case. I assume you do know that it's not just a pretty rainbow."

Claire was floored. She sat speechless. Tristan laughed so hard she had to pull off the road. "Oh, Claire, don't be upset. I didn't mean to make you mad, but your face was priceless."

"I'm not mad. I just didn't expect that at all. Don't sit there looking all smug, either. I found out about you my first day."

"Don't tell me; let me guess. It was Ellen. She always feels the need to pass that little tidbit along to anyone who crosses her path. Quite frankly, I think she's curious about what she is missing out on. She's a sweet person, and I think she means well, but she sure is fascinated with my sex life."

"You certainly have a unique way of breaking the ice with someone, Tristan Delacroix," Claire said with mock indignation.

Tristan pulled the truck back onto the roadway and headed for her favorite pizza place. Both women were more at ease and began to talk candidly. They both came to realize that they enjoyed being in the other's company.

CHAPTER THREE

Tristan pulled the red pickup into the crowded parking lot of the Pastime Lounge nestled under an interstate overpass. Claire looked at it skeptically. "Tristan, this doesn't look like a pizza parlor to me."

"That's because it's a lounge, and they serve the best pizza in Baton Rouge," Tristan said as she climbed out of the truck.

Clair reluctantly followed her into the old bar, and Tristan went to the counter to order their lunch. As Tristan suggested, Claire went off to find an empty table. Shortly after, Tristan appeared with two iced teas and took her seat.

"The pizza will be out shortly," Tristan said as she squeezed lemon into her drink.

Claire looked around the room. "This place is not so bad. Is this where you bring all of your women to impress them?"

Tristan laughed. "I have not been out on a date for so long I've forgotten how to impress anyone. With my work schedule, it's really hard to get involved. Many a relationship has died due to my sporadic schedule. I guess I have just given up."

"I can relate to that well. I have moved so often due to my job." Claire sighed. "Although it has gotten me the promotions I've desired, it's taken a toll on my love life."

Both sat in awkward silence for a few minutes until Claire changed the subject. "So, how did you get into this business in the first place?"

"My dad was a port engineer for many years. He was one of the guys they called out when a boat had mechanical problems. When I was younger and before they got so stringent on safety, I would go with him. I just fell in love with the river and the boats. When I got out of high school, much to the displeasure of my parents, I decided not to go to college and went to work for Valor, and I've been here ever since."

Claire smiled. "Tell me what it's like to be born and raised in Cajun country."

"I suppose it's not much different than anywhere else. In kindergarten, we are taught to drive boats and how to wrestle alligators when they make their way out onto the roadway. The most time-intensive training is spent on learning how to cook crawfish properly, but that's not until we take home economics in high school," Tristan said with a smirk.

"Are you naturally a smart ass, or did you undergo some sort of training?" Claire shot back, impressed by Tristan's sense of humor.

Tristan laughed, and Claire realized she liked the sound of it. "Like I said, life in Louisiana is not much different than anywhere else. I will admit that there is a very eclectic group of people who live here. New Orleans is a fine example of that.

"When I was a little girl, I used to love to listen to my grandmother tell me all sorts of tales of how she grew up in the swamp. She told me how they cooked and ate opossum and hunted alligators to make belts and shoes. I was so disappointed when I found out that she really grew up just like me out in the suburbs of Baton Rouge."

The counter called Tristan's name, and she excused herself to get the pizza. Claire watched Tristan as she walked across the room and could not help but notice that Tristan turned heads everywhere she went. What was amusing to Claire was that Tristan didn't even notice the attention. Not out of arrogance, but she was seemingly oblivious to how striking she actually was.

After eating the best pizza Claire ever had the pleasure of tasting, she and Tristan slumped down in their chairs and lit up a cigarette. Claire wanted to know more about the beautiful woman who sat across from her. As she sat there, the list of questions grew longer in her mind.

"Umm, Tris? Do you mind if I ask you some more questions?" Hopefully, by using the pet name Sam had used, Claire would be able to get her now quiet companion to open up again.

"I'm an open book. Ask me what you will." She smiled at Claire.

Claire paused and took a deep breath. "Okay, first, do you have siblings? Do you have a good relationship with your parents? What is your favorite color? Do you have another favorite food besides pizza? Why is your cat named Ralph? Would you be interested in showing me around town sometime when we are both off work?"

Tristan just sat there blinking her eyes, trying to take in all the questions that had been thrown at her. She liked the last one the most but decided to answer all in order.

"No sibs. Dad passed away two years ago. Mom and I don't see eye to eye, and when we see each other, it's usually fireworks. Blue is my favorite color. Mexican is tied with Italian. He's named Ralph because I thought it was a funny name for a cat. I would love to show you around, but that is something we need to seriously discuss."

Claire was a little taken aback by the last answer. "Discuss?"

"Claire, everyone knows about my sexual orientation. I've made no attempt to hide it. With us just working together, the rumors will fly. If we do things together after work, it will only add to the fire."

"I'm sorry, Tris, I didn't think about it that way. I don't want to make things difficult for you. I just enjoy your company and thought it would be fun."

Tristan interrupted. "I'm not saying that I don't want to go at all. My concern is for you. Unless I'm wrong, no one knows you're gay. When we start to do things, rumors will fly. I was just trying to prepare you for the onslaught. Frankly, I've been trying to think of a way to approach this subject with you, but I didn't know quite how."

"I see." Claire breathed a sigh of relief. She hated rejection.

"Since rumors will fly anyway, let them think what they will. I'm certainly not going to live my life in the shadows just because someone may talk about me. If their lives are so dull that they have to entertain themselves with my business, then I feel sorry for them. Besides, I'm not about to let what people say keep me from going out with you," Claire said with conviction, not realizing how the last part of her declaration sounded.

Tristan sat silently for a moment, and Claire could see the wheels turning behind her big brown eyes. "Umm ... will this be like a date?" She asked nervously.

Reluctant to scream, "Hell, yes!" Claire replied shyly, "What do you want it to be?"

"I asked you first," Tristan shot back.

Claire decided to take a big chance. "Tristan, I would really like to consider it a date."

Tristan grinned as her face began to color. "Good. Now, we have that settled. How about you let me make the plans since I'm the native?" she said nervously as she fidgeted with her napkin.

"Sounds good to me. I'll leave it in your hands. What do you have planned for the rest of the day?"

"Ellen suggested I take you down to some of the fleet offices and introduce you to some of the gang there, but I figured you'd rather go for a ride down River Road. They're expecting us to be out all day, and I would rather not spend it cooped up in a stuffy office listening to war stories." Tristan smiled impishly.

"Perfect! One more thing, though?" Claire asked excitedly.

Tristan finished off the last of her tea. "What would that be?"

"What night are you planning for our date? A girl has to know these things in advance. I may have to get an emergency pedicure or something," Claire said jokingly.

"Right now, Friday seems like a long way off, but I think that will have to be it. Besides, that should give us plenty of time in advance in case we need an emergency pedicure or have some sort of apparel conflict."

Tristan drove down River Road, pointing out old plantation homes and different sites along the way as she listened to Claire's excited chatter. They stopped at different fleets but remained on the levee, and Tristan gave Claire a pair of binoculars to look at the barges being set up for tow by their vessels.

"You can tell when a barge is empty by how high it sits up in the water. When they're loaded, they are only a few feet above the water's surface. When the barges are being loaded, the tankerman will open different valves to maintain an even flow of the product to keep the barge from tipping to one side, or listing, as we call it."

Tristan stood behind Claire and pointed over her shoulder at the white markers visible on the side of a passing empty barge. "When they load the barges, they sink it evenly into the water until they reach the desired 'draft.' So, if you are loading to a nine-foot draft, you will fill the compartments until the barge sinks into the water at the nine-foot mark on the bow and stern."

Claire was barely aware of what Tristan was telling her. Instead, she was distracted by the closeness of Tristan's body and the way her free hand felt on her shoulder. The sudden compulsion to turn face-to-face with Tristan was so strong that Claire had to step away, pretending that she had found something else of interest through the binoculars.

When they drifted into a comfortable silence on the drive, Claire wondered what was happening to her. She had seen so many sides of Tristan in the last forty-eight hours that the woman sitting next to her confused and intrigued her. And yet, she found herself undeniably attracted to a virtual stranger.

She glanced over at the subject of her desire and watched Tristan's profile as she smoked a cigarette. The smoke spiraled around her dark head before blowing out the window. Aside from Tristan's good looks, there was something that drew Claire to her. Something she sensed in her presence when they first met. Looking at her now, Claire realized that it was a lonely feeling the mysterious woman projected that Claire wanted to take away.

As promised, Tristan delivered Claire to her Jeep at 5 p.m. She noticed an envelope clipped to Claire's windshield when she drove up. She glanced over at Claire, who stared wide-eyed at her vehicle.

"Claire? Is something wrong?"

Claire's face was pale, and she sat staring at Tristan for a moment before she could find the nerve to speak.

"Claire, what is it? You're white as a sheet."

Claire stammered a moment. "It's ... nothing. I just remembered there was something I was supposed to do." She hated to lie, but she wanted to be alone at that very moment. She felt as though her whole world had been turned upside down and didn't want to have to explain anything.

Tristan was sure she was lying but was afraid to push the issue. She was tempted to reach over and comfort Claire, but her behavior was so strange that Tristan was reluctant.

"I'm fine, really. I've got to go. I'll see you tomorrow," Claire said as she quickly jumped out of the parked truck and shut the door. Tristan watched as Claire pulled the envelope off the windshield and got into her vehicle. Tristan noticed the troubled look on Claire's face as she started her Cherokee. She appeared to be crying as she drove off.

Claire didn't look back as she pulled out of the parking lot. She was too stunned over her find that she could barely concentrate. She lit up a cigarette in an attempt to calm herself. When traffic came to a stop, she debated opening the envelope. She stared at it for a long time, knowing what would be inside. Each time she reached for it, the car in front of her would start to move, so she decided to wait until she got home.

Once inside her apartment, Claire went straight to the room that served as her office and dropped the envelope on her desk. Then, she closed every blind in her apartment. She had goose bumps from head to toe. Now more than ever, she regretted not going to the police.

After pouring herself a glass of wine, she went back into her office. Sitting at her desk, she lit another cigarette and sipped her wine until she felt calm enough to open the brown envelope. As she reached inside, her heart sank when she felt the smooth picture paper. She pulled out the photos, and a small typed note was clipped to the stack. It simply read, "You cannot hide from me."

Claire shivered as she saw her own image walking into the Valor building. The second was taken of her getting out of her Jeep at home. The third was the most chilling. It was taken of her in the very room she sat now. Nausea welled up inside of her when she realized the unknown photographer had been standing outside her apartment.

As Claire imagined a dark figure watching and recording her actions, she was overcome. She bowed her blonde head and cried out of fear and frustration. She wanted a new start and the problems of the past to remain behind in Houston. If this person were willing to go to the trouble to follow her here, what else would he or she be capable of?

Murky Waters

Feeling utterly alone and confused, Claire drowned her sorrows in a bottle of wine. After making sure the door to the apartment was locked for the tenth time, she lay on the couch, too afraid to get into her bed. Maybe she would be too relaxed and not hear if someone tried to get in. Ultimately, she felt safer on the couch. She despised how this faceless person made her feel threatened in her own home. Feelings of anger would quickly be replaced by feelings of terror each time she heard a noise outside. She drifted in and out of sleep the entire night, jumping at the smallest noise, usually made by the icemaker or air conditioner.

The wine that Claire consumed did not keep her from dreaming. Disconnected images filled her sleeping mind. Dark figures followed her every step, but when they drew close, there was no face. She ran as fast as she could, but she was moving in slow motion. When she awoke, the same agonizing fear she felt in her nightmares clung to her as she dressed.

When Claire got out of her Jeep that morning, she was swamped with feelings of paranoia. Walking as fast as she could into the building, she glanced around nervously. Once inside, she looked back through the tinted glass windows at the parking lot to see if anyone else was out there. To her dismay and relief, there was not a soul in sight.

When she made it to the third-floor offices, Claire was relieved to see Tristan already there. Even though they were only getting to know each other, Claire felt comfortable in Tristan's presence. She silently debated whether she should confide in Tristan, then thought better of it. They hadn't even gone out on their first date. She decided not to burden Tristan with her problems until she knew where things would go between them.

Claire smiled at Tristan and went straight to her office. She put away her things and sipped her coffee as she waited for her computer to boot up. Today, she would bury herself in her work until she could work up the courage to call the police to see what could be done.

Tristan knocked softly on the open door. "Are you okay?"

Claire glanced up from her computer. "Sure. Why do you ask?"

"Well, for one thing, you were acting strange yesterday evening when we got to your car. At first, I thought you were afraid I was going to try to kiss you or something. This morning, you have dark circles under your eyes, and you look like someone who has the weight of the world on her shoulders."

Claire sighed and laughed a little. "Tristan, it didn't cross my mind yesterday that you were going to kiss me, so don't worry. I just got some bad news is all, and if you will forgive me, I am not quite ready to talk about it."

Tristan sensed Claire wanted to be alone. "Forgive me then for intruding. I'm here anytime you want to talk, no pressure. I will give you some time to relax before we begin with all the stuff we have to go over today."

"Tristan, you were not intruding. I would do the same thing. Thank you for being there."

Tristan smiled and returned to her office. She tried to busy herself with her work, but her thoughts kept drifting to Claire. Occasionally, she would glance over at the blonde going over the budget sheets for the month. Tristan watched as Claire ran her fingers nervously through her hair.

Movement in the outer room caught Tristan's attention. Two crewmen had entered and were talking with one of the crew coordinators. Tristan watched as they both stole glances at Claire, who was totally unaware of their presence. Tristan could feel her hackles rise as both men stared at Claire as if she were some new and unconquered territory. Her pulse quickened when one of them made his way to Claire's office. Her first instinct was to head him off, but she waited to see how Claire would handle herself.

Most of the men who worked the boats were decent, but a few were always on the prowl, and Tristan had no doubt Claire was the reason they stopped by before going to their assigned boat. She watched as the crewman entered Claire's office uninvited and introduced himself. Claire stood and shook his hand. Tristan observed silently as he spoke with Claire, unable to hear the conversation through the glass wall.

He talked for a while, and Claire nodded occasionally. Claire said something and looked over at Tristan and smiled. Tristan openly stared at the bold one who was standing in Claire's office, and when he glanced at her, her right eyebrow arched as she stared him in the eyes. He looked away quickly and made a hasty retreat to rejoin his fellow crewman. They left shortly after.

Claire had to fight the urge to grin when she noticed how Tristan sent them running with just a look. Tristan made her feel safe and protected, which was something she desperately needed. She gathered her reports and joined Tristan in her office. "Are you ready to go over this month's budget?" she asked as she entered the room.

"Sure, if you're feeling up to it," Tristan said as she joined Claire at the small conference table in the corner of her office. "I'm curious. Did Mister Stud ask you out?" Tristan asked with a smile.

"He sure did," Claire responded with a smile of her own. "I quickly explained to him that I was already dating someone. Although, the tan line on his left ring finger would have been a deterrent if I were interested in men."

"You will get a lot of that, I'm afraid. You're a very attractive woman, and word gets around on the river fast. Soon, many of them will be finding reasons to pay you a visit. Should it make you uncomfortable, just say the word, and I will make sure that you are not bothered," Tristan said sincerely.

"I'm very capable of handling myself, but if it does become a nuisance, I may have to enlist your help. I'm sure the look you gave him made it quite obvious that he was not welcome, so feel free to cock that eyebrow up anytime you feel it necessary." Claire said with a grin.

"Now," Claire said as she spread the work out onto the table, "this really concerns me."

Tristan joined her and looked over the spreadsheets.

"For the last two months, your crew change budget has shot up considerably. You have gone up from twenty-two thousand dollars per crew change to thirty-one thousand dollars. Do you have any idea what has caused the increase?" Claire asked as she studied Tristan's profile while Tristan studied the data.

"We really don't have any more boats up north than normal. The northern crew changes are usually more expensive because we have to fly our men getting on and off the boats," Tristan replied with her brow furrowed in concentration as she scanned the data in front of her.

"Not to change the subject, but I have been meaning to ask this since I came here. Aren't there any women who work on the boats?" Claire asked as Tristan turned to look her in the eyes.

"There are some women who do, but most of them are fleet boats that stay close to home. River towboats are really not a place most women want to work. The physical requirements are very demanding. That's not to say that a woman in good shape couldn't handle the job, but most women have no desire to spend thirty days at a time lugging rigging around and cohabitating with a bunch of sweaty, grimy men. I like to think we are just smarter than that," Tristan said with a laugh.

Claire found herself lost in Tristan's intense gaze once again. She had to shake her head to clear her thoughts. "Okay, so what is your theory on the conflicting travel budgets?"

"Well, nothing against you or your employees, but I don't think they have researched the flights well enough. For example, right here, it shows our boats just south of Cincinnati on the river, but sometimes, it is cheaper to have the guys go into Louisville and drive up to the boat. In other words, it is best to research the airports all around the boat for the cheapest fare, instead of simply flying them into the closest city."

"I see," Claire said as she made notes. "If your people can give us a time frame we can work with, I can assure you that my staff and I can save you money. Did Rhonda ever try to work this out with you?"

"The only thing I ever got from Rhonda was attitude. Let's get our people together and meet this afternoon. We can put our heads together and come up with some parameters that we can all work with and see what happens.

"Claire, aside from the fact that I am tickled pink that you are going out with me, I am truly glad you're here. I think you're going to give us a fresh perspective in here and save us money. I have to admit I'm truly impressed with what you have done so far," Tristan confessed with a shy grin.

Shortly after, Mike and Lauren arrived. Claire got busy working with the agents, going over spreadsheets and generating the reports that Tristan needed. This alone took up their entire morning. Claire was so immersed in what she was doing she had not realized that half the day had already passed until Tristan asked her to lunch.

Murky Waters

Both agreed on a deli about a block from the office. Tristan chose a spot in the far corner of the restaurant, so they would be able to talk without everyone in the deli being able to overhear. She kept the conversation light during the meal in hopes that Claire would feel comfortable enough to tell her what was troubling her so. When Claire didn't volunteer any information, Tristan decided to broach the topic as gently as she knew how when she saw Claire looking around nervously.

"Claire? Do you want to tell me what is bothering you now? Are things moving too quickly with us? Are you regretting going out with me?"

Claire laughed. "Tris, slow down, honey. Right now, you are the one bright spot in my life. I am really looking forward to our date. As a matter of fact, that has been the one thing that has helped me hold it together. What is bothering me has nothing to do with you. I am just not ready to explain it yet. I will tell you this, though: just being around you is a comfort to me. Your willingness to listen means more to me than you know."

Relieved to hear that she was not the problem, Tristan relaxed. She didn't want to push Claire into telling her anything until she was ready. Still, it bothered her that Claire would not confide in her.

The next two days flew by quickly. Tristan spent a lot of time with Claire preparing her for the crew changes that would start soon. During crew change, her department was extremely busy. Fortunately for all involved, it only lasted a week, then things would quiet down until the next one started.

Much to Claire's delight, Friday evening had finally arrived, and the butterflies in her stomach were working overtime. Tristan had told her to dress very casual, so she chose a short denim skirt and a sleeveless cotton top. True to her word, she had found the time to have a pedicure and was pleased with the results. She checked her makeup three times before Tristan arrived to pick her up, laughing at her nervousness each time she did.

She was still looking in the mirror, putting the last touches on her lipstick, when she heard a knock at the door. Even though she saw Tristan everyday, her heart leapt when she heard the gentle tapping. Claire peeked through the blind first, then opened the door for her date.

Standing before Claire was the prettiest woman she ever had the pleasure of going out with. Tristan stood there smiling, dressed in a pair of neatly pressed khaki shorts with a short-sleeved denim shirt tucked into them. Instead of her usual ponytail, her long dark hair hung down her back, blowing slightly in the gentle evening breeze. Claire felt herself trapped in the gaze of Tristan's beautiful brown eyes.

"Hey, look, we complement each other with the denim." Tristan laughed. "I even got a pedicure since it seemed so important." She thrust out a foot covered in a brown leather sandal. Claire laughed nervously and invited her in.

"I love this apartment, Claire, especially the loft up there. I could fill that whole ledge with plants. Ralph would have a blast on that spiral staircase, too."

Claire noticed that Tristan was uncharacteristically chatty. She wondered if Tristan was as nervous as she was. She gave Tristan a quick tour of her abode and offered her a glass of wine.

"I better wait on the wine, Claire. I'm on an empty stomach, and I'm afraid it will go straight to my head. I don't like to drive like that. If you would like to have a glass before we go, that would be fine with me."

Claire chuckled. "I think I will wait until we get to the restaurant, too. Besides, I can hear your stomach growling from here."

"Fine, Claire. Mock my hunger pains. I have not been able to eat a thing all day because of tonight. I may faint right here in your living room."

Claire laughed at her antics. "Come on, drama queen, let's get going. I don't want you passing out and drooling on the new carpet."

In the parking lot, Claire looked around for the red truck she had ridden in before. Instead, she followed Tristan over to a dark blue Mitsubishi 3000gt. "Is this your car, Tris?"

"Yep. The Ford is my company truck. I don't get to drive old blue around that often. She's got a few years on her, but she's still in great shape." Tristan opened the passenger side door and let Claire in.

While fastening her seat belt, Claire looked around nervously at the parking lot and grounds surrounding her apartment. She felt a twinge of panic welling up inside her as she wondered if she and

Tristan were being observed. Determined to enjoy the night that she spent most of the week looking forward to, she steeled her nerves and pushed her fears aside.

"So, Miss Delacroix, where are we going tonight?" Claire asked as Tristan started the car, hoping that her date did not hear the tremor in her voice.

"Do you like Mexican food?"

"Love it!"

"I figured I would take you to one of my favorite spots. They have wonderful food and even better margaritas. Then, I figured we could go see a movie if you're up to it."

Claire reached over and put her hand on Tristan's and squeezed lightly. Tristan seemed a little surprised at the contact but didn't pull her hand away. For someone who had such a commanding presence as Tristan did, it surprised Claire that she would be a little on the timid side.

There was a nice breeze blowing when they got to the restaurant, so they opted to sit out on the patio. One margarita and a few chips later, they were both relaxed and talking freely. When dinner arrived, they both just picked at their plates, already having had their fill of chips. Another round of drinks was ordered, and both were well on their way to getting downright goofy.

Tristan looked at Claire with glassy eyes. "Umm, Claire? Were you really looking forward to seeing a movie tonight?"

"No, not really, is something wrong?"

Tristan giggled. "Well, if we are going to one, we will have to leave now, and I'm afraid that I'm a little too tipsy to drive."

Claire laughed at her glassy-eyed companion. "I'm really enjoying myself right here. We can switch to iced tea and give our brain cells a chance to catch up. Besides, it will give me a chance to get into the mind of Tristan Delacroix."

"Well, if you were to get into my mind right now, you would find a lot of tequila and some lime juice. There are two sober brain cells in there searching for high ground. So, what is it you want to know, Claire Murray?" Tristan batted back playfully.

"Hmm, let me think." Claire paused for a moment. "Okay, got one. What is your biggest turnoff?"

Tristan giggled again. "Why do you ask? Are you about to belch or something?"

The response had Claire chuckling loudly. "No, you sick woman. Now, answer the question."

Tristan sat staring into Claire's eyes with a silly grin on her face. For a split second, Claire wondered if she was just thinking or was about to pass out. "Well?"

"Arrogance is a turnoff. People think I'm arrogant, but really, I'm very shy. It's hard for me to strike up a conversation."

"I have a hard time seeing you as shy, Tristan."

"Well, I am, and I'll let you in on another little secret. I'm afraid of the dark, too." Claire burst into uncontrollable laughter, drawing the attention of the other diners.

"Stop it!" Tristan said, laughing just as hard as Claire. "All right, it's my turn now. What turns you on?"

Claire blushed and looked across the table at Tristan, who sat patiently waiting for her answer. "Just about everything you do."

Tristan's mouth moved, but no sound came out. It took her a minute to compose herself. "I can't think of any clever comebacks."

"Wow! I have rendered Tristan Delacroix speechless. Mark this day in history!"

Tristan laughed. "Mind if I ask you an extremely personal question?" Claire shook her head as she sipped her drink. "This is an odd question, but I'm curious. Why did your last long-term relationship end?"

Claire smirked. "Tristan Delacroix, that was a smart question. You're trying to pick my brain while it is pickled with tequila. The answer is simple; she cheated on me and broke my heart."

"She was a very foolish woman," Tristan slurred. "So tell me about this moron."

"I once read in a magazine that if someone tells you that she is not good to be involved with, heed her warning and run in the other direction. She told me in the beginning that I probably didn't want to get involved with her, but I was only twenty-three at the time and very naïve. Anyway, I plunged in full speed ahead.

"Those three years were some of the most hurtful times of my life, but I did learn a lot. She was never happy with herself or anything I did. Whenever I got a promotion or achieved something, she would become jealous and berate me for it, instead of being happy for me. She seemed to be competing with me on everything. It was like having a competitive roommate instead of a lover."

"She cheated on you? After hearing all that, I wouldn't think less of you if you were the one who stepped out on her."

"Like I said, I was very naïve. I didn't understand her behavior. I spent nearly three years blaming myself for all our problems. Then one day, she admitted that she was having an affair and thought I was supposed to be understanding about it. She actually had the audacity to think I should hang around in case things didn't work out with the new girl. Needless to say, I dropped her ass like a hot rock and never looked back.

"Now, it's your turn, Tristan," Claire said with a grin. "Tell me about your last long-term relationship."

Tristan cast a sideways glance as she lit a cigarette. "You're going to be really disappointed because there is not much to tell. I have not had the pleasure of a long-term relationship. The longest lasted only a few months, and she broke it off with me."

"Are you trying to tell me that you're a hit-and-run lover, Tristan?" Claire tried to sound lighthearted, but she could not help but be alarmed by Tristan's admission.

"Don't get the wrong idea, Claire," Tristan said, seeing the tension on Claire's face. "I have not really dated a lot of women. My work schedule truly does put a cramp in my love life. The women I have dated did not take too kindly when I had to cancel dinner plans to get an injured man off a boat."

Claire was relieved by her answer, desiring more than a fling with Tristan. She was weary of the dating scene and was looking for something more substantial. Fully knowing she could get hurt, Claire could not make herself slow down. So drawn to the woman sitting across from her, she was willing to take the risk of jumping in headfirst and refused to analyze why.

After a few more glasses of tea, Tristan felt clear-headed again. They drove back to Claire's place, and Tristan accepted her invitation to stay for a while. They sat on the sofa, each with a glass of wine, and before long, Tristan began to feel the power of the grape.

Claire watched in amusement as Tristan's eyes became glassy, as they had been at the restaurant. Feeling the effects of the alcohol, as well, Claire felt her inhibitions slip away and wondered what it would be like to run her hands up and down the smooth thighs nestled so close to hers. The drink had not dulled her fear of making the wrong impression on their first date, and Claire wished that Tristan would give her some indication that she felt the same.

"I can't have any more of this, Claire. Please take it away. I would take it to the kitchen myself, but I seem to have lost some motor control."

"You are a lightweight, Tristan Delacroix!" Claire chided.

"Yes, I am and proud of it, thank you very mush ... I mean much."

"I hope you have no pressing reasons to get home, Tristan, because you are staying here with me tonight," Claire called over her shoulder as she took the glasses to the kitchen.

Tristan watched the sway of Claire's hips and bit her lip trying to stave off the feelings of desire. Claire was not someone she could simply enjoy, then walk away from. She wanted more, and she knew if she gave into her feelings of want, she would end up running out on her as she had the others.

"I don't want to impose on you. How about you let me sleep it off on the couch?" Tristan asked, hoping Claire would not think she was trying to work her way into her bed on the first date.

"It's no imposition at all. Now, you have no excuse not to have more wine," Claire said as she paused in the doorway and held up the glasses.

Tristan looked at Claire with a pair of bloodshot eyes. "Are you trying to get me drunk and take advantage of me?" she asked before bursting into a fit of laughter.

"Woman! You are really drunk, aren't you? I can't believe how easy it is to get you lit." Claire was genuinely amused.

Tristan giggled. "I know, it's pitiful, isn't it? My grandmother, God rest her soul, could drink nearly an entire bottle of bourbon and be seemingly unaffected. I drink a few margaritas, and I'm a basket case."

"Let's go get you something to sleep in." Claire chuckled as she pulled Tristan to a standing position and led her to the bedroom. She made her woozy date sit down while she dug in her dresser for a T-shirt and a pair of shorts. She turned to find Tristan lying across her bed with her arm draped across her eyes.

"Hey? You feeling okay?" Claire crawled onto the bed next to her.

"Yeah, I'm fine, but I think I'm going to be hurting in the morning. I hope I haven't made too much of a fool of myself tonight. I have never really been able to drink that much."

"I've thoroughly enjoyed myself tonight, Tristan. You've been wonderful company. To be honest, I think you're absolutely adorable when you have a buzz."

Before she realized what she was doing, Claire leaned down and kissed Tristan. Reveling in the softness of the lips that met hers, she could not resist slipping her tongue into the mouth that opened, giving her permission to continue. Lost in the taste of Tristan's mouth and the silkiness of her tongue, Claire's hands took on a life of their own. She slid her hand under the shirt that had long been untucked and enjoyed the feel of Tristan's abdomen quivering under her touch. Both women were breathing heavily when Tristan pulled away. "Claire, I don't want this."

Claire stood up quickly, stunned and hurt.

"Wait!" Tristan grabbed her arm. "That's not what I meant at all, Claire. I have only two brain cells that are sober, and right now, forming a sentence is a little tough. I think about you twenty-four hours a day. When we're together, I have to resist the urge to touch you. I'm not sure what you want from all this, but I want a relationship. You have become very special to me already, and I don't want to mess this up." Tristan sighed. "I don't want to be drunk the first time with you, either." Then, she hiccupped. "Sorry. Damn wine. Actually, I feel a lot better, and I think I should go home tonight."

Claire started to protest, but the fear she saw in Tristan's eyes was enough to silence her. "Umm, okay, I understand. I only have one request, though. I want to make you some coffee, and I would like you to wait a little while before you leave just to make sure your head is clear enough to drive."

Tristan reluctantly agreed. She desperately wanted to run at that very moment to the safe haven of her empty house where she could sort out the feelings that had just jumped from her mouth and surprised her. Claire fell asleep on the couch next to her as Tristan sipped her second cup of coffee. She gently got up, careful not to disturb the sleeping blonde. She slipped out the door into the night, eager to be as far away from Claire as she could get.

CHAPTER FOUR

Claire awoke the next morning on the couch alone. She immediately regretted kissing Tristan the night before. Obviously, she had been too forward and was furious with herself for possibly scaring away the first woman she had been interested in for a long time. Even though Tristan had babbled something about a relationship, Claire could not shake the fear she saw in Tristan's eyes. She continued to berate herself as she ate her breakfast and showered.

Pacing back and forth in front of the phone, Claire wondered if she should call Tristan first thing and do some sort of damage control. Fearful of being perceived as pushy, she decided to wait until Tristan called her. That way, she would know for sure if Tristan were really interested. Deep inside, she knew the wait would nearly drive her insane. Her heart skipped a beat when the phone suddenly rang. She snatched it up and took a breath, trying to sound casual.

"Good morning, Claire. It's Ellen. How are you today?"

"Oh, hi, Ellen. I'm good," Claire responded, trying to mask the disappointment in her voice.

"I was wondering if you would like to go out shopping today. I could give you an impromptu tour of the area if you're up to it."

Claire was hesitant to accept the invitation, not willing to leave home and miss Tristan's call — if it came at all. "I don't know, Ellen. I have so much to do around here. I'm still unpacking."

"You can do that anytime. It's a beautiful day outside, and you shouldn't waste it cooped up in that apartment."

Claire finally relented and agreed to let Ellen pick her up. She felt foolish sitting around waiting on a call that might never come.

Shopping was her favorite hobby, and she would be a fool to pass up such an opportunity.

Tristan groaned and cursed when her body refused to sleep any longer. She had been determined to stay in bed and sleep the day away in her dark bedroom. When sleep eluded her altogether, she mentally coaxed her body from the bed with thoughts of coffee and something to soothe her stomach. She pulled on her robe and walked numbly into the kitchen where the sunlight sent slivers of pain through her head.

While waiting for the coffee to brew, she pushed thoughts of Claire out of her mind as she had done for most of the night. She leaned back against the countertop and lit a cigarette, and an orange tabby circled her legs, meowing loudly. "Okay, Ralph, okay, give me a second," she scowled as she grabbed his food and poured it into his bowl.

Watching the cat eat his breakfast, she wished she would have left well enough alone and never agreed to go on a date with Claire. As bad as she wanted to have someone in her life, the thought terrified her, especially since that someone was Claire. She had to admit to herself that having just a feline as a companion did not fulfill the part of her that longed to connect with someone else.

Grabbing her coffee, she retired to the sunroom and curled into her favorite chair. Part of her wanted to call Claire and explain why she had panicked; the other part simply wanted to hide and pretend that they had never met. "I've screwed up royally this time, Ralph," she said as she scratched the purring tabby behind his ears. "She's a sweet girl. I should have never put her in this position. She needs more than what I'm capable of offering, and I'm leading her on."

"Well, I've met my match. I've never seen anyone shop the way you do, Claire." Ellen grunted as she stuffed the bags into her car.

"I can't pass up a sale, and those were some good ones. Now, after the hunt, I need to be fed. Where are you taking me for lunch?"

"I could go for a greasy cheeseburger right now. Does that suit you?" Ellen asked as she started the car and pulled onto the roadway. "I know of a great po-boy shop just up the road."

"Lead on, mighty warrior of the credit card. A greasy cheeseburger is just what I need, and onion rings, too."

The pair settled down at a table in the cramped smoking section of the sandwich shop. Claire seemed to be in another world as they made the short trip from the mall. After their orders were placed and Claire was happily sipping her iced tea, Ellen decided to find out what was going on behind the hazel eyes of her friend.

"You seem a little preoccupied; are you feeling all right?"

"Yeah, I'm fine, just a little tired, I guess. I didn't sleep much last night. "Ellen grinned. "You've been out on the town partying already?"

Claire silently debated telling Ellen about her date with Tristan. She wanted to talk to someone about her feelings, and the fact that Ellen knew Tristan would be a plus. Still, she was hesitant to come right out and tell her of her sexual orientation and that she had already been on a date with the woman she had referred to as "pepper ass."

"No, I had dinner with someone, and I didn't get home until late." Claire made the decision right then that if Ellen pressed about the date, she would tell all. She was tired of hiding who she was.

Ellen made no attempt to hide the mischievous grin that took control of her face. "Is he anyone I know? Was it Robert in accounting? He's been asking all about you since the day you arrived."

"Well, Ellen, not exactly." Claire paused, trying to find the right words.

"Not exactly?"

"Ellen, I should have told you this the first day we met. I feel like I've been lying to you. I'm a lesbian," Claire blurted out and waited quietly as the revelation sunk in.

"You ... don't ... look like a lesbian," Ellen stammered in shock.

"What's a lesbian supposed to look like?" Claire asked with a chuckle.

"I don't know. Well, maybe a mullet and some flannel for starters."

"Oh, Ellen, it's too hot for flannel right now, and the mullet is way out of style," Claire shot back, unable to contain her laughter. "Ellen, honey, there are thousands of women out there who wear makeup and feminine clothes who are lesbians. There's no official dress code. I dress the way I like to dress."

Ellen reached across the table and patted Claire's hand. "Seriously, honey, don't worry about me judging you. I like you for who you are, and whomever you date is fine with me."

"I'm glad to hear you say that because I went out with Tristan last night."

"Tristan!" Ellen yelled, then looked around in embarrassment. "Tristan? You went out on a date with Tristan already?"

"Calm down, it's not like I attacked her ... well, not exactly."

"You know, I am learning to pay close attention to when you say 'not exactly.'" Ellen didn't bother to touch her food when it was placed in front of her. Instead, she sat on pins and needles waiting for what Claire would say next.

"She took me out to dinner, and it was kind of a date. We had a great time, and she drank a little too much, so she stayed at my place until she sobered up."

"And?" Ellen asked, waiting to hear the spicy tidbits.

"Well, I was a little tipsy, too, and I kissed her. The kiss was a little heated, and she obviously became uncomfortable. She blurted out that she wanted a relationship, and I think she said things were going a little too fast." Claire rubbed her forehead in frustration. "I barely heard what she said because I was so surprised by her reaction. I made her drink some coffee before she left, and I fell asleep on the couch. When I woke up, she was gone. I think I have really screwed up with her."

"Good Lord, you girls move fast. Last week, you were pissed off at her for being rude, and last night, you go out on a date and stick your tongue down her throat." Ellen laughed and blotted her upper lip, which had begun to sweat.

"That's the problem. I'm not usually that forward, but I was tipsy, and my libido got away with me. I really like her, Ellen; she's such a sweetie when she is away from work. I don't know how to fix this."

"I don't know much about her personal life other than the fact that she's a lesbian, but I have heard rumors of her nights on the town. Tanya in personnel is also a lesbian, and she has told stories of Tristan's voracious appetite for women. Frankly, I'm a little surprised that she flipped out over a kiss. The fact that she mentioned something about wanting a relationship might mean that she really does want to settle down. Maybe she really likes you, too, and wants something more substantial."

"You didn't see the look in her eyes. It was stark terror. I thought I was going to have to pin her down just to keep her there long enough to sober up. I want to talk to her about it, but I'm afraid it'll just make things worse."

"You'll just worry yourself silly if you don't." Finally finding her appetite, Ellen took a bite of her food. "You went on a date with Tristan. I'm still floored. Here I was thinking I would have to be a referee, and you two have gone out on your first date."

Tristan woke up in her favorite chair with Ralph still curled up in her lap. "Oh, my neck." She groaned out loud, waking her feline friend. Her stomach grumbled loudly, protesting her decision to skip breakfast.

She wandered into the kitchen and decided on a peanut butter and jelly sandwich. Between the sandwich and the tall glass of milk, she was pleasantly full. She went back to her bedroom and crawled into bed. Sleep had become her only defense against the depression to which she was accustomed.

Claire's stomach tied up in knots as she approached the door to the crew dispatch office. Torn between wanting to see Tristan and dreading the encounter, she opened the door and plunged right in. She sighed audibly with relief when she noticed that Tristan was not in yet. Nevertheless, she wondered why Tristan wasn't already there because she normally was in before her.

Settling into her office, Claire switched on her computer and signed in. Out of the corner of her eye, she saw someone enter her office, and the butterflies in her stomach took flight. Looking up, she realized that Mike, not Tristan, was standing before her desk.

"Good morning," she greeted him cheerfully.

"And good morning to you. We're a little slow in there right now, so I was wondering if you needed help with anything." Mike took a seat in front of Claire's desk. "I wasn't sure if you felt a little overwhelmed by all this." He gestured around the dispatch center. "I certainly was when I first came here."

"That's so sweet of you, Mike. I am a little taken aback by it all. I have a lot to learn in a very short time."

"I learned a lot by sitting out there with the crew coordinators. Watching them work gives you a good sense of what they're going to need. They're extremely helpful because they know that the more you understand of what they do, the better equipped you'll be to help them.

"I noticed last week you got all the reporting down quickly, and that will make Tristan very happy. You always want to keep her happy. Rhonda didn't quite grasp that concept."

"Reporting is a no-brainer for me. Learning this business will be a daunting task, so anything you can teach me will be welcome," Claire replied with a smile.

Mike spent a few hours with Claire going over details of the job. She took nearly an entire notepad of notes. Engrossed in what Mike had to say, she never noticed Tristan walk into her office.

The lunch hour rolled around fast, and since it was the slow week, Claire offered to take her agents to lunch. Both happily accepted, pleased with the idea of a free meal. When Claire picked up her purse, her eyes met Tristan's through the glass partition between their offices. Tristan gave her a slight smile and nod and turned back to her work.

Claire debated asking Tristan to accompany them to lunch but changed her mind when she thought the tension between them might become evident to Lauren and Mike. She grabbed her things and led the two hungry agents out the door without casting another glance Tristan's way. It tore her apart knowing that Tristan saw her leave without saying a word.

Tristan leaned back in her chair and watched as Claire briskly walked out of the dispatch center. Her heart sank, knowing she had hurt Claire's feelings. Perhaps it was for the best; in her heart, she believed that she didn't deserve someone as open and kind as Claire. She packed up her things and went home to work. There, she wouldn't have to come face-to-face with what she so deeply desired and was too afraid to pursue.

"So, what have you been doing with yourself when you're not at work?" Mike asked as he stabbed at his salad.

Mike was the only one who ordered a salad. Claire noticed that he had put on quite a few pounds since she had last seen him. He was still sporting his trademark crewcut that took away from the fact that his dark hair was thinning and turning gray. "I've been unpacking and trying to get things squared away around my place. Ellen took me shopping Saturday, and we really had a great time. Other than that, not very much." She decided to keep her private life just that — private.

"Well, if you would ever like a tour guide to show you around, just let me know. I've become well acquainted with Baton Rouge and would be happy to give you a tour," Mike said as he noticed Lauren roll her eyes.

"What?"

Lauren set down her sandwich and looked at him with a grin. "You got us lost last week when we were trying to find that pizza place. You don't know jack shit about Baton Rouge."

Mike waved off Lauren's comments. "So, how about it, Claire? When would you like to take a tour?"

"That's sweet of you to offer, Mike, but I can't go anytime soon. I still have a lot to do right now. Maybe after I get things settled," Claire lied. Her apartment was finally in order, but there was something about Mike's persistence that told her he may be interested in being more than a tour guide.

When Claire returned to the office, her heart sank when she was informed that Tristan had gone home for the afternoon. She regretted not asking Tristan to lunch and wondered if the offer would have been rejected anyway. She was miserable for the rest of the day.

The entire time she sat in traffic on her way home, she debated calling Tristan. "Get it together, Claire; you've only just met the girl. Focus on the new job, not the gorgeous woman in the office next to you," she said aloud to herself, just to hear the words come out of her mouth. She smiled as she continued to encourage herself to forget Tristan Delacroix. Taking a deep breath, she could feel her resolve flowing through every inch of her being.

"Forget this!" Claire growled as she stomped into her new apartment. "Ready or not, Tristan, we're gonna talk." Before she could lose her nerve or debate the wisdom of her decision, she dialed the number she had stared at for two days.

The annoying noise of the phone ringing beside her brought Tristan from a deep sleep. Knowing it was the office, she grabbed the cordless and barked into the phone. "Yes!"

Claire felt anger, and with it came boldness as Tristan's angry voice greeted her. "Tristan, this is Claire. I hope you don't have plans for tomorrow night because we are going to try this again," she stated huskily, leaving no room for argument. "I'm cooking dinner, and I expect you to be here at six ... okay?"

Tristan lay staring at the ceiling in stunned silence as Claire ordered her to have dinner with her. "Umm, okay. What can I bring?"

"Nothing. Just you and your appetite. See you tomorrow ... bye." She hung up the phone with an ear-to-ear grin. "Now, that is how you take the bullheaded Tristan by the horns," Claire stated triumphantly.

The dial tone startled Tristan as she lay there with the phone still pressed to her ear. Many women had asked her out, but that was the first time she had ever been commanded to dinner. A smile broke across her face, envisioning the blonde dressed as a drill sergeant. "Well, Ralph, I've been ordered to dinner. I guess I better heed the order, or she may make me do pushups."

The following morning, Claire marched down the hall and entered the dispatch center feeling like she was truly in charge. When she noticed that Tristan was already in her office, her insides turned to Jell-O and began to quiver as she approached her office. In the presence of the woman she desired, Claire felt her courage slip away and felt like a nervous teenager with a powerful crush.

Tristan glanced up from the reports she had begun her day reviewing and saluted Claire as she walked in. The smile she was rewarded with made Tristan's stomach flutter. She was torn from her feelings when one of the dispatchers came running into her office.

"Tristan, we have a situation on one of the boats. One of the face wires broke free of the tow and caught a deckhand across the arm.

He's bleeding pretty badly, and Chuck is on the phone with the captain now."

Tristan jumped up from her desk and walked briskly to where Chuck was trying to tell the captain what to do for the deckhand until the ambulance arrived. She calmly placed her hands on the dispatcher's shoulder and whispered into his ear to put the call on speaker phone. Chuck complied, and the room was filled with the captain's nervous chatter.

"I think they need to put a tourniquet on that arm. He is bleeding all over the deck, and his color doesn't look too good." Chuck glanced up and shook his head and looked to Tristan for confirmation.

"Bill, let's try some things before you do that. If you put a tourniquet on, he is going to lose everything below it. Let's do what we can to save his arm and go with the tourniquet as a last resort," Tristan said as she stood behind Chuck.

Claire heard the commotion and watched as everyone in the room gathered around the cubicles. She could see the intense concentration on Tristan's face as she spoke. "Where is he hurt?"

"He's on the deck of the barge," the captain replied, nearly shouting.

"No, Bill, where on his arm is he cut?" Tristan asked again as Claire walked over to hear more of the conversation.

"Oh, it's on his lower forearm," the flustered captain replied.

"First, you need to apply direct pressure to the wound with clean bandages."

"See if you can get someone to put pressure on the brachial artery. That will help reduce the blood flow," Chuck added.

"What the hell is a brachial?" the captain asked in exasperation. The cries of the injured man could be heard in the background.

Chuck rubbed his hands over his face. "You can put pressure on the brachial artery by digging your fingers into his upper arm until you feel the bone. Have someone try that now while one of the guys holds pressure on the wound."

Tristan leaned down and whispered into Chuck's ear. "Bill is freaking out. He can't think straight right now, and even though he has had the same training as we have, you are going to have to talk him through this."

"The blood has stopped spurting," the captain shouted back into the phone. The cries of the wounded man grew louder as his co-workers put pressure on his injured extremity.

"Y'all are doing good then. Keep holding that artery and keep pressure on the wound. See if you can find something to prop his feet up on, keeping his legs elevated above his body. That will stave off shock until the ambulance can get there," Chuck coached as Tristan stood behind him, quietly telling the rest of the dispatchers to make the proper notifications when such an incident occurred.

"The ambulance is on the levee, and the fleet boat is getting ready to bring the crew out to us now," the captain informed them as his voice began to calm.

"Good, keep doing what you're doing until they get there. How does his color look now?"

"He's still pretty pale, but he's not thrashing around as much. He's getting tired, Chuck."

"I'm going to stay on the phone with you until the ambulance crew arrives. Keep doing what you're doing. I know he's hurting, but it's all we can do until help comes."

Tristan patted Chuck on the shoulders and gave him a pleased smile. "Good job," she whispered and stepped into the neighboring cubicle and called Cameron Hughes. "Mr. Hughes, are you aware of the emergency situation we are having on the motor vessel *Achilles*?" She paused as Cameron hit her with a barrage of questions. "The paramedics will be boarding the boat in a minute. We are on the phone with the captain now, and for the moment, they have the situation under control. I'll advise you as soon as I know what hospital they will be transporting him to." Tristan answered a few more questions and returned to stand beside Chuck as he hung up the phone, now that the ambulance crew had arrived.

"Excellent job, Chuck. Let's step outside and smoke a cigarette." Then, she addressed the rest of the crew coordinators. "Please wait to notify the injured crewman's family until we know what hospital he will be transported to. If his family lives out of town, please make all the arrangements to fly them over.

"Claire, will you personally oversee his family's travel arrangements? Regardless of the cost, get them here as quickly as you can."

"Don't worry about a thing. We will take care of it all as soon as we find out where he lives and who will be coming," Claire assured Tristan as she took Chuck out for a much-needed break.

Once the deckhand was en route to the hospital, Claire and her staff got to work. They made arrangements for the young man's wife and parents to be flown into the Baton Rouge airport. When Tristan and Chuck returned, Claire gave her the flight arrangements, pleased that her staff produced so quickly.

"Would you come into my office when you get a moment? I've got to call Mr. Hughes and give him this information, then I need to talk to you for a minute."

When Claire saw that Tristan had finished the call, she joined her in the office. "Claire, I'm really looking forward to dinner tonight, but I need to be at the airport when this man's family arrives. Do you want to do this another night, or will you be willing to have a late dinner?"

"As much as I would like to spend the evening with you, I understand that you have work to do. Why don't you call me when you leave them, and if you're hungry, I will be happy to feed you. If you're tired, we will make it another night."

"Sounds like a good plan to me. I'm going to the hospital now. I'll call you later this evening." Tristan gathered her things as she made a hasty retreat from the dispatch center.

Claire watched Tristan as she walked out. Even though Claire had grown to respect and admire Tristan in such a short time, her desire for the statuesque beauty drove her to distraction. Never had she met such a captivating woman who dominated her every thought. No one person had ever evoked the feelings of lust and desire as this woman had in such a short time. Claire silently prayed she would have the strength to rein in her raging libido, lest she ruin the budding relationship.

She spent the rest of the day wondering if Tristan would grace her with her presence later that evening. When it came time to go home, she breathed a sigh of relief and left the office, hoping she would not be alone for dinner. She paced around the apartment like a caged animal, hoping that Tristan would call soon and say she was on the way.

At 9 p.m., she had nearly given up hope when the phone rang. Tristan sounded exhausted, and Claire felt her heart sink. "I'm sorry to call so late, Claire. I felt like I should stick around until his parents were ready to go to their hotel. I hope you didn't go to a lot of trouble."

"Nope, no trouble at all." Claire did her best not to sound disappointed. "I made spaghetti, which is easy to warm up if you're hungry."

"I'm starved. All I've had to eat was a candy bar. If it's not too much trouble, I'd love a home-cooked meal."

"Then, come on over. I'll have it on the table by the time you get here." Claire's heart started to thud in her chest at the prospect of being allowed even a little time alone with Tristan.

When Tristan arrived, the exhaustion was evident on her face. She had spent most of the time at the hospital on her feet, fetching coffee for the worried family members of the deckhand who had spent the afternoon in surgery. She and Cameron Hughes had done their best to make sure the family had everything they needed. During the drive to Claire's place, Tristan felt the last of her adrenaline fade away.

"Are you sure this is not too much trouble? I could just grab a plate to go, so you can go to bed," Tristan offered as Claire waited on her.

"Sit down, Tris. This is no trouble at all." Claire set a glass of red wine next to a steaming plate of spaghetti and meatballs. She sliced a couple of pieces of French bread and set them down in front of Tristan, who looked like she was about to fall asleep at the table.

"Tristan, I want you to stay here tonight." She held up her hand to silence the protest forming on Tristan's lips. "I'm not talking about sex. You're exhausted, and I'm worried about you getting back out on the road. While you eat, I will run you a hot bath, and I have clothes you can wear to sleep in. You can take my bed, and I'll be happy to take the couch."

Tristan's big brown bloodshot eyes stared at her for a moment. She was truly whipped, and dinner and a hot bath were just what she needed, but she didn't want to run Claire out of her own bed.

She opened her mouth to protest, but Claire put up her hand again, silencing her.

"I won't take no for an answer. You've spent the day taking care of that man's family, and it's time you allowed someone to pamper you for a change," Claire stated resolutely.

Tristan was too tired to argue, and she figured that Claire knew she was too tired to do more than sleep, so she reluctantly gave in. "Okay, but I am not taking your bed. I will be just fine on the couch." Claire left to run the bath. "We'll debate that after you've had a bath."

Tristan had nearly eaten the entire plate of spaghetti by the time Claire returned to the room. She was enjoying the relaxing effect the wine was having on her aching body. "You're an excellent cook, Claire. Thank you so much."

"The pleasure was all mine. I'm sorry I couldn't wait for you. After smelling the food, I had to eat it." Claire gathered up the dirty dishes and waved off Tristan's attempts to clean up after herself. "You go soak in the tub. I've put some clothes in there for you, and there's a new toothbrush on the counter. Make yourself at home."

Tristan did as she was ordered. She quickly stripped off her clothes and settled into the soothing hot water. She sighed as she lay back in the tub and looked at her surroundings. She estimated that there were at least twenty bottles of hair care products on the surrounding ledge of the tub. "She's a high-maintenance woman," Tristan chuckled to herself as she bathed.

Emerging from the bathroom clean and relaxed, Tristan found Claire curled up on the couch with a book. "Feel all better?" Claire asked as she set the book down.

"I feel like a new woman. Thank you again for all of this, Claire." "There's no need to thank me. I'm happy to have your company." Claire jumped up from the couch, grabbed Tristan by the hand and led her to the bedroom. "What time do you want me to set the alarm for?" she asked as she turned down the king-sized bed.

"I bet you look like a fly in a bowl of soup in this big bed," Tristan teased.

"I like to have lots of room when I sleep." Claire grabbed the alarm clock and looked at Tristan with a questioning expression.

"Set it for five, I need to get up early enough to go home and get dressed, and I will have to spend some quality time with Ralph because he is going to be pissed when I don't show up tonight. The last time I stayed away, he murdered two house plants in protest."

"Five it is. We can't have Ralph taking out his anger on your plants. Now, get into this bed, Miss Delacroix."

"I'm not taking your bed." Tristan folded her arms across her chest. "We can share, or I'm taking the couch; that's my final offer." She hoped Claire would relent and allow her the couch.

Claire's heart hammered inside her chest. The thought of curling up against Tristan for the night was almost too much to bear. "Okay, but only if you promise to behave yourself," Claire teased, wishing Tristan would not.

"I may cuddle up against you if that is acceptable, but I am way too tired to misbehave." Tristan climbed into the bed and groaned when her head met with the soft pillow. Claire rushed off to brush her teeth and cut off the lights. The sound of Tristan's groan sent shivers up and down her spine.

She crawled shyly into bed, smiling at Tristan, who was now lying on her side facing her. "Claire, thank ..."

Claire pressed her fingers to Tristan's lips. "I should be the one thanking you for allowing me such delightful company."

"That was good. You get two brownie points for that line," Tristan teased with a smile.

"How many brownie points do I have to earn for a prize because I have tons of those lines. And what kind of prize do I win when I meet the quota?" Claire's face flushed with her boldness.

"Well, you've already earned a bunch, which entitles you to a night of cuddles. I'll get back to you on the rest of the prize package." Tristan yawned, and her eyelids grew heavier.

Claire switched off the bedside lamp and scooted closer to Tristan, who rolled onto her back and draped her arm around Claire when Claire rested her head on her shoulder. Almost immediately, Tristan's breathing became deep and regular, and Claire knew she had fallen asleep. They lay that way for a long time as Claire listened to the slow steady rhythm of Tristan's heart.

Murky Waters

Tristan eventually rolled onto her side, facing away from Claire, who snuggled up against her back. She buried her face in the long dark brown locks, enjoying the smell of her soft hair. Claire smiled as she held onto Tristan. Tonight, Claire would sleep better than she had in a long time. She felt safe and protected with Tristan there.

CHAPTER FIVE

Tristan's entire body jerked in surprise when the unfamiliar alarm clock sounded and jolted her into consciousness. She felt Claire pull away from her and heard her slap the clock. "I hit the snooze," Claire said sleepily as she snuggled back against Tristan's warm body.

As Tristan lay in Claire's arms, she felt the old familiar feeling creep over her. As she had done in the past, she wanted to jump from the bed and run as far and as fast as she could from the woman with whom she'd spent the night. She felt her pulse race as she noticed the possessive way Claire held onto her. She fought the urge for as long as she could before she untangled herself from the sleeping woman and quickly got out of bed.

"Tris, honey, my alarm is set fifteen minutes fast; you don't need to rush." Claire's empty arms fell across the warm bed where Tristan had occupied it.

"I really need to go," Tristan said brusquely as she gathered her things. "I'm sorry, I guess I'm not a morning person. I'll wash your clothes and get them back to you quickly. Don't get up." She left the bedroom and was out the front door before Claire could respond.

Tristan threw her clothes and purse into the passenger seat and jumped into the truck, wincing as the cool leather came in contact with the thin boxer shorts she was wearing. Pulling out of the driveway, she never looked back at the apartment; the need to distance herself from the woman she had just spent the night with was too urgent.

Claire lay in bed, staring into the darkness as the dawning day turned her room to gray. She was hurt and bewildered by Tristan's behavior. The night before, Tristan had been so warm and affectionate, but this morning, cold and distant. Had she pushed her too far again by insisting that she stay? Tristan's hot and cold behavior confused her and filled her with self-doubt. Nevertheless, she was determined to find out why Tristan behaved this way. It would just take a little time, and she was willing to wait. The prize was too precious to give up on.

Claire's heart sank when she was informed that Tristan had already gone to the hospital to check on the injured deckhand and his family. Her mood had turned sour when Tristan had not returned at the end of the day. She decided on the ride home that she would give Tristan a little time alone, but she would make it a point to try to talk to her when she felt the time was right.

Tristan only came into the office for a couple of hours for the rest of the week. She spent most of her time with her staff, catching up on what had taken place during her absence. Her contact with Claire was minimal, and when they did speak, it only pertained to business. By Friday, Claire was beginning to wonder if Tristan were truly busy or simply ignoring her. She had choked back the hurt while at the office but spent her evenings sulking, trying to figure out the mysterious behavior of the woman who was worming her way into her heart.

Saturday morning was spent doing laundry and household chores. The phone call she got from Ellen was a welcome relief. "Let's do lunch," Ellen chirped into the phone. Claire happily accepted, looking for a break from her thoughts.

Claire met Ellen at a popular bar and grill in midtown Baton Rouge. Ellen had already gotten a table in the smoking section and was happily sipping a margarita when Claire arrived. "I started without you. I saw a waiter go by with one of these, and it just called to me." She giggled as she sipped the frozen drink.

"It's calling to me, too," Claire said as she flagged down their waiter and ordered one of her own.

"Claire, as your friend, I feel the need to say this ... you look like shit. What's wrong with you, honey?"

Claire tucked a piece of hair that had escaped her ponytail behind her ear. "I've just been out of sorts lately. I think it's getting used to a new job and new surroundings."

"Save that for the folks at the office and tell me what is really bothering you." Ellen patted her hand and lit up a cigarette, waiting expectantly for Claire to answer.

Claire thanked the waiter as he set the frozen concoction in front of her. "It's Tristan," she answered as she sipped the frozen drink.

"Are you two fighting again?"

"I wish we were, then I'd know what was going on in that head of hers. We spend time together, and everything is great, then she shuts me out, and I don't see her for a while. I don't know what to make of it."

Ellen grinned mischievously. "I've been playing Scooby-Doo. I've been asking around, just trying to gather tidbits of info on her." She grinned again when Claire's eyebrows shot up.

"You look more like Velma," Claire teased, causing Ellen to give her the one-finger salute.

"Don't worry. I haven't found out much. She's a very private person. She doesn't talk much to anyone at work about her private life. This is what I know so far. Her dad used to work here before he passed away. Apparently, he and Cameron Hughes were very close friends. A few of the older employees attended his funeral and said that Tristan and her mom behaved very peculiarly.

"During the graveside ceremony, Mallory, her mother, sat stone-faced. She showed no emotion whatsoever. When Tristan broke down and cried, her mother constantly hounded her to stop acting like a baby. They said it was awful; the woman would not let Tristan grieve at her own father's funeral. Rumors surfaced later that she and Mallory got into a huge argument in the parking lot, and Tristan refused to ride with her. Obviously, Tristan and her mother do not get along."

"That might explain why she runs hot and cold all the time. She may have some intimacy issues. I know she likes me; I'm just not sure she knows it yet." Claire sucked down half her drink and felt her dark mood begin to lift.

"Give her a little time, Claire. You've only just met, and although you are comfortable with a relationship, this might be something she will have to work into.

"While we are talking about family, I'm curious to know about yours. What does your family think about your sexual preference for women?"

"I have no family, really. My mom, dad and sister were killed in a car accident when I was younger. My grandmother, who took me in after their deaths, passed away a few years ago, so now, I guess it's just me."

"Oh, Claire, I am so sorry." Ellen's face filled with compassion. "Please forgive me for prying and churning up painful memories."

Claire smiled, but the pain showed through in her eyes. "I'm okay. There's no need to apologize."

"Well, consider yourself adopted into the Comeaux clan. I'll stand in as your big sister if you'll have me."

Claire raised her glass in a toast. "Then, it's official. You're my new big sister, just as long as I don't have to baby-sit my nieces and nephews."

Ellen raised her glass and tapped it gently to Claire's with a chuckle. "You've got a deal, sis. Besides, my kids are too old to need a babysitter. You're off the hook."

Claire spent the afternoon pouring out her heart to Ellen well after they had switched to coffee. Her new sister listened intently and tried to give advice and encouragement when she could. On her ride home, Claire felt better, and it seemed like a load had been lifted off her shoulders. She hoped that the new workweek would bring about something positive between her and Tristan.

When she walked into the busy dispatch center on Monday morning, Claire's heart did a flip when she saw the vase of flowers sitting in the middle of her desk. Tristan was nowhere to be seen. She tried to look casual as she plucked the card, tore it open, and read it silently.

Dear Claire,

I hope these brighten your day.

Your Friend,
Mike

Claire did her utmost best to hide her disappointment when she looked into the neighboring office where Mike sat grinning. She had assumed they were from Tristan and suddenly felt embarrassed and silly.

Claire buried herself in her work. Crew change was in effect, and she helped Lauren and Mike set up the numerous travel plans that came through their email in abundance. She gave Tristan a slight smile when she arrived and went back to work, determined to concentrate on something that did not revolve around the woman who sat in the office next to her.

Phones in the work area of the crew coordinators rang incessantly. They talked back and forth to one another as they lined up the boats for crew change. Claire thought it sounded a lot like the New York Stock Exchange. Occasionally, one of the coordinators would lose his temper with an obstinate crew member and yell out a string of curses at which the other coordinators would shout their agreement.

Claire watched in amazement at how the quiet dispatch center came alive. She struggled to keep up with the constant demand for rental cars, flights, and hotels. At 2 p.m., the center seemed to quiet again, and she was surprised when Tristan called her on her extension and asked her to lunch. She glanced through the glass partitions at Tristan, who stood with her purse draped over her shoulder, motioning for Claire to hurry up.

Within minutes, they were downstairs and climbing into Tristan's truck, which felt like it was well over a hundred degrees inside. "Whew, I had to get out of there for a little while. I leave the office for lunch whenever I can during crew change just to get away from those damn phones," Tristan said as she pulled the truck onto the road.

They chose a popular restaurant close to the office and relaxed a bit as they waited for their food. Tristan seemed nervous, as though she had something on her mind and didn't know how to convey what she was thinking. Tension formed a knot in Claire's stomach as she wondered if Tristan were about to give her the "let's just be friends" speech.

"Claire, I was wondering if you would like to have dinner with me Saturday night?" Tristan slowly raised her eyes and looked at Claire shyly.

Relief flooded every inch of Claire's being when she heard Tristan ask her out. She was so thrilled that she didn't immediately answer as she rejoiced in her head. Tristan became nervous again and started to fidget with her cigarettes as she waited impatiently for a reply.

"That sounds wonderful, Tristan. I'd love to have dinner with you. What did you ...?"

"Well, hello, strangers," Mike said as he walked up to their table. "I see that Tristan has brought you to the lunchtime hot spot." Mike's words were friendly, but his eyes were cold when he regarded Tristan.

"Hi, Mike. Oh, and thank you for the flowers. With all the commotion this morning, I didn't have time to thank you," Claire responded cheerfully, trying to break some of the obvious tension rolling off Mike in waves. To add to the awkwardness of the moment, Mike seemed to be waiting to be asked to join them. And when Tristan showed no intention of extending an invitation, Claire thought it would have been improper if she did. Mike picked up on the hint and went off in search of his own table.

Tristan cleared her throat when he walked away. "That was awfully nice of Mike to send you flowers." Though she tried to sound casual, Tristan could not hide the sarcasm in her voice.

"He's just trying to make me feel welcome, I guess."

"Are you sure that's all he has in mind?" Tristan looked directly into her eyes.

"No, I'm not totally sure, but I can assure you I have no interest in him if that's what you're implying."

"Sorry, Claire, I didn't mean anything by that comment."

"Yes, you did." Claire returned Tristan's gaze. "And I like it. Does this little hint of jealousy mean you like me more than a friend?" Claire was surprised by her own boldness.

Tristan's face turned a bright red. "I'm sorry that I have not done a very good job of showing you that I want more from you than just friendship. I know I have a lot of explaining to do, but please just be patient with me."

Claire felt bad that Tristan seemed to be struggling so hard with their budding relationship. "Tristan, I'll always be patient with you. There is no need to try to explain anything until you're ready.

And when you do, just know that I will be here ready to listen and be here for you."

Claire was on a high when she returned from lunch. She had something to look forward to Saturday night. She sat down in her chair and went over the ticketing screen to make sure everything had been issued when Lauren tapped lightly at her door.

"Claire, do you have a minute? I really need to talk to you privately."

"Sure, come on in and close the door." As Lauren took a seat, Claire pushed away from the desk and gave her undivided attention. "What's on your mind, Lauren?"

Lauren looked around nervously. "It's about Mike. Claire, I don't think you realize how infatuated he is with you. He talks about you incessantly. It's obvious to me that you don't feel the same about him, but he has had the biggest crush on you since the last time we worked together. Let him down easy, Claire, and do it quickly before he starts planning an engagement party."

Claire was floored. "I had no idea. I knew he seemed interested, but I never dreamed he thought of me that way." She stopped short when Mike walked into the dispatch center.

When Lauren saw the expression on Claire's face, she sunk down into her chair. "Oh, dear Lord, that's him, isn't it? Ask him to come in and make up something quick, so I don't have to explain why I'm in here with you."

Claire waved Mike in and asked him to close the door. "Please have a seat, Mike. I just wanted to take this opportunity to thank you both for the fine job you've been doing. Your help has made my transition go very smoothly. Tristan seems to be very pleased with us, and I owe it to your diligence and hard work. If there is anything I can do to make your jobs easier, please let me know."

Claire silently applauded herself as her agents left her office; she'd been quick with that little speech, even though it was well deserved. She glanced over at Mike while he worked, and for a split second, she felt pity for him until Lauren's words replayed in her mind. *He has had the biggest crush on you since the last time we worked together.* Pieces of the puzzle were coming together, and she felt the anger rise in the pit of her stomach, thinking that her tormentor had been right under her nose all along.

Murky Waters

The next morning, she decided to take the bull by the horns and talk to Mike. She felt safe talking to him in her office with Tristan on one side and a roomful of people on the other. She used her anger to instill the courage she would need to initiate the unpleasant conversation.

"Mike, the gesture of these lovely flowers was very kind of you, but I feel the need to be honest with you. I like you as a co-worker and a friend, but that's as far as it can go with me. Most importantly, I am your boss, and a relationship above anything but friendship would be considered improper. And to be blunt, I'm not interested in exploring a personal relationship with you. I just wanted to bring this out in the open now, so there will be no miscommunication between us." Claire paused as she noticed the color drain from Mike's face.

"I've stepped over a line with you, haven't I?" His voice was barely a whisper. "I'll be very honest with you since you are being so open with me. I have wanted to date you for a long time, but I cannot stand the thought of making you uncomfortable around me. If that is what I've done, then I am truly sorry. You don't have to worry about me misconstruing your kindness or friendship from here on out. And I sincerely hope that we can continue to work together like we always have."

It can't possibly be him. He looks like he is going to cry, Claire thought to herself as she listened to Mike's heartfelt apology. "I'm sorry to have been so blunt, Mike, but I was afraid that if I was not completely candid, it might cause tension that neither of us needs right now."

"No, don't apologize, Claire. I appreciate your candor, and I will give you my word that this will not affect our working relationship." He finished with an uneasy smile.

"Thank you for being so understanding," Claire offered as Mike left her office.

Claire glanced toward Tristan's office where Tristan sat with her eyebrows raised in question. From Tristan's vantage point, she could see the expressions on Mike's face, and she wondered what they could have been discussing to elicit such a response. Claire gave her a reassuring smile before getting back to work on the morning reports.

When Claire's hungry stomach had just begun to complain, her phone rang, and she could see on the ID that it was Tristan. She glanced over as she picked it up. "Get your purse and start heading for the door. I could eat the ass out of a bear right now," Claire said as she stared at the grinning brunette on the line.

"Yuck, no kissing after lunch then. I'm gonna have a hard time finding a place that serves bear ass, so be thinking of some alternatives."

The alternative was a small restaurant that boasted home cooking. Claire ate like a bear; her appetite had returned with a vengeance. She had not been able to eat breakfast because her nerves were wreaking havoc on her stomach preceding the conversation with Mike. "Oh, Tris, this is so good," she purred between bites.

"Obviously," Tristan kidded. She was about to open her mouth to speak when a familiar voice addressed her.

Claire looked over Tristan's shoulder to see a woman standing just behind her. Claire knew instantly that this was Tristan's mother. Her long, dark hair had streaks of gray, but otherwise, they were the same height and build. Mallory Delacroix was a beautiful woman, and it was obvious where Tristan got her looks from.

"Aren't you going to speak to your own mother?" the woman asked, staring into Claire's eyes. There was no mistaking the disapproval Claire saw there. Mallory glanced down at Tristan, who sat speechless, her neck covered in red splotches.

"Hello, Mother," Tristan responded, without turning to look.

"Since you have forgotten the good manners I taught you, I'll invite myself to join you." She pulled a chair out and sat down, looking her daughter in the face. "I haven't seen or heard from you in a while. You can't pick up the phone and make a call?"

"The phone lines work both ways. If you wanted to talk to me, you could have called." Tristan's voice was cold as she stared back at her mother. Her body language spoke volumes. She held her fork so tightly that her fingers turned white. Muscles in her jaw twitched as Mallory spoke.

Ignoring her daughter's remark, Mallory turned her attention to Claire, who sat transfixed by the exchange. Mallory continued to speak to her daughter as her eyes bore into Claire. "You must have found *something* to keep you occupied." She put great emphasis on the word something.

"Is there a reason you interrupted a pleasant lunch, or do you have something to say to me?" Tristan snapped, making Claire jump at the hostility in her voice.

Mallory slowly turned her head back to Tristan. "Normally, when mothers and daughters see one another in public, they do speak, Tristan." Her voice dripped with sarcasm.

Tristan leveled her eyes on her mother's. "That's assuming they have a normal relationship, Mother."

"You're a fine one to speak about what is normal, little girl."

"In case you haven't noticed, I am no longer a little girl, and I will not allow you to sit here and insult me and Claire. Get up from this table and leave, or I will, and stick you with the check," Tristan hissed.

Mallory stood and looked down at them for a moment. "So, it's Claire, is it?" She turned and walked away without another word.

Tristan set down her fork and immediately lit up a cigarette. Claire thought it wise to allow her to speak first, when she was ready. Claire thought she had seen Tristan angry before, but she was wrong. Tristan went off for nearly five minutes straight and was shaking from head to toe when she finished. Still, Claire felt flattered because the main reason Tristan was so angry was because of the way Mallory referred to her.

Claire tried to stifle the chuckle that rose within her, resulting in a snort. Tristan looked at her as though she had lost her mind. "What are you laughing at?"

Claire broke into fits of laughter. "Did you see the look on her face when you said you were gonna stick her with the check?" Claire continued to laugh until Tristan finally chuckled with her.

On the ride back to the office, Tristan was lost in thought. Uncomfortable with the silence, Claire tried to get Tristan's mind off the encounter with her mother. "So, where are you taking me to dinner Saturday night?"

Tristan smiled. "It's a surprise. I hope you'll enjoy the cuisine; it's simple but pretty good. I know the cook personally."

CHAPTER SIX

Claire's eyes grew wide as she and Tristan pulled off the highway onto a small gravel road leading into the woods. Soon, a clearing came into view, revealing a well-manicured yard surrounding a large Acadian-style house that backed up to a lake encircled by cypress trees. Spanish moss swung lazily in the breeze, making the place look like a picture from the Old South.

Claire's heart skipped with joy when Tristan divulged that she was cooking dinner. She was excited at the prospect of seeing Tristan's place. She'd always believed that you could tell a lot about a person by how they lived. A person's home contained all sorts of tidbits of information just waiting to be observed.

"I feel like I'm being taken to Batman's cave," Claire said as Tristan pulled the car to a stop.

"Yeah, well, there is no butler waiting to serve us," Tristan answered playfully as she climbed out of the car.

"Let's get all this stuff unloaded, and I will give you a tour of the outside before we lose daylight and the weather hits," Tristan said as she gathered up the groceries. Both women unloaded the car quickly, managing to get everything in one trip. Tristan opened the back door to the house and set everything just inside. She turned to Claire, who was tiptoeing, trying to get a peek over her shoulder.

"You can see the inside in a minute. I want you to see all my handiwork first. We're going to have to do this quickly, though. With this wind picking up, the rain will be on us before we know it." Tristan looked out at the western sky, seeing the storm clouds moving in.

She led Claire down a cobblestone path leading from the back door to a wooden deck. Trellises that were completely covered in confederate jasmine bordered two sides of the deck. The deck itself overlooked the back yard and the lake on one side and butted up to the house on the other. Just to the right was a small herb garden, and beyond that was a well-maintained vegetable garden.

Claire marveled at the maze of flowerbeds that were spaced throughout the yard, one of which held at least a dozen varieties of butterfly-attracting plants. Butterflies were in great abundance around the beautifully maintained bed. Tristan had greatly reduced the area of her yard to be mowed by building flower beds divided by small gravel pathways. The centerpiece was a fountain feeding a small goldfish pond.

"I think I forgot to mention my other hobby. I love to grow things," Tristan said. "In the last couple of years, I've discovered that I have a green thumb. Every spring, I find myself making new flower and vegetable gardens, but by late summer, I am swearing I will never do it again."

Claire stood transfixed, taking it all in. "Tristan, this place is a little slice of heaven. If I lived here, I would find a million ways to work from home."

Tristan nodded. "I'm so glad you like it. I love it here. It gets a little lonely sometimes, though."

Tristan blushed at the admission that slipped from her mouth. It was the truth, however, and she wondered why admitting it to Claire came so easily. The woman standing before her had changed so much about her so quickly that she hardly noticed it. In the past, she would have never dreamed of inviting someone to her home, but she did it without thinking. Realizing that she was standing there with an awestruck expression on her face, Tristan struggled for something to say.

Just as Tristan opened her mouth to speak, a fuzzy bolt of cat lightning flew out of the nearby butterfly bushes. Tristan reached down and picked up the orange tiger-striped tabby cat. He gave her a few love nips and two licks to the chin and began to purr.

"Claire, I would like to introduce you to Ralph. He's my patrol cat. He patrols the perimeter of the property, making sure all is well while I'm away."

Claire laughed and scratched Ralph behind the ears. "So, you have a watch cat instead of a watch dog. How does he alert you to trouble?"

Tristan stroked her protector lovingly. "He doesn't alert me unless it's too big for him to handle. That doesn't happen very often, though. He's one bad little dude."

Claire found this funny. "What kind of security issues have you had out here?" Tristan began to explain the incident that had earned the cat his title. Ralph looked at Claire as though he was insulted that she doubted his skill. He jumped out of his owner's arms to further investigate the new intruder. He circled her, sniffing her shoes, but shied away when she reached down to pet him.

"Earlier this spring, I was planting the vegetables. I was really into what I was doing, not paying much attention. Ralph ran up to me and started hissing. All the hair was standing on his back, head to tail. I thought he had gone crazy from the heat. I took a step back to go get him some water, and I saw what all the commotion was about. Three feet from where I was standing was a snake about four feet long. I killed it with the shovel. If not for Ralph, I may have been bitten. Hence, the title 'patrol cat.'"

Ralph circled Claire's feet, staring up at her as his beloved owner gave the details of his heroism, his facial expressions conveying what he thought. *Yeah, take that, lady.* Claire could not help but find humor in the story of the great rescue, but her laugh was cut short as the rain began in earnest. Tristan grabbed her by the hand and made a dash for the house. The orange tabby sped past them and waited at the back door for the slower bipeds.

Once inside, Tristan took Claire on a tour of the interior of the house. The décor was simple but tastefully done. Every room was impeccably neat. The entire house was devoid of dust down to the baseboards. Claire thought it odd when they came to one of the bedroom doors that was locked with a padlock. "Tristan, do you have a roommate?" Claire asked in confusion.

"That is kind of a storage room," Tristan explained when she saw the bewildered look on her companion's face. "I keep my dad's belongings in there. I rarely ever go in. It reminds me too much of him, and I miss him all over again. I keep the lock on there because I still have his gun collection, and it would break my heart if it were stolen.

"How about you and Ralph get acquainted while I get dinner started? I'm going to make you one of my house specialties, and it takes a little while to cook. Once I get it under way, we can start watching some of the movies we rented."

"Sounds great to me. Can I help you with anything?"

"No. Let me spoil you tonight, Claire. I don't get the opportunity very often to spoil someone besides Ralph, and he isn't nearly as cute as you are. Don't tell him I said that, though. Would you like anything to drink?"

Claire blushed at the offhanded compliment and declined the drink offer. As Tristan disappeared into the kitchen, Claire wandered into the sunroom just off the main living area. Enjoying the tropical appeal of the room, a shiver made its way up her spine when she noticed all the open windows. All thoughts of the stalker had been pushed into the deep recesses of her mind until she entered that room and felt like she was on display.

Could someone have followed us here? she wondered to herself as she slowly backed out of the room. Feeling her heart rate kick into overdrive, she took deep breaths to get herself under control. She had no desire to ruin what so far had been a perfect evening by freaking out and having to explain her behavior.

Instead, she tried to make herself comfortable on the living room sofa. She picked up the TV remote and surfed the channels for something to keep her occupied. Nothing grabbed her attention, and her thoughts drifted to the woman cooking her dinner. Her heart was warmed by the fact that Tristan wanted to spoil her, making her feel contentment and happiness she had not known in a long time.

She looked around the room, studying the surroundings. There were a few pictures scattered about of Tristan with a man Claire assumed was her father. There was none of her mother to be found. She ran her fingertips over the replicas of antique sailing ships that adorned the mantle over the fireplace, wondering what Tristan's mother could have done to be excluded from her daughter's life, aside from the fact that she was an asshole.

Her mind wandered as she stared at nothing in particular on the television. Movement caught the corner of Claire's eye. She stared for a moment in that direction. Seeing nothing, she resumed her channel surfing. A minute later, an orange ball of fur came flying through the air and pounced on the remote that she was idly swinging. Claire leapt from the couch, screaming at the top of her lungs before she realized that it was Ralph.

Tristan ran into the room with a dishtowel slung over one shoulder and a wooden cooking spoon in her hand prepared to do battle. The furry culprit fled the scene of the crime before she could see him. Tristan found a very disheveled Claire standing in the middle of her living room.

"Are you okay? What happened?" Tristan pulled Claire into her embrace.

"I'm fine. Your patrol cat pounced on the TV remote. He scared me half to death. I haven't been around cats much. Do they always do stuff like that?"

Tristan laughed. "I'm afraid so. That is kind of a cat's way of getting to know you. He's playing with you. If you dangle something in front of a feline, it will pounce." Tristan had to hide her face as she returned to the kitchen to keep from laughing in front of Claire.

"Crazy-assed cat," Claire murmured under her breath.

Claire rolled up a cable guide as she sat back down and waved it a little. "Come on, buddy, pounce this. I owe you one," she said low enough for only the cat to hear. Ralph knew a trap when he saw one and stayed in his favorite hiding place under the couch.

After dinner was left to simmer, Tristan joined Claire on the sofa. They spent the better part of the evening snuggled up together watching movies. Tristan served their dinner on the coffee table in front of the TV. Claire was delighted to eat a home-cooked meal, and the spicy fare was right up her alley. She was even more delighted that Tristan could cook so well, an attribute that ranked very high with her.

"Oh, my God! Tristan, this is delicious! What is it?"

Tristan blushed a little. "Sophisticated folks call it steak and gravy. We call it meat and gravy. We, meaning coon-asses."

"Coon what?" Claire laughed.

"You've never heard of a coon-ass? It's another name for Cajun. It's about the only time you can call us an ass and not insult us," Tristan said in a heavy Cajun accent.

"I can see now that I will have to invest in a Cajun French dictionary. Louisiana seems to be a world all its own. Do you speak Cajun French?"

Tristan shook her head. "I am ashamed to admit that I know very little. My dad spoke it fluently. You would figure that I would have learned more than I did. My mother is not from here and did not favor the language. She swore my grandmother was always insulting her when she spoke it. The funny thing about it was, my grandmother was doing exactly that."

Claire seized the opportunity to ask about Tristan's mother. "Why are you and your mother on such strained terms? Is it your sexual orientation that causes the friction?"

Tristan's face became solemn. "That among other things. There is nothing I can do to please that woman, so I stopped trying."

Tristan didn't offer any more information on the subject and got up to collect the plates from dinner. Claire jumped up and helped her take the dishes to the kitchen. As Tristan rinsed off the plates, Claire wrapped her arms around her waist. She felt Tristan stiffen.

"I'm sorry, Tris. Was that being too forward?"

"No, not at all. I just get a little tense whenever I think about my mom. It's not you."

After the dishes were put away, Tristan and Claire settled in front of the TV once again to watch another movie. Both were cuddled together on the sofa enjoying the closeness when the storm released its full fury and knocked the power out.

Tristan sighed. "So much for the movie. I'm glad we weren't at a pivotal point. That would have really pissed me off."

Claire gave her a mischievous grin when she returned from lighting candles throughout the house giving it a warm glow. "Do you know what we could do here in the dark all alone?"

Tristan gave her best innocent look. "Umm, knit?"

"That's not exactly what I had in mind. It involves you taking off your shirt. Don't worry; I will honor your request to take things slow. I just wanted to give you a back rub."

Tristan laughed. "You make me sound like a prude!"

After a while of playful banter, Claire finally coaxed Tristan out of her shirt. She spread a blanket down onto the floor and had Tristan lie on her stomach. Claire straddled Tristan's hips and began to massage the soft flesh under her fingers. When she got to Tristan's bra strap, she quickly unhooked it before her subject could refuse.

Claire marveled at the softness of Tristan's skin. She began to think this was really not a good idea for her. The skin under her fingertips made her crave more. Her attraction to Tristan grew more intense every time she looked at the dark-eyed woman. Now, with her hands on her warm skin, it was becoming almost unbearable to resist a more intimate touch.

Tristan could not contain the groans that issued from her while Claire's talented hands worked over her back. She was seriously regretting her declaration to take things slow. With each touch, she debated taking advantage of the sensuous moment. All her resolve faded away. Just as she had made up her mind to act upon her desires, she felt a searing pain in her right foot.

"Oh, my God!" Tristan cried out.

Claire knew she gave great back massages, but she did not expect this sort of reaction. Tristan kicked her feet and screamed. Claire turned to see an orange fur ball firmly attached to Tristan's foot.

"Let me go, Ralph! You furry bastard!" As Claire moved off of Tristan, Ralph shot off to a safe hiding place. His attack achieved the desired effect. The stranger was off of his beloved pet.

"I cannot believe that little fart bit me! What on earth has gotten into him?" Tristan rubbed her hands over her ankle, noticing she was bleeding.

"Has he ever done anything like that before?"

"Never! I don't know what has gotten into his fuzzy little ass. When I catch him, I may have to beat it out of him!" Tristan hissed, as she remembered she was naked from the waist up and clutched her discarded shirt to her chest.

Claire felt a familiar heat consume her when she caught a glimpse of Tristan's breasts. For a split second, she was overcome with a desire to see the rest of what Tristan had to offer. However, if she acted on that desire before Tristan was ready, she feared her actions would send Tristan running to the hills again.

"We have to get these cuts cleaned up before any cat killings commence." Claire stood and pulled Tristan to her feet. They went into the bathroom where Tristan sat with her injured foot hanging over the bathtub and her shirt held to her chest. Claire gently washed the blood away with soap and water, then applied some antibiotic ointment. Last but not least, she put on a Band-Aid and kissed it for good measure.

Murky Waters

It wasn't until Tristan felt the warmth of Claire's mouth that she fully realized that she had initiated a kiss with the blonde sitting so close to her. The kiss deepened, and she felt Claire's tongue responding to hers. Tristan was quickly losing the battle with her good intentions. She wanted Claire more than she could remember wanting anyone else.

This time, Claire pulled away. "Tristan, if we keep this up, I'm going to have a hard time stopping. Just like you, I want more from this relationship than just sex. I am only human, though, and extremely attracted to you."

Claire stood back and offered her hand for Tristan to take as she stepped from the bathtub. Tristan didn't immediately release Claire's hand as she stood in front of her. Instead, she gently brought Claire's fingers to her lips and kissed each fingertip.

Claire closed her eyes when she felt her breath leave her. The sensation of Tristan's lips and occasionally the tip of her tongue on her fingertips was more than she could stand. Tristan was well aware of the effect it was having on Claire by the way the blonde's face and neck flushed. Tristan pulled Claire closer and wrapped her arms around Claire's waist as she backed her into the bathroom cabinet. Claire wove her fingers into Tristan's hair as her tongue filled Tristan's mouth, making every fiber of her being feel like it was on fire. Aware that Tristan had dropped the shirt that she had been holding protectively to her chest, Claire allowed her hands to roam over the smooth skin of Tristan's back, causing her to involuntarily grind her hips against Tristan's.

As Tristan's lips kissed a searing trail up Claire's neck, Claire lightly ran her nails across the skin of Tristan's back, causing her to moan in Claire's ear as she kissed and nibbled it. Claire did what she had only dreamed of until that moment and ran her hands over Tristan's firm rear end, causing her to press her body even closer into Claire's. Their bodies melded together, separated only by the clothing they still wore.

Tristan pulled back and looked deep into Claire's eyes. "You're trembling. Are you sure you're ready for this? We don't have to hurry anything."

"I'm very nervous," Claire replied with a shy smile. "But that's not the only reason I'm trembling, and you're shaking as much as I am."

Tristan buried her face in Claire's neck. "I'm nervous, too. You've become so special to me in such a short time that it's overwhelming."

Touched by Tristan's admission, Claire gently pulled her into another kiss so intense she barely realized that Tristan had already reached up the back of her shirt and unclasped her bra. However, when Tristan ran her fingers under the garment and stroked her nipples lightly, Claire gasped against Tristan's mouth at the sensation that sent shivers up her spine.

Tristan released her hold on Claire's body and stepped back. Claire immediately tensed, fearing that Tristan would tell her she was not ready to continue what they started. Instead, Tristan looked at her neck and smiled. "Your skin blotches when you're aroused."

Claire turned and looked at her reflection in the mirror. Even in the glow of the candlelight, she could see the telltale signs of what she was experiencing clearly displayed on her face and neck. Tristan moved in close behind her, staring into her eyes in the reflection, as she slowly unbuttoned her shirt. Claire's eyes dropped from Tristan's and watched as each loosened button revealed more of her own flesh.

Claire observed as Tristan slid her shirt down her shoulders and dropped it to the floor. Her eyes slowly drifted back up and locked with Tristan's as she did the same with her bra. Feeling exposed, Claire watched as Tristan's eyes left hers and roamed over her body, following the trail her hands blazed across her bare skin.

Claire could feel and hear Tristan's erratic breathing as she pressed her bare breasts into the skin of Claire's back. Tristan's hands moved over Claire's quivering abdomen, reaching for the clasp of her shorts. Their eyes met again as Tristan slid Claire's shorts and underwear together over her hips until they dropped freely to the floor. The roughness of Tristan's jeans rubbed against Claire's oversensitized skin as she freed her feet from her discarded clothes. Reaching behind her, Claire longed to free them of the last barrier of clothing that separated them when Tristan caught her hand and led her into the bedroom.

Tristan bent slightly to turn down the bed, and Claire took full advantage of the vulnerable position by grabbing Tristan around the waist with one arm and unzipping her jeans with her free hand.

She felt Tristan stiffen against her. "Is there any reason why these are still on?" she whispered against Tristan's ear. The word "no" had barely escaped Tristan's lips when Claire tugged the last of Tristan's clothes from around her feet.

Grinning shyly, Tristan tugged Claire to her feet before lowering her body to the bed and lying on top of her. Both shuddered and groaned when their bare bodies pressed together for the first time. Unable to resist the urge to pull Tristan closer, Claire wrapped her legs around Tristan's as Tristan slowly ground herself against the part of Claire's body that craved her the most.

As Tristan nibbled Claire's bottom lip, she felt Claire's body become tense beneath hers, and her erratic breathing made her acutely aware that Claire was close to going over the edge. Tristan pulled back as Claire whimpered, wanting the first time the blonde came for her to be put off as long as her partner could stand.

Kissing her way down Claire's heaving chest, Tristan took her lover's right nipple into her mouth and sucked gently as Claire writhed beneath her. Clasping Claire's hands against her sides, Tristan held her in place as she made Claire nearly crazy by softly teasing both breasts mercilessly. Releasing her grip, Tristan kissed and nibbled her way down Claire's stomach, slick with sweat, enjoying how the muscles quivered under her mouth and the salty taste of her skin.

Nestling between Claire's legs, Tristan ignored the blonde's pleas as she took her time reveling in the taste that was uniquely Claire. Wrapping her arms around the thighs that trembled against her face, Tristan relented and brushed her tongue over the place she knew would give Claire the release she was desperate for.

Claire was near the point of physical exhaustion, and every muscle in her body strained with tension. She had no control over the way her back arched off the bed. When Tristan's roaming tongue concentrated on her clit, she was powerless to contain the scream that came from deep within her as her orgasm claimed her.

Tristan realized as she kissed and caressed Claire's body that this was the first time she could consider sex making love. She was startled when she realized that this woman had already won her heart. With each kiss and caress, she was determined to make Claire feel what she could not bring herself to say yet.

Climbing up to lie upon Claire's limp body, Tristan positioned herself between Claire's legs, ignoring her weak protests as she slowly ground herself against Claire's wetness until she felt Claire respond by wrapping her trembling legs around hers. "Come again for me, Claire, I know you can," Tristan whispered seductively in her ear as Claire's body tensed beneath her, and another orgasm built within.

As Claire lay with her head on Tristan's shoulder regaining her strength, Tristan nuzzled her hair, enjoying the scent of it. "It's a good thing you're in such good physical shape because I am far from finished with you," Tristan whispered with a grin.

"Are you trying to kill me? I'm not sure I'm going to survive making love with you, Tristan," Claire said as she sat up to drink the water that her lover had fetched for her.

"I want our first time to be memorable for you," Tristan said with a chuckle as she stroked Claire's nipple, causing her to nearly spill the water she was thirstily gulping.

"You have to allow me to conserve some energy, sweetie. There's so much I still want to do to you," Claire said as she set the empty glass on the bedside table.

"There is something you can do for me right now," Tristan said smugly as Claire's brow raised in question.

"Straddle my hips," Tristan said with a wicked grin.

Claire eagerly complied, looking forward to having the taste of Tristan's skin in her mouth. As Claire bent down eagerly to devour the body beneath her, Tristan put a hand in the middle of her chest and pushed her upright. "That's not what I have in mind, baby," she said, slipping her hand between Claire's legs. The blonde moaned at her touch.

Slave to her desires, Claire gave in to Tristan, and her eyes fluttered shut as her lover filled her. Claire gasped when Tristan filled her completely. "You feel so good, Tris," she said breathlessly as her body welcomed the intrusion.

"Move with me, Claire. Slowly. I want to see your face." Allowing Claire to set the pace, Tristan moved her fingers in time with her hips. She intently watched Claire's expressions, illuminated by candlelight, which so easily mirrored the ecstasy she felt inside. Claire opened her eyes and stared into Tristan's. It was at that moment that Tristan felt Claire contract around her fingers. When Claire closed her eyes again, Tristan watched as her pleasure overtook her.

Claire lay on top of Tristan for a while, recovering from another powerful orgasm. It felt so perfect being with her like this. She knew at that moment that she did not want to ever be apart from this woman with whom she felt so connected.

Once her strength returned, Claire kissed Tristan, teasing her by letting her tongue graze her bottom lip but not slipping it into her mouth. She sucked Tristan's lip as she ran her fingertips over her swollen nipples. Tristan moaned and bucked against her, and Claire wasted no time. She slipped down and drew Tristan's right nipple into her mouth. She sucked and teased until she had Tristan panting and clutching the sheets.

Tightening her legs around Claire's, Tristan tried to prevent her from moving any farther down her body. "You can't control me, Tris. I can kiss and nibble wherever I please," Claire said playfully as she demonstrated by moving to the left nipple and treating it with the same care with which she had lavished the other one. Feeling Tristan trembling under her touch, Claire began her descent down Tristan's body again when Tristan clamped her legs tighter around her, preventing her from moving.

"Tris, let me go." Sympathizing with her lover's nervousness, Claire kissed the skin just beneath her. "I have been dreaming of this since we met. I want to taste you."

Tristan slowly relaxed her legs, letting Claire slide lower down her body. Claire had no intention of delaying one of the things she wanted most. She nestled her shoulders between Tristan's thighs and tasted for the first time the woman who had stolen her heart. Tristan gasped at the touch, making Claire desire her more. She circled the sensitive clit slowly, enjoying the way it made Tristan's hips move. Claire wanted to be inside Tristan when she brought her to the same heights of ecstasy. She slid a finger inside and met resistance. Claire froze.

Tristan's voice was tempered with emotion. "Claire, please don't stop. I want it to be you."

Unprepared for the revelation, Claire took a moment to recover from the surprise. She continued to stroke Tristan with her tongue, distracting her from the discomfort she knew was to come. She slid a second finger into Tristan's opening, testing the membrane with her fingers. As the pace of Tristan's hips became more insistent, she buried her fingers deep inside, tearing through the soft barrier, causing Tristan to cry out in pain and surprise. Claire did not stop her movements, and soon, Tristan matched her pace again.

Unaccustomed to the things Claire was making her feel, Tristan was lost in the sensation of it all. Claire's insistent tongue swirled over her, making her body convulse uncontrollably. The pain she initially felt when Claire entered her was now replaced with a feeling of ecstasy she could hardly fathom. Helpless to stop the tidal wave of pleasure that Claire was drawing from her, she succumbed to the most intense orgasm she had ever experienced, leaving her emotionally and physically exhausted.

Only when Tristan's body went limp did Claire pull away from her. Moving up to lie next to Tristan, Claire could see the tears glistening on her lover's cheeks. She pulled her into her arms, and with so many questions unanswered, she reluctantly gave in to her own exhaustion, and sleep overtook her.

Tristan however, lay awake watching the candlelight fading into the darkness. She'd allowed Claire to touch her in a way that no one had been allowed to before, and myriad emotions flooded her. She accepted that she was in love with the woman who lay sleeping in her arms, and with that, she felt so vulnerable and fearful that she may one day lose what had become so precious to her.

During their first night together at Tristan's place, Claire got a taste of what it would be like to be in Tristan's shoes when the phone rang at 3 a.m. She felt Tristan pull away from her as she reached for the phone. "Hello?" Tristan answered groggily.

"How bad is he?" Claire heard Tristan ask in the darkness. "What hospital is he being taken to? Notify his port manager, and let me know what the hospital says after they look him over. Thank you for the notification." Tristan dropped the cordless phone and groaned.

"Do you have to go out to the boat?" Claire asked, hoping that the answer would be no, as she snuggled up against Tristan.

"No, they are way up on the Ohio River. If he is admitted to the hospital, one of the port managers will go up."

"Good," Claire mumbled as she drifted off to sleep with her lover cocooned in her arms.

An hour later, the phone rang again. Tristan untangled herself from Claire and answered it. "What?" Tristan sat straight up in bed. "He knows better than that! We do not stop a boat to wait on a crew change!" She remained silent for a minute, and Claire figured the person on the other line was doing some serious explaining. "Tell him to get that boat back in gear, and the crew will catch up with them!" Tristan barked into the phone and hung up.

She lay back down, and Claire snuggled up next to her, trying to soothe her annoyed lover. "Is there anything I can help you with?" she asked as she ran her fingers through Tristan's hair.

Tristan sighed. "I shouldn't let them get me so angry. They just pull the most moronic stunts sometimes, and I get so aggravated. I'm sorry I woke you up. I can go sleep in the living room if you want."

Claire tightened her hold. "Not a chance, Tris. The calls aren't bothering me enough to let you out of this bed."

Blissful sleep claimed them once again, but just before sunrise, the phone rang for a third time. "Hello!" Tristan barked into the phone. "Yes, I remember. The guy with the chest pains, right?" She sat quietly for a moment, listening to the report. "So, you're telling me it was gas, and he was not having a heart attack, he just had to belch or something?" Tristan paused a moment before speaking again. "Chad, I'm sorry. I didn't mean to blow up on you. I know you're just the messenger."

Claire rolled over and buried her face in the pillow and laughed until she cried. She never got to hear the rest of the conversation and was still laughing when Tristan lay back down. "You can stop that laughing, you little brat," Tristan snickered.

CHAPTER SEVEN

Tristan woke up and untangled herself from Claire and spent a long time admiring her sleeping lover before getting out of bed. She pulled on a pair of shorts and a T-shirt before making her way to the kitchen to feed her tiny tiger and start the coffeepot. For a fleeting instant, Tristan felt the familiar fear and apprehension well up inside her. Pausing for a moment, she leaned against the wall, fighting the nausea that accompanied her panic. The compulsion to run nearly overwhelmed her, and she silently questioned her decision to allow Claire to stay.

Glancing down at the orange tabby awaiting his breakfast, Tristan realized how foolish it would be to flee her own home. For the first time she could ever remember, she put someone else's feelings before hers, knowing it would devastate Claire to be left alone again. "Not this time," she whispered to the cat. The fear receded after her admission, making her believe that she had won a pivotal battle in the war against herself.

Lost in thought, she sat down at the kitchen table, ignoring the cat's demands to be fed immediately. Wincing as she rubbed the back of her neck, her entire body ached from the previous night. She had taxed muscles she didn't even know she had. One part of her body in particular was sorer than the rest.

In all the dalliances she had enjoyed, she had never allowed anyone to touch her there. Feelings of fear and vulnerability kept her from giving that part of herself to anyone. Claire had obviously been shocked to discover her secret, that much had been evident on her face in the pale light. Yet, she was gentle and introduced Tristan to feelings that she had craved for so long. A grin made its way across Tristan's face at the memory.

Ralph had grown impatient with her silent reverie and slapped at his empty bowl, breaking her from her thoughts.

Relieved to see that the power had come back on during the night, Tristan sleepily started the coffee brewing and filled Ralph's bowl of food. "I shouldn't even feed you after that stunt you pulled last night." She thrust her foot out at the cat dining on his morning meal. "Look what you did to me! I should wring your fuzzy little neck. If you weren't so cute, things would be much different around here!"

Her tirade was interrupted by a knock on the door. Tristan's heart sank into her stomach. With everything going on the night before, she had forgotten about her ritual Sunday morning breakfast date. She opened the door to Cameron Hughes and his wife, Lucy.

She hugged them both as they entered. They exchanged glances as they appraised Tristan's lack of apparel. "Why aren't you dressed yet, Tris?" Lucy asked.

Tristan began to stammer. "Well, I, umm ..." At that moment, Claire stumbled into the kitchen, wearing Tristan's robe. Her eyes grew wide, and her mouth moved without making any sound. Tristan looked at Claire and the couple with a sheepish grin.

"I'm sorry, Cam and Lucy, I just forgot," Tristan said with a shrug.

Lucy seized upon the moment to make the girl she had come to accept as a daughter squirm. "Tris, honey, we've had the same date for the past three years. What on earth have you been up to that you would forget?"

Claire's face turned crimson; she dared not look Cameron in the eye. Tristan, overwhelmed with the situation, just began to laugh. Lucy held a straight face for as long as she could before falling into a fit of laughter of her own.

"You must be Claire," Lucy said as she took the embarrassed blonde into her arms. "Cam has told me a lot about you already, and I'm looking forward to getting to know you." Claire returned the warm embrace, stealing a glance over her shoulder at Tristan, who stood grinning.

Lucy made her way to the coffeepot. "Well, Cam, it looks like there will be four of us for breakfast this morning."

Claire began to object. "Oh, I don't want to intrude ..."

Before she could get another word out, Cameron spoke up. "Nonsense, Claire. We would love to have you. Matter of fact, we insist." Claire accepted the invitation as gracefully as she could under the circumstances, relieved that she had forsaken her earlier plan to walk into the room naked.

"Tristan, honey, go get in the shower, and let us have a cup of coffee with Claire," Lucy said as she grasped a very nervous-looking Claire by the hand and led her to the table.

"Oh, no! I'm not leaving her alone with you two!" Tristan objected. This in turn made Claire even more nervous.

"Do as I say, missy," Lucy said with mock indignation.

After she was sure Tristan was in the shower, Lucy spoke to Claire. "Sweetie, I know you are embarrassed, but don't be. Being your boss, Cam here cannot discuss this with you, but I sure can. We don't make our relationship with Tristan public knowledge. We don't want anyone at Valor to think she gets preferential treatment. She has earned her position with the company.

"Though she is not our flesh and blood, we consider her our baby, and we love her very much. We were at the hospital the day she was born. Her father, Mitchell, grew up with Cam, and when her father died, we became her adopted parents, in a manner of speaking. The reason I am telling you all this is because we do not want her hurt. She has never brought anyone to her home, so you must be extremely special to her. If she doesn't mean the same to you, please let her down gently and quickly."

Claire suddenly realized that even though Tristan was not Lucy's daughter, she had gotten her bluntness from Lucy. Claire looked Lucy in the eyes and chose her words carefully. "I feel exactly the same for Tris. I won't do anything to intentionally hurt her. I realize how this must look to you both, especially with me just starting with the company."

Lucy interrupted. "Darlin,' Cam and I met at Valor. No need to explain that to us. We just want to protect Tris from being hurt, even if it is not our place."

At this, Cam interrupted. "I'm sure we seem overprotective. After all, she is a grown woman, but she's had a very rough life." Cam hesitated and looked at Lucy, searching for the right words. They both looked down the hall to make sure the coast was clear.

Murky Waters

"What Cam is trying to say is that Tris had a very tumultuous relationship with her mother. That woman has beaten her down all her life. She has told Tristan from the time she was a baby that no one would ever want her. Tristan is just now starting to get a sense of self-worth." Cam reached over to calm his wife, who was well on her way to a tirade. Lucy would never forgive Mallory for the abusive treatment of someone she held so dear.

"She told me that her relationship with her mother was terrible but has not gone into detail. I've been afraid to push her; I can tell the wounds go very deep," Claire said with concern. "I know she is doing her best to cope with what has been dealt to her, and I will be there for her as long as she will allow me."

Knowing that Tristan would be back soon, Lucy reached across the table and took Claire by the hand. "I believe you will be good for our girl. I didn't mean to pry, but she is very special. Thank you for putting up with us."

As if on cue, everyone at the table began talking about the weather when they heard Tristan coming down the hall. Tristan entered the kitchen with a suspicious look on her face. She got herself a cup of coffee and joined the group at the table.

Lucy focused her attention on Tristan. "What took you so long, baby? Did you have to shave both of those long legs twice?"

"As a matter of fact, just once," Tristan shot back with a grin.

"Did you ever tell Claire the story of the weekend you stayed with us and decided to shave your legs for the first time?" Lucy asked laughing.

"I cannot believe you are going to bring that up!" Tristan said as her cheeks blushed.

"Oh, Claire, it was so funny. Tris came to stay with us one weekend when she was around ten. Cam and I had no children, so we really didn't know how to childproof our house. Anyway, Tris was having her bath and decided to shave her legs. She grabbed my razor and lathered up. Poor baby was covered with so many cuts she could barely rinse her legs, but that wasn't good enough. She decided her arms needed to be done, too. Not the armpits, mind you, but her forearms," Lucy said chuckling.

Tristan looked at Claire with a grin. "It was awful. The hair grew back thicker on my arms, and I looked like a woolly mammoth. I had to go through high school with arms that were hairier than most of the boys. Thank God for laser hair removal."

Cam joined in on the conversation. "Remember when you got on that pork and beans kick and that was all you wanted to eat?"

Tristan buried her face in her hands. "Don't listen to them, Claire, it's all lies," she said as Cam and Lucy teased her mercilessly.

"She came to the house one weekend, and all she wanted were the beans. Of course, we obliged her. They upset her little stomach so bad that the dog wouldn't even sit next to her!" Cam said as they all burst into a fit of laughter.

"Claire, if you have any feelings for me whatsoever, have mercy and go shower while I deal with these two," Tristan pleaded, refusing to look Claire's way.

Claire excused herself from the table and went to bathe. She was still chuckling as she made her way down the hall. Tristan narrowed her eyes and tried her best to glare at the two sitting across from her. "The first woman I ever bring home and you two have to tell her stories of how I farted on the dog." Cam and Lucy tried to apologize, but the chuckles belied their sincerity.

Tristan did her best to maintain her scowl, but a smile tugged at the corner of her mouth. "Try to behave yourselves at breakfast, and if you dare tell her the story of me getting my Easter dress caught in my stockings, I'll kill you both."

The group went to breakfast at a café a few miles from Tristan's place. The conversation was light, and Claire found herself enjoying the company of the older couple. She noticed that Tristan was at ease in their presence, and there was a sense of peace about her. Claire could tell that Tristan cared just as deeply for them as they did her.

Cam and Lucy could have very easily passed for Tristan's biological parents, especially Lucy with her dark hair and eyes. Claire wondered if Tristan would have been a different person had she been raised by such loving people. On the exterior, Tristan seemed self-confident, but Claire was quickly learning that Tristan bore many insecurities inside, no doubt caused by her upbringing.

A feeling of melancholy settled over Claire as she watched the three of them talking and laughing. At seventeen, she had lost her parents and only sister in a car accident, and times like these made her heart ache for them. Her grandmother had taken her in after the accident, and although she was warm and loving, she could not fill the void. With the passing of her grandmother shortly after she finished college, Claire had been on her own, with the exception of a few relationships.

She smiled as she remembered the day she told Tristan of her loss and how her brown eyes filled with tears of compassion. Watching her now with Cam and Lucy, Claire wondered if this would be her new family.

Tristan and Claire spent the remainder of the day basking in the sun on Tristan's deck. They lay sprawled out in the chaise lounges, each lost in her own thoughts, when Claire noticed that Tristan had dozed off. She looked at the woman lying next to her in silent wonder. Her skills in the bedroom were amazing, but how she had maintained her virginity was a mystery. Claire had been too exhausted to press the issue the night before, and now, curiosity got the better of her.

She stuck her hand into her water glass and sprinkled it across Tristan's stomach. The sleeping woman squirmed but didn't wake up. Claire's face lit up in an evil grin as she fished out an ice cube and carefully dropped it down the front of Tristan's baggy shorts. Seconds later, Tristan lurched forward and grabbed at her crotch.

"Whoa there, missy! No self-pleasuring in front of Ralph, you might warp his innocent mind," Claire teased as Tristan stood and tugged at the leg of her shorts until the ice fell onto the deck.

"After last night, I thought I was special, then you pull this," Tristan said, poking her bottom lip out.

"Aw, baby, you are special," Claire said mockingly. "Come sit down here, and I'll show you how much."

Tristan straddled Claire's chair and sat in the pit of her stomach. "Is this good?" she asked with a wicked grin as Claire's eyes bulged.

"You're heavier than you look, must be all those muscles," Claire croaked under her weight.

"I'm thinking there's a compliment in there somewhere," Tristan said as she folded her arms across her chest for a moment before having mercy on Claire and moving to sit beside her.

Claire ran her nails lightly over Tristan's back. "Yes, dear, take it as a compliment." Listening to Tristan's chuckle, Claire decided to take advantage of the moment and ask what she was dying to know. "Can I ask you something, sweetie?"

"Uh huh," Tristan responded as she scratched Ralph behind the ears while he lay in the shade of Claire's chair.

"Last night, when we ..." Claire paused, trying to choose her words carefully.

"I never let anyone touch me that way until now," Tristan answered softly, already knowing what Claire was trying to get at.

"I have never been comfortable with being that vulnerable with anyone, except you." She glanced nervously over her shoulder at Claire as Ralph took off at maximum speed in pursuit of a butterfly foolish enough to cross his deck.

Claire sat up and wrapped her arms around Tristan's shoulders. "That really means a lot to me, Tris. My feelings for you are so strong." Claire wanted to say more, but the words caught in her throat. She was afraid to spring her real feelings on Tristan too soon. Afraid to indulge in the conversation any further for fear of getting her heart broken, Tristan changed the subject. She ran off to refill their water glasses, and when she came back, the topic took a lighter turn.

Ralph would appear occasionally, bringing his pet presents, the first of which was a half-eaten grasshopper. Tristan fawned over him as though he had brought her a pot of gold. The ritual continued for most of the afternoon. Both women made a big deal of each dead bug he brought up until he brought his last gift — a small grass snake.

It took Tristan a while to coax Claire down from her precarious perch on top of the patio table. "Look, Claire, it's dead, I promise. Besides, it was only a grass snake. As disgusting as it is, it's not poisonous." Tristan could not help but laugh at the situation, which perturbed Claire even more. To top it all off, Ralph was pissed off that he had not gotten the praise he had become accustomed to when he brought his gifts.

"What in the hell is wrong with that cat? I mean, is he crazy? Why on earth would he bring a damn snake up here?" Claire hissed through clenched teeth.

Tristan chuckled despite herself. "We've been out here long enough anyway. Your skin is starting to get a little red." She held out her arms and assisted Claire down off the table. They went inside to cool off, leaving a bewildered cat in their wake.

After Claire had a few sips of iced tea, she began to calm down a bit. "Tristan, I'm sorry I got so upset out there. I cannot stand a snake." She shook in disgust. "My nerves have been a little on edge lately with the new job and all; I guess I just flew off the handle. Although I have to admit, if he ever does that again, I will jump on top of the closest thing I can find, which might just be you."

Tristan looked at her thoughtfully. "Sounds to me like you need a little break. I have to go up to St. Francisville tomorrow to meet one of the boats at the ferry landing to deliver some paperwork. We don't have crew change this week, and your department will be slow, except for a few reports that I am sure your agents can handle. Cam expects me to show you all aspects of our business, so you will have a broader understanding of what we do. We'll kill two birds with one stone. You can accompany me on the trip and visit another one of our boats. Then, we will be free for the afternoon.

"Aside from it being a quaint and historical little town, St. Francisville is home to one of the most notoriously haunted plantation homes. We could have lunch there and take a tour of the place. I hear it's really very spooky. So what do ya say? Want to see some ghosts?"

"As long as you don't plan on spending the night in any haunted house, it sounds great to me. Umm, do I have to wear those steel-toed boots? If so, I don't see us walking very far. The last time you made me wear those things, my calves ached for a week, and I had to get a pedicure to fix the damage to my toenails."

The next morning, they climbed into Tristan's work truck and headed north to St. Francisville. After they were out of Baton Rouge, Claire paid more attention to the landscape. It was similar to Texas with all the pine trees that lined Highway 61. Just before they got into the city limits of St. Francisville, she noticed that the land became a little hillier. Old live oak trees lined the roadside. It seemed as though they were in a different world entirely.

Being with Tristan made her fears of the stalker fade into the background, but occasionally, those thoughts would break through the joyous haze she had been wrapped up in and smack her in the face. Often when they were in public places, she would feel the hair rise up on her neck, as though someone was watching her every move. The panic would rise in her until she would find Tristan in the crowd watching over her.

Lighting a cigarette, she inhaled the smoke, waiting for it to calm her nerves. So far, she had not received any more unwanted envelopes. The appearance of the menacing packages had always been sporadic, and she was certain a new one would arrive soon.

She longed to confide in Tristan about the nightmare that had pursued her from Houston, but she was afraid of divulging her problem so early in their relationship. She was forced to admit to herself that she was simply in denial, hoping that one day it would all just go away, but each time she thought that happened, a new envelope would arrive.

Tristan broke Claire from her thoughts when she spoke. "Normally, the port managers do this kind of stuff, but I love taking short road trips. It gets me out of the office for a while and gives me a chance to just think about things and enjoy being outside."

Claire looked at her for a moment. "What kind of things do you think about when you make these trips?"

"I don't know, really. It's just nice to let my mind roam free for a while. I purposely don't think about anything concerning work until I get to where I'm going. It's kind of refreshing," Tristan said with a grin.

"Can I ask you something off the subject?" Claire glanced at her nervously.

"Sure. What's on your mind?"

"I know you told me that you wanted a relationship, but I am just curious about whether you intend to date anyone else or just me exclusively."

Tristan steered the truck down the steep ferry landing. Once she had the vehicle in park, she turned to look at Claire. "I want to be very honest with you."

Murky Waters

Claire felt her stomach tighten. She was afraid of the ominous tone in Tristan's voice. Up until that moment, she thought she and Tristan were on the same page. Now, she was not so sure.

"I've never really been in a serious relationship. I have dated a few girls but only for a short time. I've never really committed myself to anyone ... until now," Tristan said. "I hope you feel the same way about this, but I am not interested in seeing anyone else. For the first time in my life, I have found in you someone I'd like to share my life with."

Claire hugged Tristan and held her close for a moment. "I am so glad you feel that way. I was so afraid you were going to tell me that you still wanted to date other people. Once I find someone I really like, I have no desire to see anyone else, and I really like you. I grow fonder of you each minute I spend in your presence, and I would love to commit myself to you and this relationship."

Tristan drew back from Claire to kiss her, but just as their lips brushed together, a loud horn startled them both. The *Taylor Nichole* made its presence known. Tristan growled low in her throat at the captain for interrupting them.

Tristan made a call to the boat on her cell phone. She and the captain talked a moment and decided it would be unsafe for her and Claire to try getting out to the vessel since fog had settled over the water. Tristan didn't want to take a chance with Claire in the small launch boat called a skiff.

They both stood on the landing and watched as the craft was lowered into the water. The towboat itself was too large to come any closer to shore. Claire and Tristan walked to the water's edge to meet the deckhand who brought the tiny boat on shore. Tristan introduced Claire and gave him the needed paperwork. They watched the skiff make its way back to the boat before being hoisted onto the deck.

"Now, the day is ours." Tristan grinned and led Claire back to the truck. "It's still a little early for the first tour. Why don't we take a drive around town? Should you see anywhere you want to stop and look around, just let me know."

As they drove, Claire noticed a small graveyard next to an old church. It gave her the creeps the way it was surrounded by trees whose moss hung down over the old stone crypts. "Tristan, why do they have all those crypts above ground? It looks so creepy."

"When I was a little girl, my dad told me it was because of the water table. Most of the graveyards in New Orleans have aboveground crypts because the city itself is below sea level. Whenever there is a flood, the water table rises and pushes the soggy coffins up and out of the dirt. So, they just started to put them on top of the ground in crypts.

"This graveyard here was thought to be high enough above the water table. There is an old tale that one year we had real high waters on the Mississippi, and the water table rose high enough to push the coffins buried here out of the ground. According to the stories I have heard, the townsfolk did not take too well to seeing the long dead back above ground."

Claire shuddered. "Can you imagine waking up and seeing something like that, or worse, seeing it actually happen? It gives me the creeps just thinking about it. I can tell you right now, if I had seen something like that, I would have shit a kitten. Hell, maybe a whole litter!"

Tristan burst out laughing at Claire's colorful banter. Claire cast her a sideways glance. "What are you laughing at?"

"Shit a kitten? Sheesh, you Texans can come up with some stuff!" Tristan continued to laugh.

Claire looked at her mockingly. "Texans, huh? I learned the 'shitting a kitten' thingy from one of your crew coordinators, and I happen to know for a fact that he is a native of Louisiana."

They drove around admiring the town and bickering over which state was best. Neither really cared but enjoyed ribbing the other about what her state did and did not have. The playful banter came to a halt when they pulled through the iron gates of the Myrtles Plantation.

The day had become overcast and added to the eerie appeal of the Myrtles. Claire instantly began scanning the windows of the old house trying to catch a glimpse of ghostly activity. From just the brief history Tristan had given her on the ride up, she already had a good case of the creeps.

They decided to have lunch since the next tour would not start for an hour or so. Tristan refused to have wine with her meal, reminding Claire that she was a lightweight and would not be able to drive home. In addition, she wanted her mental faculties about her in case they encountered anything strange. They both settled on iced tea.

"Do you believe in ghosts, Tristan?" Claire asked with a smirk.

Tristan returned the smirk. "I've never seen a ghost myself, but I suppose that doesn't mean they don't exist. Frankly, I don't know what to make of all the things people have claimed to see. Maybe they want to see something so badly that their mind plays tricks on them." Tristan shrugged her shoulders.

"What would you do right now if you looked out that window and saw a ghost?" Claire widened her eyes, attempting to appear dramatic.

Tristan laughed. "I can assure you of two things if I saw a ghost right now. First, I would wet my pants. Second, I would run out of this place like I was on fire, and may God help the person who got between me and my car. You better hope that if that happens I have the presence of mind to grab you and take you with me!"

Claire roared with laughter, so much so that the other patrons turned to look at her. Tristan gave them her most charming smile and shrugged her shoulders as if to say she didn't know what Claire's problem was. Claire was still chuckling when their lunch was brought to the table. The waitress gave her an awkward glance before departing.

Tristan had gotten a case of the giggles, as well. She did her best to control herself and asked Claire if she could compose herself long enough to eat. "Claire, are you going to be all right? You still have tears in your eyes."

Claire choked a couple of times before she could speak. "I'm sorry, but I just had a mental picture of you running out of here with wet pants and waving your arms like a mad woman. I bet you my next paycheck they would put that in their brochure!" The couple giggled all through lunch with no regard for the amused glances thrown their way.

After lunch, they stepped outside with a few others to smoke. They listened as some of the tourists talked excitedly about hopefully catching a glimpse of one of the famous ghosts known to haunt the house. Claire found herself drawn into the conversation and had learned all about Chloe, the slave who was hanged there for poisoning two children and the wife of the master of the house. Someone in the crowd mentioned that she had heard the poison was made from oleander leaves from a popular flowering plant found in yards everywhere.

The tour guide joined the group and called their attention to the house. "The Myrtles Plantation was built in 1796 by General David Bradford and carries the dubious distinction of being one of the most haunted plantation homes in America. According to legend, the house is built on an ancient Indian burial ground. No less than ten murders have been committed here."

The guide drew their attention to the intricate ironwork that surrounded the veranda. Claire poked Tristan in the ribs, causing her to jump. She giggled as Tristan spun around to glare at her. Claire raised both hands in the air. "I didn't do it. Are your pants still dry?" The antics started a whole new round of giggles from both of them, despite the glances they received from the rest of the group.

Tristan paid more attention to the beautiful old live oaks and the grounds, while Claire looked up at each window hoping to get a glimpse of something or someone peering back. Occasionally, they would glance at one another and wink as the guide told stories of ghostly children wandering and playing on the grounds.

As they entered the foyer, Claire and the rest of the group admired the three hundred fifty-pound Baccarat crystal chandelier that graced the entrance. "Oh, Tristan, look how beautiful."

Tristan yawned. "What's the big deal? It's just like the one in our dining room," Tristan said a little louder than she intended. The entire group turned around and looked at her, including Claire.

Tristan shrugged. "Wow, tough room. It was a joke, people." She and Claire burst into another fit of laughter. They decided to hang back from the group since they were having such a hard time behaving.

Pamphlet in hand, they decided to conduct their own tour. "Tris, it says here that this grand piano plays by itself in the night until someone comes into the room. The ghost apparently plays the same chord over and over. Wouldn't that just piss you off at some point? I wonder if you requested something by Elton John if it would give it a whirl."

Their next point of interest was a portrait of a man that had been said to change facial expressions and his eyes would follow a person around the room. Both women stared at the portrait intently, waiting for something to happen.

"I think he is kind of smiling," Tristan declared after a moment of intense study.

"You do? I think he looks a little sad. I dare you to fart and see if his nose twitches," Claire said as she studied the portrait while walking backwards to see if the eyes moved.

Tristan scratched her head. "How old are we again?" They both acknowledged that their humor was crass and juvenile, which made them laugh all the more.

They meandered through the home, admiring and commenting on various antique pieces. Both were equally impressed with the plaster ceiling medallions, none of which were the same. Claire admired the antique furniture found in each of the rooms. Antiques did not impress Tristan, but she followed the blonde dutifully as she roamed from room to room of the beautifully decorated old house.

Claire frowned. "I wish we brought a camera with us. We might have captured a ghost on film."

"I'm not much for taking pictures. I always seem to forget to bring a camera with me, and when I do remember, I get so into what I'm looking at that I forget to use it. Matter of fact, I don't even own a camera anymore," Tristan said ruefully.

The ghostly aura was accentuated by moss-laden live oaks that swayed on the breeze, casting shadows. Tristan walked about the grounds, commenting on different plants and trees. Claire walked beside her, but her eyes were drawn to the house. She had hoped to see something unexplainable but had been disappointed thus far. She was staring up into the windows when she caught her foot on a tree root protruding from the ground. She stumbled forward and nearly fell to the ground before Tristan caught and steadied her.

In all the confusion, they didn't notice the man dressed in clothes that appeared to be from the 1800s approaching them. "Careful, Miss" were the only words he spoke. He smiled and walked past them toward the house.

When he was out of sight, Tristan pulled Claire close and kissed her. "I have been waiting to do that all day."

Claire gave Tristan one of her most seductive looks. "Don't do that again unless you want to be rolling around in the shrubs."

"As tempting as that may sound, I cannot do it with ghosts watching. I'm sure I'll have performance anxiety. Besides, I am willing to wait for a nice big soft bed ... or the kitchen table. I'm not that particular," Tristan said, wiggling her brows suggestively.

"Well then, we need to be going!" Claire grabbed Tristan by the arm and nearly dragged her to the parking lot. As they drove down the driveway back to Highway 61, they noticed the same man who had spoken to them earlier. He waved as they passed, then seemed to vanish into the mist. Claire was not sure if she was seeing things or not. She stared at the spot where he had been as Tristan drove down the drive.

"Did you see that?" Claire exclaimed.

Tristan slowed to a stop. "See what? Did I run over a squirrel or something?"

Claire stared out the window confused. "I thought I saw that guy we passed earlier. He was standing right over there, then he just disappeared."

"Funny, Claire, real funny." They drove on, and Claire tried to no avail to convince Tristan that she really did see the man disappear.

The old groundskeeper laughed hysterically at Claire's facial expression. He had been scaring the hell out of people for years pulling that stunt. He always looked forward to the fog rolling in late in the afternoon. The look on Claire's face would have him laughing well into the night.

As they left the city limits of St. Francisville, Claire drifted off to sleep, leaving Tristan alone with her thoughts. Tristan glanced over at the slumbering blonde and wondered what it was about this woman that captured her so. She conjured feelings in Tristan that she thought were impossible for her to have. Not only did Tristan physically desire Claire, but she also hungered just to be in her presence. It occurred to her that she actually craved her company, something she had never experienced before.

Love is fleeting played through Tristan's mind. It was a dangerous thing giving this woman her heart, and what if she broke it? She was torn between the feelings of elation and fear. If one day Claire rejected her, Tristan wondered if she would be able to recover from such a blow.

Murky Waters

Tristan lit up a cigarette and rolled down the window a bit to ventilate the truck. She glanced quickly at Claire, hoping that she had not woken her. Confirming that Claire was still asleep, Tristan stole another glance at her and silently mused to herself. "What have you done to me, Claire? I don't know if I should do this. You're the only woman I have ever met who has made me feel like a real person, someone who could be loved."

CHAPTER EIGHT

After a quick stop at Claire's place to pick up some clothes, they arrived at Tristan's house just before dark. Tristan was pleased that Claire enthusiastically agreed to stay with her another night. They ordered a pizza for dinner and relaxed in front of the TV for the better part of the evening. Ralph decided to be cordial for a change and curled up in the pit of Claire's stomach. All three of them spent the evening as couch potatoes.

Tristan internally questioned her sanity when she had asked Claire to stay with her again. The question flew out of her mouth before she had given any thought to it. She felt as though she had reached a milestone. The old fear that she had suppressed was still lurking deep below the surface, and she wondered how long she would be able to keep it at bay.

The following day, Tristan walked into Claire's office midmorning. "Claire, I have somewhere I have to be around lunchtime. Would you like me to pick something up for you?" Claire thought Tristan's behavior a little odd when she didn't elaborate on where she was going. Since Claire had been at Valor, they always had gone to lunch together.

Claire smiled. "No, don't go to any trouble. I'll order a sandwich or something; I'm not really that hungry."

Tristan nodded. "I'll be back soon. Call me on my cell phone if you change your mind."

Tristan knocked at the door of the two-story brick home of Cameron and Lucy Hughes. She didn't wait long before Lucy opened the door and invited her in. Walking into the spacious gourmet kitchen, she could smell the aroma of Lucy's famous chicken spaghetti. Tristan grinned. Lucy always cooked her favorites when she came to visit.

"Sit down, sweetie. I have already made a plate for you. Your iced tea is coming up," Lucy said as she filled the glass with ice.

The conversation was light as they ate. As usual, Tristan complimented Lucy on her culinary skills, at which Lucy would scoff and laugh. Tristan told her all about the trip to the Myrtles, and Lucy thought she recognized a gleam in Tristan's eyes that wasn't there before.

After lunch, Lucy refilled their tea glasses and invited Tristan out to the patio because she knew Tristan liked to smoke after she ate. Lucy also had a feeling that something was up with her adopted daughter because Lucy was always the one to invite Tristan over. This time, Tristan had called her.

Tristan sat down at the wrought iron patio table and lit her cigarette. Lucy sat across from her, waiting for Tristan to open up and say what was on her mind. Tristan made small talk about the weather, toying with the cigarette in her hand. Lucy couldn't stand the suspense any longer.

"Tristan, baby, what is going on in that head of yours? I know you like my cooking, but there is something on your mind, and to be honest, I will reach over this table and choke you if you don't tell me what it is right now."

Tristan was quiet for a few minutes. She stared at the table, hoping to find a way to express what she was feeling. "Lucy, I am so afraid of what is happening between me and Claire. I've never met anyone like her. Unlike so many I have dated, she makes me feel like she really cares for me. I'm so afraid she will wake up one morning and decide she doesn't want to be with me, and I don't think my heart can take it. I'm to the point that I want to break things off with her out of fear that will happen." When she did look up at Lucy, Tristan's eyes were rimmed with tears threatening to spill over.

Lucy reached over and took Tristan's hand. "Baby, we all fear that going into a relationship. There are no certainties in life or love. I will tell you this, though. I think Claire really does care for you, and I think given a little time, that will develop into love."

Tristan fought against the lump in her throat. "Lucy ..." Tristan stammered a moment. "Why would she love me? Why would a woman like that want to stay with me?"

"Baby, why on earth would you even think that? You have a lot to offer her. The problem is, you don't see that in yourself. I know your mother did a lot to undermine your self-confidence. As long as I live, I will never understand why she did that. Tristan, you are a beautiful woman inside and out." Lucy's eyes welled with tears as she spoke; her heart broke because of the pain radiating off the woman sitting before her.

Tristan broke into sobs. "You and Cam have always been so supportive and loving. You've both told me that all these years, but it is so hard for me to believe."

Lucy got up and went to Tristan's side of the table. She took her into her arms and held her until the tears subsided. "Tristan, listen to me, honey. There is no way to sugarcoat this; I have to say it plainly. Your mother is a mean-spirited woman. Frankly, I think she hated herself; therefore, she couldn't really love anyone else.

"Tristan, Cam and I couldn't love you more if you were our own flesh and blood. We used to lie awake at night trying to figure out a way to keep you with us. That's why we came and got you for the weekend so often. We were so afraid of hurting Mitchell because he loved you with all his heart, but we always dreamed of taking you and running away."

Tristan looked at Lucy incredulously for a moment. "I honestly had no idea you and Cam felt that way. Don't get me wrong, I knew you loved me, but I always thought it was because of your loyalty to my dad. I don't mean any disrespect by that, but I know how close you were with him."

Lucy pulled Tristan back into her arms. "Baby, we spent time with you because we loved you as though you were our daughter and still do. I still have all your pictures throughout your school years, and when you graduated high school, we could not have been prouder. We love you, Tristan, just because you're you."

Tristan hugged Lucy back, finally accepting in her heart that someone aside from her dad truly loved her. The tears began anew.

Murky Waters

Lucy chose her words carefully. "Tris, honey, you have kept a lot bottled inside. I have never pushed you to talk about your mother, but I think it's time you let it all out. I know you have harbored a lot of guilt and pain, and unless you let it go, it will continue to affect you all your life. If it is not dealt with, it could very well cause you problems in your relationship with Claire."

Tristan held on to Lucy a little longer before she spoke. "If I'm going to talk about this, I will need to smoke. It makes me a nervous wreck."

Lucy returned to her seat but pulled it closer to Tristan. She waited patiently for Tristan to calm herself enough to speak. Lucy looked at the woman across from her and felt her stomach tie in knots. Deep in her heart, she dreaded what she was about to hear. Lucy silently wished Cam had been there for both of them.

Tristan lit a cigarette and sipped her tea. "I have no pleasant memories of my mom. I used to cry in my room when Dad left to go out on work trips; I hated to be alone with her. When he was away from home, I stayed in my room or outside for as long as I could.

"When she would call me into dinner, I would run in and wash my hands and face. Then, I would sit at the table praying that I would not spill or drop anything. One time, I accidentally knocked over my milk. She slapped me hard enough across the face to knock me out of my chair. She didn't hit me very often, but when she did, it made a lasting impression on my memory, as well as my skin. Her words, however, were more painful than any slaps she could deliver."

Lucy did not want to start crying again, but the far-off look and pained expression in Tristan's eyes broke her heart into pieces. She watched Tristan's hands shake as she lifted her cigarette. Lucy could not fathom how traumatic it must have been for a small child to endure so much. She swallowed the lump in her throat as Tristan went on.

"I was such a tomboy. I loved climbing trees and building clubhouses. She would usually find me with a group of friends, and she would make a spectacle out of me. She would ridicule and berate me in front of all those kids and drag me in the house. I was so humiliated that I stopped seeking out other kids to play with.

"Whenever we went somewhere, she would complain the whole time that I looked like an orphan, even though she chose the clothes I wore. I was told every day of my life that I would never amount to anything, and if she ever had the chance to do it over again, she would have never had me."

Lucy knew that she needed to let Tristan unload the horrible things that had burdened her throughout her life, but hearing it was tearing her up inside. More than once, she had to remind herself to be calm in front of Tristan, but what she really desired was to get a piece of Mallory Delacroix.

"When I was in my teens and my body began to fill out, she was especially harsh," Tristan continued. "We went to the home of a friend of hers. She had a son my age, and he invited me to shoot pool with him in the game room. During our game, he came on to me. I didn't entertain his advances; there was nothing appealing about him at all. I suppose he got tired of being put off, when he pushed me against the table and started pawing at me.

"Of course, my mom and her snooty friend came into the room at that moment. His mother told us that he had pulled that stunt before with another girl. She apologized profusely for his behavior and assured my mother that he would be dealt with.

"When we got into the car, my mother demanded to know what I had done to provoke him. She never gave me the benefit of the doubt. She was certain that I had enticed him, even after his mother told her that he had done the same thing to someone else. She told me she would not have a slut living under her roof.

"I could go on for hours telling you what it was like to live with her. You know yourself she didn't even attend my high school graduation. To be honest, I am glad she didn't. That was one day I just didn't want to be humiliated."

Tristan felt true anger rise within her toward her mother for the first time in her life. "How can a child have self-esteem when her own mother hates her? The only thing that kept me from killing myself was knowing that it would bring her satisfaction."

"Oh, God, Tristan. I knew she was hard on you, but I had no idea. Honey, you have to believe if I had any idea it was that bad, I would have taken you, damn the consequences. How could Mitchell have let this go on?" Lucy asked in tears.

Murky Waters

"Dad knew she was rough on me, but she saved most of her hatefulness for the times he was on the road with work. She behaved herself when he was home, but she released her fury on me when he left. The times she did haul off and hit me, she made sure I kept the marks covered. I was just too afraid to tell Dad because of what she might do to me when he went on his next trip."

This time, it was Lucy who needed comforting. Tristan gathered her in her arms and held her until they both stopped crying. They spent the better part of the afternoon together, and Tristan continued to pour her heart out. Instead of feeling vulnerable and weak, she felt like a new woman. Someone she trusted was there for her and supported her.

CHAPTER NINE

The afternoon had gotten away from Tristan and Lucy. Tristan realized that Cam would be home soon. There was no way she could hide the fact that she had been crying, and she didn't want him to see her that way. Lucy assured her that she would not tell Cam what they had discussed until Tristan was ready for him to know.

Lucy hugged and kissed Tristan before she left. "Sweetie, as long as I live, I will be here for you, and so will Cam. We love you very much. In my eyes, you are my daughter, and nothing will ever change that." Tristan smiled and kissed Lucy goodbye and left before she started crying again.

When Tristan arrived home, Claire pulled in behind her. Tristan was still collecting her things when Claire walked up to the truck. "I was wondering if you would like to have dinner with me tonight." Her voice trailed off when she got a look at Tristan's face.

"Oh, God, Tristan, what has happened? Are you okay?" Claire asked as she pulled Tristan into her arms. Tristan made no attempt to explain. She welcomed Claire's embrace and allowed herself to be held. Claire took the keys from Tristan and opened the door. She led Tristan into the house where she took her into her arms again. "Tristan, are you all right, baby?"

"I know I look like crap, but I really am all right. I spent the afternoon with Lucy. We discussed some things about my childhood, and it really upset me, but I feel better now that I got it off my chest. Please forgive me, but I am not emotionally up to rehashing any of it right now."

"That's okay, I understand. Would you prefer to be alone tonight, or would you like some company other than Ralph?" Claire asked with a smile.

"I would love it if you stayed with me again. I don't feel very much like going out, though. You mind if I cook for us instead?" Tristan said.

"I have to run home and get some more clothes for tomorrow. While I'm out, I'll pick up dinner. You will open a bottle of wine and go soak in the bath until I get back. It will relax you, I promise. If I return to find you still in these clothes, there's gonna be trouble, missy!"

Tristan smiled and kissed Claire. "Yes, ma'am! I only have one request." Claire raised a brow inquisitively. "I would like Chinese. Either cashew chicken or sesame kitten with fried rice," Tristan said as she made her way to the bathroom.

Claire laughed. "You better hope Ralph didn't hear that kitten comment, or you may be missing some more skin tonight."

Tristan splashed her tear-stained face with the water from her bath. What she really wanted was a shower but opted for a soak in the tub. Claire was right, it had soothed her nerves.

Tristan lay back in the tub, letting the hot water surround her and remembering her conversation with Lucy regarding Claire. As much as Tristan wanted to guard her heart, she realized Claire already owned it, and it wouldn't matter if Claire walked away today or ten years from now, it would still hurt the same. She had toyed with their relationship, thinking she could enjoy Claire and not allow herself to lose her heart.

She had really only considered her feelings until then, but the look in Claire's eyes that night had spoken volumes. It would kill her to break Claire's heart. And with that in mind, she resolved herself to hanging on to Claire as long as she could. All plans to run away went down the drain with her bath water.

When Claire returned, she fixed their plates and had them on the living room coffee table when Tristan emerged from her bath. Claire opened a bottle of white wine, hoping that the drink would relax Tristan. She was determined to comfort her obviously emotionally drained lover.

Tristan took a few bites of her dinner before speaking. "What did I miss at work this afternoon?" "Nothing at all, really. It was very uneventful. I spent most of the day renewing hotel accounts to assure that Valor would get the best rates. The crew coordinators seemed to be having a quiet day, as well. They only requested two rental cars for some crew swaps, and that was it. The afternoon was really boring. I think I would have enjoyed the downtime, but Mike set up camp in my office the latter part of the day."

Tristan glanced up from her plate. She didn't like the way Mike stared at Claire, and she felt her hackles rise at the mention of his name. "So, what did he want? Was he hitting you up for a raise already?"

"He was hitting on me, all right, but it was not for a raise. He asked me out, even though I told him a while back that I was not interested and would not date an employee. It's like he forgot all about the conversation."

Tristan set down her fork and looked at Claire. "I can't believe he did that. He must have a brass set of balls to ask you out after you've made yourself clear. You did make it clear, didn't you, Claire?"

Now, Claire felt *her* hackles rising; she didn't like what Tristan was implying. "I can assure you that I made it explicitly clear. I reaffirmed that with him today."

Even though Tristan knew Claire had no interest in Mike, it made her stomach turn. She was unaccustomed to the intense feelings of jealously it caused. She didn't like the idea of someone trying to compete for Claire's affections.

Tristan changed the subject, not wanting to discuss the topic any longer. "I have to do some work on the travel budget tomorrow. I was supposed to have done it today. I will need you to run some reports for me first thing tomorrow morning, so I can get a look at the numbers and make sure we are still on track."

Claire welcomed the change in conversation; her anger was too close to the surface. She was more than capable of handling her staff. "I'll have them on your desk first thing. If it's slow for me tomorrow, I will be happy to assist you. Maybe we could split the boats in half and work the numbers that way."

For the remainder of the evening, they sat quietly in front of the TV. Tristan laid her head in Claire's lap, and Claire ran her fingers through the dark locks, soothing her partner. As the evening passed so did Claire's anger.

With the wine and Claire's attentions, Tristan relaxed and drifted off to sleep. Claire woke her after a while, and they went to bed. Claire lay for a long time with Tristan in her arms, regretting her anger earlier in the evening. Tonight was not the night to discuss the problems she was having with Mike.

Tristan pulled away from her and sat up in bed, startling Claire, who thought she was asleep. "I made you mad earlier tonight, didn't I?" Tristan asked softly.

"Yes, you did, but I understand your concern. Just give me some time to deal with him in my own way. I need to prove to Suarez and myself that I can handle this position. If I can get it through Mike's thick head that I'm not interested, maybe I can salvage a decent agent."

"I don't have any doubt in your abilities, Claire, and if it means anything, I am truly impressed with what you've done with that department. He just gets under my skin," Tristan said as she lay back down and stared at the ceiling as the feelings of anger and jealously crept back.

Both lay in silence for a while until Claire rolled onto her side and stroked Tristan's hair out of her eyes. "Tonight is not the night to worry about Mike and his antics. You've obviously had one hell of a day, and I wanted to be a comfort, not bring you down further."

Tristan took Claire's hand into her own and kissed her palm. "You are always a comfort to me, Claire."

What was intended by Claire to be a tender good night kiss turned into something altogether different. The moment her lips brushed against Tristan's, a fire ignited inside her, and the flames quickly spread to Tristan.

Claire soon realized that one kiss was not going to satisfy her as her hands roamed over the body of her lover, who tried to roll over and take control. Claire broke from the kiss and looked into Tristan's eyes glistening in the darkness. "Tris, you've never been tied up, have you?"

"Of course not." The surprise was evident in Tristan's reply.

"Well, if you don't lie back and relax and let me do what I want, you will be tonight," Claire said with impish glee.

Claire reached over and switched on the bedside lamp, filling the room with a soft glow. She kissed Tristan until she was compliant to her touch. Hoping to make Tristan feel more at ease, Claire stripped off her own clothes before doing the same to her nervous lover. She lay back down fully on top of Tristan, who looked a little uncomfortable with being the one taken.

Covering Tristan's neck with kisses and soft bites, Claire was determined to make Tristan relax and enjoy what she had in store for her. She grinned, pleased with herself when she sucked Tristan's earlobe, making her whimper. "What do you want me to do to you, Tris?" she whispered seductively in her ear.

"You specifically told me to lie here and let you do what you wanted, and now you ask me what I want?" Tristan replied with a snort of laughter.

Beat at her own game, Claire could not help but laugh with her. "Okay then, roll over on your stomach," Claire whispered.

"Huh?" came the startled reply.

"Tris, I'm right next to your ear, so I know you heard me. Roll over." Claire shifted her weight, giving Tristan room to move. Tristan reluctantly obeyed.

"Just relax, I'm not going to take you anywhere you don't want to go." Claire murmured as she kissed a hot trail up Tristan's spine, making Tristan squirm under her touch. "Get up on your knees," she commanded softly and was pleased when Tristan complied.

Tristan's arousal was evident when Claire slipped one finger inside her and began to move in a rhythm that Tristan eagerly responded to. Claire slowed her pace and added a second finger, feeling Tristan shudder as she did. This time, she slowed her pace, teasing Tristan, who had forgotten all her inhibitions in the moment.

"Please, Claire," she pleaded as Claire continued to tease her. The desperation in her voice turned Claire inside out, and she quickly gave in to Tristan's desires. Only when Tristan sank down onto the bed did Claire stop. They both lay in an exhausted heap, gasping for air.

Murky Waters

"I'm so gonna walk funny tomorrow," Tristan said, her voice muffled by the pillow. That was the last thing Claire remembered before drifting off to sleep.

The next day at work, Tristan paid close attention to Mike. She felt the hair on her neck rise every time he found a reason to go into Claire's office. Claire was of course professional, but it grated on Tristan whenever Claire smiled at him. Tristan mentally assured herself that Claire was not entertaining Mike but simply doing her job.

Tristan spent the remainder of the workweek verifying that her department was still in line with the budget. Claire worked closely with her, going over the numbers and double-checking her figures. On Friday afternoon, they both breathed a sigh of relief when Tristan emailed her findings to accounting.

At lunch that afternoon, they decided they would spend the weekend at Tristan's place relaxing. Tristan promised to teach Claire how to fish in the lake behind her house. Both were looking forward to spending some alone time together, and Tristan's secluded property was the perfect place to do just that.

Claire wondered if Tristan would be ready to confide in her about her childhood. She knew that whatever it was had to be extremely painful for Tristan. Claire almost dreaded the conversation because she knew she would lose all emotional control if Tristan broke down, and she hoped that she could be the support Tristan needed.

Claire had toyed with the idea of telling Tristan about the stalker. No new envelopes had come recently, and she took it as a good sign. Maybe that chapter in her life was over, and there would be no need to trouble Tristan with it.

On Saturday morning, Tristan was up just after sunrise. Ralph was fed and the coffee was brewing when she woke Claire. "Tristan, why on earth are you up already? It's Saturday, for goodness sake!"

"The fish bite best in the morning. Your fishing lesson isn't going to be any fun if you don't get a bite. Now, get up." Tristan poked Claire in the ribs until she couldn't stand it any longer. Claire ran to the bathroom, fussing the whole time and refusing to come in contact with any bait.

After breakfast, they went down to the water's edge, dragging two lawn chairs behind them. Once they had picked a shady spot, Tristan prepared the rod and reels. She stuck her hand in the cricket can and found the perfect specimen for catching a bream, known as a perch by non-Cajuns.

"Eww, Tristan, do you have to put the hook through its back like that?" Claire thought the little insect was too gross to touch, but she felt bad about the way it was speared onto the hook.

Tristan stood up. "Now, watch me, Claire, it's all in the wrist." Tristan flicked her wrist and released the line. The orange bobber landed about ten feet out into the water. She handed the pole to Claire. "Watch the bobber. If it gets pulled under, pull back, then start reeling." Claire took the pole and kept her eyes locked on the float.

Tristan baited her line and cast it out, as well. She glanced over at Claire, who was admiring the pretty multicolored lures in the tackle box. Her float was nowhere in sight.

"Claire? Where is your float?" Tristan asked calmly.

Claire looked at the spot she last saw the bobber, and it was gone. "Oh!" she exclaimed. She jerked the rod back, nearly knocking herself out in the process, reeling as fast as she could until she saw the small fish breaking the water's surface.

"Okay, what do I do now?" she asked excitedly.

"Keep reeling him in. When he gets close to the bank, grab the line with your hand, set the reel down, and grab the fish by the bottom lip. Then, you can take the hook out of its mouth," Tristan said as though Claire had done this all her life.

Claire froze. "You want me to touch it?"

Tristan laughed. "Of course, girl, they don't bite. Just be mindful of the fins."

"Tristan Delacroix! I am so NOT touching that fish!" Claire exclaimed.

Tristan grumbled, "sissy," under her breath as she put her own rod down and helped Claire with her first catch. She grabbed Claire's line and guided the fish over to them. She gently put her thumb in the fish's mouth and took the hook out. She then held it up for Claire to see.

"That's close enough, Tristan. Don't touch me with that thing, or I will freak out on you," Claire warned as she backed up.

"Baby! You don't mind touching them when we eat them! Now, be a big girl and come get your fish," Tristan said jokingly.

"Are we going to eat him? He looks like he's just a baby," Claire said with sad eyes.

Tristan decided to quit tormenting the fish and Claire and tossed it back into the water. "No, my love, we will not eat him, he is way too small. Now, put a cricket on your hook and catch our dinner."

The slip of the tongue was not lost on Claire, and she wondered if Tristan were even aware of her words.

Claire glanced at her empty hook, then at the cricket can, then back at Tristan. "Tris, darling ..." She began with a sly smile. "You look so sexy when you bait my hook. How about you bend over again and get another cricket and put it on my hook as only you can?" She batted her eyes for an added bonus.

Tristan laughed at Claire's antics. "Oh, Claire, you are dealing with the wrong sex with that tactic. I'm not a man, so you can stop trying to stroke my ego."

"Fine then. I'll get my own cricket." Claire marched up to the can and thrust her hand in without a moment's hesitation. As she tried to catch the next victim, another used her arm as an escape route to freedom. Claire jumped up and flailed around like she was on fire, slinging the escapee into the grass.

Tristan made no attempt to disguise her laughter. Claire glared at her but began to laugh herself. Tristan baited Claire's hook for her for the rest of the morning. Between the two of them, they caught enough fish for a decent dinner. Tristan, of course, would be the unlucky person to clean the catch, knowing that Claire would not touch one much less gut it.

She pulled a small table over to the water's edge and began the messy chore. Ralph stood nearby, waiting patiently for the delicious morsels he knew his pet would throw him. Claire brought Tristan an iced tea and stood by with a disgusted look as Tristan performed the tedious task.

Bored with just standing around, Claire decided to entertain herself by teasing Tristan, who could not defend herself with her hands full of fish guts. Claire nibbled her ears and neck and ran her hands over her body as Tristan tried to keep her mind on her work.

They were both laughing and didn't hear the approach of an uninvited visitor making her way across the lawn. "Tristan! What the hell are you doing?" Mallory Delacroix shouted as she stormed across the yard. Tristan and Claire looked up in surprise as the woman launched into a tirade.

"Your sick lifestyle should be kept behind closed doors, not out in the open for everyone to see. I am so ashamed of you. If your father were still alive, he would disown you on the spot!"

Tristan calmly looked at her mother. "My lifestyle is none of your business. If I choose to make love to this woman in the middle of my front yard, that, too, is none of your business. Most importantly, if my dad were still alive, he would never disown me because, unlike you, he loved me regardless of what I did."

Mallory opened her mouth to speak, but Tristan cut her off. "Not another word, Mother. I am very calm at the moment, but if you make the mistake of trying to push any more of my buttons, you will not like the result." She accentuated her point by stabbing the fish-cleaning knife into the table. "You never just drop by. What's on your mind, or did you just come to see what your 'sick' daughter was up to?"

"I wanted to talk to you about what you're doing with your life. You've accomplished your goal, Tristan. You have embarrassed me by parading around town with the likes of her!" Mallory pointed a finger in Claire's direction. "In the past, I have tried to overlook your little escapades, but carrying on with a woman you work with is going too far."

To Claire's relief, Tristan left the knife on the table as she stood toe-to-toe with her mother. "I don't give a shit what embarrasses you. I stopped caring a long time ago what you thought. If you want to be embarrassed of something, be embarrassed of your own behavior!"

Mallory tried to respond but was cut off by the icy tone in her daughter's voice. "It would be wrong to hit you, Mother, but I swear if you open your mouth, I will start swinging and not stop. Do not ever come back here. As of today, we no longer know one another. Now, leave before you get the beating you so rightfully deserve."

Mallory Delacroix stared at her daughter in disbelief before she turned and left.

Murky Waters

Claire watched Mallory storm across the yard and noticed the way Tristan stood seemingly rooted to the spot, her entire body trembling in anger. Claire was hesitant to approach Tristan; the tension and hostility flowing from her was like static electricity.

Tristan turned slowly, and the look in her eyes was one that Claire would not soon forget. "She has made me stoop to levels I never dreamed possible, and she has the nerve to say that I am embarrassing her? Had you not been here, Claire, I may have hurt her."

Claire approached Tristan cautiously. "Had you not been here, I may have been tempted to hit her myself. I think you handled yourself very well. One day when you're ready, I'd like to hear the whole story of your relationship, but only when you're ready."

Tristan leaned over and kissed Claire gently on the lips. "I will tell you all about her, but not today. I have to finish cleaning our dinner, then get myself cleaned up. I want this weekend to be nothing but pleasant, so we'll go on with our day as planned."

Tristan seemed to take her ire out on the fish as she cleaned them. By the time the task was complete, she was calm again, and her face and neck were no longer flushed with anger. Claire sat quietly watching and wondering what all was in Tristan's past and if the hurt would ever be fully healed.

Aside from the interruption of Mallory Delacroix, the weekend went exactly as they hoped. They spent Saturday outdoors, and in the cool of the evening, they fried the morning's catch on the deck. On Sunday, they kept the traditional breakfast date with Cam and Lucy, after which they napped and watched movies, and spent the evening making love.

CHAPTER TEN

For several months, Claire and Tristan were inseparable. Some nights they would spend at Claire's apartment. Most of the time, however, was spent at Tristan's house. Claire was relieved that she had not received any more of the mysterious packages. She had still not reported them to the police; she would put that off as long as she could. Since so much time had elapsed, she hoped that the unknown photographer had just given up.

Claire's presence had improved the work environment at the office, and she took special care in mending the problems that Rhonda had created. She worked closely with Tristan and the crew coordinators, and their combined efforts sharply decreased travel costs. Cameron Hughes was very pleased, and this in turn made Tristan happy. Even Cameron noticed the harmonious relationship between travel and crew coordination. No one person was more affected than Tristan. Her stress level had dropped to a minimum, and the department flourished as a result.

In addition to affecting Tristan's life at work, Claire had a profound effect on her personal life, as well. Tristan had found it easier to deal with her feelings of anxiety and fear in their relationship. She was letting go of the part of herself that no one had ever been able to tap into. She often wondered if Claire knew that she was holding her tender heart in her hands.

There was one last hurdle that Tristan had yet to cross, and that was her jealous feelings of Mike. Each smile that Claire gave him gnawed her to the bone. She felt as though Claire toyed with her when it came to the overbearing man by entertaining him with her cheerful and polite demeanor. Had Tristan been in her shoes, she would have been as cold as ice where he was concerned.

Murky Waters

One Friday afternoon as Tristan was walking Claire to her car, she noticed a brown envelope on Claire's windshield. Claire stopped dead in her tracks and stared at the envelope with a look of pure dread.

"Claire, don't you think we should discuss this now? This is the second time you've found something on your car, and judging by your reaction, it can't be good."

Claire looked at Tristan dumbfounded. "Yes, I think we should." Her hands shook as she reached up to retrieve the package. "Tristan, do you mind if we park my Jeep in the back and I ride home with you?"

Tristan readily agreed, seeing the expression on Claire's face. "Let's go to my house tonight. I'll cook you dinner, serve you wine in a hot bath, and when you are relaxed, we'll talk about this," she said, indicating the envelope.

The ride home was quiet. Claire didn't say a word. Tristan figured she was not up to talking, so they drove in silence. She watched as Claire smoked one cigarette after another.

After dinner, Tristan filled the large garden tub in the master bath with hot water. She dropped in some bath salts to make it even more relaxing, lit a few candles, and dimmed the lights. She left a bottle of red wine and two glasses on the ledge of the tub and went to find Claire.

Tristan found her sitting on the couch in the sunroom, still clutching the unopened envelope. Tristan sat next to her and pulled her close. "Claire, what inside that envelope has you so upset?" Claire stared at her absently for a moment and handed it to her.

Claire watched as Tristan pulled two photos out of the package. There was no note this time. Claire shuddered; she knew that the pictures would be of the two of them. She was afraid of how her lover would respond. Now that they were in this together, the stakes had gotten even higher.

Claire wondered how Tristan would react to finding out what she had done her best to keep so well hidden. Would she be offended that it had taken her so long to confide in her? What would Tristan demand of her?

Tristan glanced at Claire and studied the photographs. Both were taken at the Mexican restaurant they went to on their first date. They were taken at an odd angle as if the photographer had difficulty capturing them. Whoever took the pictures was very close by.

Confusion registered on her face as she looked over at Claire. "What's going on?"

Claire could not contain the tears that had threatened to fall. "Tristan, I have no idea. I've been getting them for a while now, even when I was living in Houston. For the life of me, I cannot figure out why anyone would do this to me."

"This has been going on that long? Have you gone to the police?"

"No," Claire said dejectedly. "At first, I didn't want the scrutiny of my personal life. I suppose I was in denial. I hoped it would just go away."

Tristan looked around at all the windows in the sunroom and decided that it would be better if they went inside. She took Claire by the hand and led her to the bathroom. As Claire undressed, Tristan added more hot water, and after undressing, she climbed in herself.

Once she had Claire wrapped in her arms, Tristan broached the subject again. "Claire, honey, you have no suspects at all? Maybe an ex-lover?" She intentionally avoided bringing up Mike, waiting to see if Claire would.

Claire sniffed back the tears. "I confronted my most recent ex. I am certain it's not her. I have searched my mind for anyone I thought could be remotely responsible and have come up with zip."

"Did you say this started while you were in Houston?"

"Yes. The envelopes started coming almost a year ago. Since I have been living here, I've gotten two. Whoever it is knew exactly where to find me in Houston and now knows where I live and where I go. I know this sounds terrible, but I have been wondering a lot about Mike and Lauren."

Tristan poured them each a glass of wine. "Did you know them before you got here?"

Claire thought for a minute as she sipped her wine, hoping it would calm her frazzled nerves. "I've worked with Lauren a couple of times when she was a floater. I've worked with Mike also on a couple of accounts."

"Did either of them live in Houston the same time you did?"

"I know that Lauren lived in Beaumont for a while. Mike lived in Houston until he got the job here. I know you suspect Mike, but I can hardly believe he would be capable of such behavior."

Tristan sighed. "I don't want to accuse anyone, but they are both the most likely suspects in my mind. Especially Mike."

Claire drank half her glass of wine, and Tristan topped it off for her. The wine was having a relaxing effect on Claire. She leaned back into Tristan, feeling comforted by her closeness.

"I suppose that stands to reason, but I can't imagine why either of those two would do something like that to me. I would hate to go to the police and have them investigated. Can you imagine the scandal that would cause, especially if they were proven innocent?"

"Something needs to be done. I understand your reservations about going to the police. Either way, I will support you in your decision, but I don't want him with you alone. No matter how mundane the conversation, you should always have someone else present when you talk to him. I'm doing my best to stay out of it and let you deal with him, but I'd really like to get my hands around his neck."

"I just need a little time to make up my mind on that, Tristan. I'm so thankful I have you in my life now. It's such a comfort to have your support." Claire turned in Tristan's arms to face her. "I don't know if you're ready to hear this or not. I have tried so hard to convey it to you without words, but I have to tell you that I love you very much."

With hands covered in suds, Tristan caressed Claire's face, giving her a bubble beard. "I love you, too, Claire. Now that I have you, I won't let you go. You're stuck with me for life."

The conversation continued into the bedroom, where both women expressed their feelings for one another. Claire lay with her head on Tristan's shoulder as she ran her fingers through her hair. She marveled at how different it had been that night. Tristan caressed her with a tenderness that she had never felt before. Through each kiss and touch, they communicated the feelings that words alone could not convey.

Both were pleasantly exhausted and on the verge of sleep when Claire noticed something in Tristan's bedroom that she had not paid much attention to before. A picture hung on the wall, beautifully framed and matted. Through sleepy eyes, Claire could tell it was of a towboat on the Mississippi. The boat itself was just a shadow silhouetted by the setting sun. She was about to ask Tristan about it but found her sound asleep. Claire turned off the bedside lamp and burrowed close to the warm body that made her feel safe.

The next morning, Tristan left early to finish up some reports in the office. Claire used the excuse that she needed to catch up on laundry. She had argued that since she nearly lived there, she should help out with the household chores. She watched as Tristan drove down the driveway before she quickly dressed.

As she sat on the hard metal chair waiting for the detective who had been assigned to handle her complaint, Claire regretted not bringing Tristan with her. She tapped her tennis shoe nervously on the tile floor and clutched the brown envelope with the pictures and letters to her chest. She needed to do this herself, and she didn't want Tristan to know how really terrified she was. This was something she needed to do on her own.

An attractive female detective approached her. "Miss Murray?"

"Yes." Claire stood and accepted the hand extended to her.

"I'm Detective Salmetti. Please follow me to my office, and we will take down your complaint. Can I offer you something to drink? Coffee, maybe?"

"Yes, please, that would be great," Claire accepted graciously. She waited in the small office while the detective retrieved the coffee. Plaques of special recognition hung on the walls behind the desk. Claire admired the picture of a teenage boy sitting next to a little girl, noticing that they both strongly favored the detective.

"Those are my kids," Salmetti said as she entered the room.

"They're beautiful," Claire responded.

"Yes, I think so, too, when I look at that picture, but when I get home and see what they've done to my house, I tend to look at them differently." The detective chuckled as she took her seat. "I've been informed that you have someone stalking you, Miss

Murray. May I have a look at the pictures?" Salmetti asked, getting down to business.

Claire passed the envelope over the desk with shaking hands. "These are the originals. You can keep them. I've made copies, as well. As I've stated in my report, this has been going on for nearly a year now."

The detective glanced up at her. "I imagine this has really been a trial for you. Why have you waited so long to report this?"

"When I moved from Houston, I hoped that this would all be over, but this person has followed me here." Claire took a sip of her coffee and set the steaming cup on the desk when her hands shook too much to hold it.

The detective thumbed through each picture. "How many people have looked at these, besides you and me?"

"My girlfriend has looked at them, but no one else."

The detective glanced up at her for a split second, then went back to the pictures. "Most of the time, the stalker knows his victim quite well. Do you have someone in mind who you think may be capable of this?"

Claire chewed at her bottom lip. "There is a guy I work with who has been a little pushy about going out with me. My girlfriend suspects it may be him, but I'm not ready to accuse him yet. If I name him, will you question him?"

"This man has continued to pursue you, even after you have made it clear you don't want to see him?"

"Yes, he has, but to be completely honest, if you question him, it is going to stir up a lot of controversy at the office, and I have just taken this job."

"Miss Murray, that is a risk I think you ought to take. Perhaps if we will talk to him, he will lay off, even if he isn't the one who has been stalking you."

The detective set the pictures down on her desk and leaned back slightly in her chair, crossing her legs. "You've mentioned having a girlfriend twice. Is this woman someone who happens to be just a friend, or is she your lover?"

"What does that have to do with anything?"

The detective smiled. "There are two reasons I ask. First, if you are a lesbian, you are accustomed to controversy, and I think you will be able to handle the fallout when we question your co-worker. The second reason is, I want to know if you or she has an ex who might not be happy with your relationship."

"I confronted my ex when I was still in Houston. After she pleaded with me to go to the police, I believed she was innocent. I can give you her name; I doubt she'll mind speaking with you. I don't know anything about Tristan's exes."

The detective's eyebrow shot up at the revelation. "How long have you been involved with this woman?"

Claire's face flushed with anger. She was embarrassed because she realized that she really didn't know that much about Tristan's past lovers. "We've been together for a few months, and I don't think I like where this is going."

"Why not?" the detective asked pointedly.

"Are you including my girlfriend as a suspect, just because we haven't been together that long?"

"I'm just covering all the bases."

"If a straight woman came in with the same complaint, would you suspect her boyfriend?" Claire fought hard to keep her anger at bay.

"Miss Murray, it's my job to suspect everyone around you. It doesn't matter to me what the sex of your lovers is. There have been cases where we have overlooked the obvious," the detective stated kindly.

"I didn't meet Tristan until I moved to Baton Rouge, so you are safe to cross her off the list," Claire asserted calmly. "My employee Mike is the only plausible suspect in my mind because I worked with him on other accounts in the Houston area."

The detective jotted notes on a tablet. "Let me run these for prints, and I will forewarn you when we go to question Mike. I promise we will do it away from the office and do our best to avoid causing you any embarrassment at your place of business."

Tristan finished her work in record time and was happy to be headed home. She missed Claire in the short time they were apart. She marveled that she had not had the compulsion to run from Claire anymore. She'd purged her soul of the hurt that she had harbored for years and now felt free to let someone in. For the first time in her life, she wanted someone to be there when she woke up each morning, and that someone was Claire. Nearly all her dark secrets had been revealed, and she knew she had one more hurdle to cross before Claire could truly be hers.

Claire eventually relaxed and spent a lot more time than she planned going over all the details with the detective. When she returned to Tristan's place, Claire was surprised to see that Tristan had already beaten her there. She wondered if Tristan would be angry that she didn't include her in the plans to go to the police.

When Claire opened the door, the smell of spicy food cooking filled her sinuses. Making a beeline for the stove, she lifted the lid to find seafood gumbo simmering. "Don't even think about digging in yet, missy. It needs another hour." Tristan laughed as the startled blonde dropped the lid onto the pot.

Tristan gave her a peck on the cheek. "Where have you been, honey? You didn't leave a note, and I was beginning to get a little worried."

"I had some errands to run. I got the laundry started, then I went out. Did you get caught up on your paperwork?" Claire asked, changing the subject.

"Yep, I did, and I rushed home because there is something I really want to talk to you about."

"Oh, honey, I'm sorry I wasn't here when you got home. I'm all ears now."

Tristan poured Claire and herself a cup of coffee and sat down at the kitchen table. "I was thinking about this on the way home today, Claire. I have to tell you ... I ... umm ..." Tristan's nervousness was evident, and Claire reached across the table and took Tristan's shaking hand into her own.

"I've never discussed this with anyone, and it's so hard." Tristan bowed her head, struggling with what she knew must come next.

"Is it about your mother?" Claire asked, trying to help.

"No, it's not about her at all. Claire, I love you with all my heart. Will you move in with me?" Tristan blurted out in a burst of words, knowing if she didn't get it out quickly, she would lose her nerve.

Claire tucked her fingers underneath Tristan's chin and lifted slightly until Tristan's nervous eyes met her own. "Are you really in love with me, Tristan, because I am head over heels in love with you."

Tristan smiled faintly. "I've never been truly in love, so I have nothing to compare it to. I can tell you, though, that I've never felt anything like this in my entire life."

Claire jumped up from her chair and settled on Tristan's lap. "I love you, too, sweetie, and I would love to move in with you." Tristan buried her face in Claire's chest and breathed a sigh of relief.

"I do think we need to discuss a few things, though," Claire said as Tristan looked up at her. "If you're ready, I'd like you to tell me about your mother. I know it's hard to talk about, but I want to know how to deal with Mallory should she ever show up here again."

Tristan nodded and reached for her cigarettes. "Up until recently, I've never told a soul about my childhood." She painfully explained the same things about her mother that she told Lucy. It was still a struggle but less of an effort this time around. Claire openly wept as Tristan relived the trauma.

"How could anyone treat her child that way?" Claire asked as tears poured down her face.

"I would like to know the answer to that and a million others. I think part of it was she was jealous of the relationship I had with my dad. We were always so close, and she was always left out, mostly of her own choosing." Tristan wiped her eyes. "I'm a grown woman now, and I can't let the ghosts of the past rule my life. My first step was allowing you to get close to me, and I am so glad I did."

"Tris, while we're bearing our souls, I need to tell you the truth about what I did today. I went to the police with the pictures and letters. The detective is going ..."

"You did what?" Tristan jumped up from the table, nearly throwing Claire to the floor. "Why ... Why did you go behind my back?"

Claire was shocked by Tristan's reaction. "Baby, I didn't go behind your back. I decided on the spur of the moment, and I went before I lost my nerve. Besides, I felt it was something I needed to do on my own."

Murky Waters

Tristan stood staring at Claire, her eyes easily conveying the hurt and betrayal she felt. Claire got up and took her into her arms. "I'm sorry, love. If I'd known that it was this important to you, I would have taken you with me." She felt Tristan's arms encircle her, but her body remained rigid. Claire closed her eyes and silently prayed that she had not set their relationship back by her misjudgment.

Claire spent the evening trying to make it up to Tristan. Tristan verbally accepted her apology, but Claire could tell there was something brewing behind her brown eyes. Later that evening as they lay in bed, both trying to sleep with the specter of hurt feelings hanging heavily upon them, Tristan confirmed for Claire that she did indeed still want her to move in. It was her first attempt to get back to the happy decision they made earlier in the day.

"If you would prefer, we can use your sofa, and I can move mine into the storage room. Whatever belongings you have that you would like to see in this house, feel free to tell me where you want them, and I will move my stuff out of the way. I want this to look and feel like your home, too, Claire. All I ask is that you leave the storage room to me. It hurts to go in there. That's the real reason I have it locked. Dad's stuff is in there."

Claire rolled over and lay her head on Tristan's shoulder. "Then, that will be your room, Tris. I have no reason to go in there. I wouldn't want to invade something you keep so private anyway."

CHAPTER ELEVEN

Tristan decided to spend the remainder of the weekend relaxing with Claire. She had put off finishing her weekly reports until Monday and regretted that decision when her alarm went off at four-thirty that morning. She looked over at Claire, who was sleeping peacefully, and did not have the heart to wake her up. Knowing Claire didn't have to be at work until eight, Tristan let her sleep in.

Claire awoke later when she heard a sound in the room. She was aware that Tristan had already left, and she could sense that she was not alone. She lay very still, hoping against hope that she was wrong. She barely opened her eyes and scanned what she could see of the room without moving. Every muscle in her body screamed in protest. Claire tensed when her eyes met his. Both waited for the other to make the first move. She reasoned in her head that if she sprung up first, she would at least have the element of surprise on her side.

His pupils began to dilate. Claire knew he had the same thought. As he jumped into action, she sat straight up. His tooth caught her across the bridge of the nose, and Claire fell back onto the bed in pain. As she lay there with tears streaming from her eyes, she saw him prance across the room, his little orange tail held high in victory. The score was cat one, Claire zero. His victory would be a hollow one because today Claire would toss his favorite catnip toy down the garbage disposal.

Tristan noticed the small cut immediately when Claire arrived at work. "What happened to your nose? Are you okay?"

Claire frowned. "Ralph happened to my nose. I was lying in bed this morning, and he decided to act as my alarm clock. He pounced on my face and bit me!"

Tristan tried her best not to laugh and add insult to injury. She comforted Claire as best she could under the circumstances; however, she quickly returned to her office, where she could be heard laughing hysterically.

The events of the morning did distract Claire for a while, but before long, her thoughts went back to Lauren and Mike. She watched them through the glass walls of her office. She could not fathom how either of them could be a stalker. Claire took into account that she didn't really know much about them personally. She figured that anyone could work next to a person for years and not really know him or her.

Claire studied Lauren's profile as Lauren typed on her computer, unaware that she was being scrutinized. Claire wondered if the slightly overweight young woman would be capable of scurrying around snapping pictures cloaked in darkness. Her young and innocent features would not raise suspicion of anyone who passed by. Claire was unwilling to believe that Lauren, who had always been so kind to her, would do such a thing.

She focused her attention on Mike, who also sat at his desk working at his computer. He would be more likely to stoop to such a level. He wasn't a bad-looking man, but Claire suspected that no one who passed him on the street would do a double take. It had nothing to do with his thinning hair, but more with the way he carried himself. His clothes never seemed to fit right, and it was obvious that he did not care much for personal hygiene.

He was the more likely suspect, especially since he paid Claire so much attention and was undaunted by her continually brushing him off when he asked her out. He seemed surprised each time Claire declined his offer as if he were certain she wanted to go out with him. Whether he was the stalker or not, he was well on his way to a harassment suit.

"I've been staring at them all morning, too," Tristan said as she walked into the room. "I was tempted to go through their desks when I was alone in here."

"What did you hope to find?"

Tristan furrowed her brow. "I don't know, really, maybe something that would solve the mystery."

Claire sighed and sat back in her chair. "I'm going to drive myself insane trying to figure out who is doing this."

"Sweetie, you need a break. Why don't we go away for the weekend? We could go to the beach in Gulf Shores. Cam has a condo there, and I'm sure he will let me use it. We can just go there and relax."

Claire nearly purred. "That sounds heavenly."

"Great! Leave all the planning to me. We will discuss all the details over lunch."

Friday could not come soon enough for the both of them. They had taken the day off to make a long weekend. Claire put the last of their things in the car and joined Tristan on the deck, where she was giving Lucy feeding instructions for Ralph.

Lucy smiled at Claire as she approached. "Hi, sweetie. Tristan tells me that Ralph has been a pill lately. I'm going to leave my water gun here for you when you get back. When he gets out of line with me, I pop that fuzzy ass with a blast of water, and it straightens him right up."

Once they were on their way out of town, Claire began to relax and enjoy the trip. She glanced over at Tristan, who was the picture of relaxation. Her long hair was in a ponytail protruding from the back of a baseball cap. She had kicked off her tennis shoes and had one foot tucked underneath her thigh. She was sporting an LSU T-shirt complemented by a pair of purple gym shorts. Claire thought at that moment that she had never seen Tristan look more lovely.

Tristan glanced from the road to Claire. "What are you thinking about?"

"I was thinking about how adorable you look," Claire said with a wink.

Tristan laughed. "I hope you weren't looking forward to dressing up for anything because this is the dress code for the weekend. I plan for us to be bums the whole time. Our biggest decisions should be what to eat and which bathing suit to wear."

"You have a deal on that. I might not want to go home after a weekend like this." Claire rubbed Tristan's neck as she spoke. "Tris, I have been meaning to ask you about something. There is a picture of a towboat taken at sunset in your bedroom. Did you take that picture?"

Murky Waters

Tristan looked at Claire for a moment with an odd expression on her face. Her voice took on a dreamlike tone when she spoke. "Actually, my mother took that picture years ago. It used to hang in my dad's office. My mother has become a very popular photographer in the last few years. She's done a few wildlife features in local magazines."

"I wouldn't have figured her for a photographer. She seems more like a banker to me."

Tristan chuckled. "Yeah, she does look like one of those tight-assed business types, ready to pounce if you miss a payment."

"Oh, Tris, that's not what I meant. She just didn't strike me as a photographer. What about you? Did any of that creative talent rub off on the little apple?"

"Nope, I'm afraid not. I've always been more like my dad, not an artistic bone in my body."

They rode in silence for a while, both deep in their own thoughts. Tristan fought the tears that threatened to spill from her eyes. Remorse filled her heart because she had lied to her first love. She was learning to cope with the raw feelings of her past, but the memories that flooded her mind brought a new kind of pain that she struggled to deal with. Pain that she was not ready to give voice to.

Memories of the day that picture had been taken had not been skewed with the passage of time. Tristan could still remember running down the levee with "Uncle Cam." The light was perfect when she snapped that picture. She took many photographs that day, waiting for her father to finish his work with the boat in dry dock. It was a perfect afternoon spent with those who truly loved her.

She sat watching the sunset next to Cam. With his arm draped over her shoulders, he told her of the humorous antics of his Cajun grandmother. Tristan burrowed closer to Uncle Cam; he was just like her dad. He made her feel loved. Unfortunately for the ten-year-old, all her happy feelings would desert her when she returned home.

Tristan chattered excitedly about her adventures with Uncle on the ride home. Her dad never seemed to tire of hearing her stories and was content to listen as she relayed the day's events. "I took a bunch of pictures, Dad. Do you think Mom would develop them for me?" Her innocent face rose to her father, waiting expectantly for an answer.

Mitchell, Tristan's father, sat silently for a moment. "I'm not sure, sweetie. She may be busy with her work when we get home. Why don't you let me ask her about it?"

When they arrived at the modest Delacroix home, Tristan became quiet and sullen once more. Mitchell grieved for the way his wife treated their only daughter. The change in Tristan's behavior when she was around her mother had not escaped his attention. He had attempted to reason with his wife to no avail; she was a hard woman, and any suggestions made to her about her child were always taken as an insult. Mitchell did what he could to keep peace in the household, but he feared what effect it might have on his daughter later in life.

Mallory Delacroix was setting the table when Tristan and Mitchell walked in. Instead of a hug and kiss for either of them, she went about her tasks and suggested that they wash up for dinner. Mitchell complimented his wife on her cooking, as he always did, while they ate. Tristan, as usual, did not say a word at the table but sat listening to the conversations between her parents.

When he had finished most of his meal, Mitchell patted his wife on the hand and asked her about developing Tristan's film. "Mallory, Tristan took a lot of pictures down at the work site of the boat we put on dry dock today. I would like to see what she captured on film. Would you minddeveloping it when you get a chance?"

Mallory looked up at her husband. "If you wanted photos of the boat, why didn't you have an adult take them? I am sure that whatever Tristan took will not be suitable for what you are looking for. You will be lucky if she were able to get a shot of anything that would be useful to you."

Mitchell chose his words carefully, hoping not to spark his wife's temper. "I would like to see what Tristan captured. She may have taken after you and may have an eye for photography. Who knows, your daughter may follow in your footsteps."

Mallory set her fork down and pushed her plate back. She looked at Tristan, who refused to meet her eyes. "Like I said before, if you were hoping to get some decent photos, you should have had them taken by an adult. I see no reason to waste my time and effort on developing something taken by a child."

Tears formed in Tristan's big brown eyes, but she refused to look at her mother and give the hateful woman the satisfaction of knowing she had hurt her. When she was confident that she had her emotions under control, Tristan asked to be excused from the table. She took her plate to the sink and went to take a shower. Only then did she allow her tears to flow freely.

CHAPTER TWELVE

Tristan and Claire agreed not to discuss the issue of the stalker while they were on their trip. Instead, the conversation moved to food. By the time they exited the interstate onto the highway leading to Gulf Shores, they were famished. About twenty minutes later, they came upon a restaurant that looked interesting to Claire.

"Hey, how about that place?" Claire asked excitedly. 'Home of the throwed roll.' How can a girl pass that up?"

"Claire, I am not sure I want to eat in a place where they throw the food."

"Come on, Tris, be a sport," Claire pleaded while bouncing up and down in her seat like a child.

The atmosphere of the restaurant was casual and relaxed. The cuisine was mainly Southern home cooking, which appealed to both women. After they had placed their orders with the waiter, they sipped iced tea and ate the rolls that Claire had bravely caught until their plates arrived heaped with food. The staff walked around the dining room with hot pots of side items and ladled huge helpings for anyone interested.

The food was wonderful, and Claire ate like there was no tomorrow. Tristan was enjoying her meal until she was knocked in the head by a rogue roll, which put a damper on her dining experience. Claire laughed all the way through dessert.

Claire was impressed with the small town of Gulf Shores. There were plenty of tourists but not so many that it was overwhelming.

She rode along, grinning from ear to ear, pointing out all the places she wanted to explore.

Late that afternoon, they arrived at the condo. After unpacking, Tristan and Claire agreed that they were still too full from their late lunch to consider dinner. Instead, they opted for a sunset walk down the beach. When they came to a picnic pavilion, they sat and talked. Except for an occasional beach stroller, they were alone.

Tristan chose one of the picnic tables in the corner, where the large beams obscured them from sight. She began to kiss and nibble Claire's ears and neck while slipping her hands underneath Claire's shirt when Claire stopped her. "Tristan! Are you nuts? Someone is going to see us out here. Not to mention, I have some nut running around snapping off pictures of me."

"You have a good point. I'm sorry, Claire, I wasn't thinking. Sometimes when I'm around you, I get a little carried away. Besides, this atmosphere is so romantic. I feel frisky." Tristan wiggled her eyebrows up and down.

Claire pulled Tristan close and nuzzled her neck. "Nothing to apologize for, my love. We can continue what you started when we get back to the condo. Matter of fact, we can spend the entire weekend doing that if you want."

Tristan gave her a mischievous grin. She and Claire made their way back down the beach, walking a little faster than before. Most of the hike back was spent in the surf as they kicked water and sand all over each other. When they did eventually make it back to the condo, they were soaking wet and covered in sand.

Tristan gave Claire a seductive look. "Why don't we conserve some water and shower together? That way, we won't get sand all over the place. I assure you, my intentions are entirely innocent."

Tristan's jaw dropped when she got Claire's answer. Without saying a word, Claire stripped off every piece of clothing and dropped it at Tristan's feet. Then, she ran upstairs naked as the day she was born, leaving Tristan to stare wide-eyed after her.

Tristan joined Claire in the shower as Claire was shampooing her hair. Tristan stood back and watched the water and suds cascade down Claire's shapely body. The beauty of her lover never ceased to amaze her. To Tristan, Claire was as pretty on the inside as she was on the outside.

Tristan made no effort to resist the temptation of touching her lover's slick body. She soaped her hands and ran them lovingly over Claire, watching as Claire responded to her touch. Once both women were free of soap and sand, they continued to explore one another's bodies with their hands and mouths.

Tristan turned Claire to the wall and kissed her way down her spine. Claire gripped the slick wall, attempting to hold herself up, despite her weak knees. Tristan continued to blaze a trail of kisses down the back of each thigh and across Claire's firm buttocks until she had showered the entire back of her body with kisses and nibbles.

"Claire, there is so much I want to do to you," Tristan whispered hotly in her ear as she ran her nails lightly over Claire's backside, grinning as she felt Claire's body trembling against her. "Claire, tell me that I can do anything I want to you." Claire simply nodded her head in agreement. Not satisfied with the answer, Tristan pushed a little further. "Tell me that I can do with your body anything I please, Claire, say it." Tristan pinched Claire's nipples to accentuate the point.

Claire lay her head back on Tristan's shoulder as her body shuddered in Tristan's hands. "Yes, the answer is yes. You can do anything you want with me, Tristan. I trust you completely."

Tristan turned Claire around and looked in her eyes, seeing the truth revealed in their depths. "I will never make you do anything you're not comfortable with, my love."

Tristan continued kissing and nibbling Claire's neck, igniting a fire in Claire that the now cool water could not suppress. They kissed passionately as Tristan lightly ran her fingertips down Claire's body, teasing her, barely brushing against all the places Claire pleaded with her to caress.

Claire responded by weaving her hands through Tristan's wet hair and pulling her closer. Tristan slid two fingers into Claire; the strokes were fast and hard. Claire dug her nails into Tristan's back, encouraging her to continue. When she knew Claire was close to orgasm, Tristan stopped and pulled away.

Claire wrapped her arms around Tristan, pleading for her to continue. Untangling herself, Tristan pulled away and grinned. "Sweetie, I'm not finished with you, but I do plan to make you beg."

Murky Waters

Tristan turned the water off and stepped out of the shower. She smiled at Claire as she toweled off, then Tristan did the same. Tristan took her lover by the hand and led her to the bedroom. She stood behind Claire, kissing her neck and fondling her breasts. Claire nearly went to her knees when Tristan pinched her nipples and whispered in her ear all the things she planned to do to her. Fortunately, the condo next to them was unoccupied, or its residents would have heard Tristan's name screamed repeatedly.

Claire had drifted off into the most peaceful slumber and was sleeping soundly when she heard a noise in the room that jolted her into consciousness. She opened her eyes and wondered if she had been dreaming or if there had been a noise. Tristan, who was snuggled beside her, was breathing heavily and whimpering softly. Claire realized that it was the same noise that had woken her.

She lay beside Tristan, debating whether to wake her from the obvious nightmare. Tristan stirred and mumbled something in her sleep that Claire could not distinguish. Seconds later, Tristan began to thrash and moan Claire's name in a pleading tone. "Please, no, Claire."

As Claire reached over to soothe her lover, Tristan bolted upright in bed. "Tris, honey, it's okay. You were having a bad dream." Even in the darkened room, she could see Tristan's eyes opened wide in terror.

"You were dreaming, baby. It's okay," Claire said as Tristan looked around confused for a moment before relaxing. Claire pulled her into her arms and could feel Tristan's heart beating erratically against her own skin.

"What was the dream about?" Claire asked as she held her trembling lover. She heard Tristan swallow hard, but she said nothing in response.

"Tristan? Talk to me, sweetie," Claire said, stroking Tristan's dampened hair from her brow.

"You died, and there was nothing I could do to stop it," Tristan said as hot tears rolled down her cheeks onto Claire's shoulder.

"Baby, it was a nightmare. I'm here safe and sound. There is nothing to worry about." Claire soothed Tristan until she was sure she had fallen back to sleep. Claire lay there in the darkness, waiting to drift off again, enjoying the feel of Tristan in her arms. She had not stopped to think how the stalker business might be affecting her lover. She knew that Tristan was not one to open up and discuss the things that troubled her, but the dream confirmed to Claire that she was equally scared.

"Oh, Tristan, look what you did to this room!" Claire said as daylight filled the space. The bed was torn apart, and the blankets and linens were on the floor. The bedside table had been knocked over, and the alarm clock and phone were nowhere to be seen.

"I think I may have swallowed one of your earrings," Tristan replied in a raspy voice. "Besides, it's not like I was alone, Miss Innocent. You had your tongue in my ..." Tristan was interrupted by a pillow hitting her face.

Claire lay back down and burrowed against Tristan, her face coloring as she remembered what had taken place in that room the night before. No stranger to sex, she still blushed remembering how Tristan had pushed her beyond her limits and how she reacted. She was certain that Tristan's back would be covered with scratches.

"I wish this place had room service," Tristan sighed. "I'm too lazy to go downstairs for food. We could spend the whole day in this bed, and that would be fine with me. Of course, we wouldn't get any sun, and we would have to explain why we don't have tans."

Claire's stomach growled at the mention of food. "Let's go grab breakfast somewhere quick and go to the beach. Then, we can explore Gulf Shores and have lunch at one of the places on the coastline."

Tristan smirked. "When you say 'explore,' I'm sure you mean shopping. I bet you will drag me to every one of those shell shops you pointed out on the way in."

Claire laughed. "You know me so well, baby. Get up and get dressed. I'm starving!"

CHAPTER THIRTEEN

Tristan and Claire decided to eat breakfast at a place called Hazel's Nook. The restaurant was bustling with locals and tourists. Tristan loaded her plate up at the buffet, and Claire opted for an omelet prepared with all her favorites. They enjoyed their breakfast in the relaxed Southern home-style atmosphere.

Tristan ate oblivious to her all surroundings but Claire. Several of the patrons openly appraised Claire's beautiful partner, and she smiled to herself, thinking that she was with one of the most beautiful women she had ever seen. The attention paid to Tristan only confirmed what she believed.

Afterward, Tristan took Claire on a tour of the Gulf State Park where Tristan had camped at the campground for years. They drove through the scenic park that stretched for a few miles down the Gulf when Claire noticed a warning sign that read, "Do not feed or molest the alligators."

"Who the hell would want to feed an alligator, much less molest one? Although, I suppose they had to put up the sign because someone was foolish enough to try it."

Tristan laughed. "Claire, don't you find them sexy? I often fantasize about taking one to dinner. Looking across the table at those big eyes and stroking that green skin, it just makes me hot thinking about it."

Claire shook her head. "Tristan, I love you very much, but, honey, you have one sick sense of humor. Guess that's why I love you so."

After finding a parking spot, Tristan and Claire trekked down one of the public piers to the beach. They picked a spot close to the water's edge away from the rest of the sunbathers. Once they got everything set the way they wanted, both women were sweating profusely. Tristan was the first to jump into the emerald-colored water with Claire close on her heels.

Feeling refreshed, they returned to their spot on the sand and relaxed in the chairs they brought with them. They watched as children splashed in the surf and dug in the sand along the beach. One child in particular caught their attention. He looked to be only four or five, and his head was full of light blond hair. He sat shirtless in a little hole he had dug with his plastic shovel.

A wave washed up on the shore and filled his spot with water. He giggled and laughed and splashed, then jumped up excitedly and proclaimed, "Mom, I farted in the water hole, and it made bubbles." He ran toward his embarrassed mother, singing his discovery at the top of his lungs.

Claire and Tristan could not help but laugh at his antics. "Tris, have you ever thought about having kids?"

"It crosses my mind every now and then. How about you?"

Claire nodded. "I think about it all the time. Even the mundane things like cooking dinner for them or helping with homework. I think children are wonderful."

Tristan gave Claire a big grin. "If by some miracle I manage to get you pregnant, I will be happy to let you do the cooking and homework. I'll do the fun stuff like building tree houses and playing softball. Of course, we'll have plenty of time to do all that stuff. We'll be the richest women in the world and be immortalized in every scientific journal on the planet."

"Who says I have to be the one to carry our children? What if I get you pregnant?" Claire asked smugly.

"Okay, let's get back to reality. Neither of us is able to impregnate the other. So that brings up the issue of a sperm donor. I personally think I'm allergic to sperm because it makes me sick to think about it. Therefore, it will have to be you, Claire."

Claire laughed uncontrollably at Tristan's supposed allergy to sperm. The conversation, however, made Claire more excited about her life with Tristan. For the first time, she had met someone with whom she believed she would have a future.

Claire lay back in her chair, reveling in the soft sea breeze that blew in off the water, pondering a life with Tristan. She pictured them having and raising children together. Having a family life once again filled her with a peace she had not known for a long time.

When Tristan's stomach began to growl, they decided to go in search of a place to have lunch. She and Claire decided on Hooters, which had an open deck that welcomed wet bathing suits. They ate their fill of hot wings and fries as they relaxed, enjoying the shade of the deck.

Claire gazed at Tristan while she sipped her tea and stared out at the coastline. In this light, Tristan looked so different from the first day they met. She looked happy, especially in this environment. Claire made a promise to herself then that when they encountered problems in their life together, this place would be their safe haven. They would come here to work out their difficulties.

"Claire, have you ever been snorkeling?" The question broke Claire from her ponderings.

"I've always wanted to try it but never really knew anyone who could teach me. Why? Do you know how?"

Tristan smiled. "There's a place up the road from here near Orange Beach. I've been there a few times. Not much to see underwater, but it is fun to collect shells near the jetties. I have my gear in the back of the car, would you like to give it a try?"

Claire enthusiastically agreed, and they were on the road to Orange Beach in a matter of minutes. The dark-tinted windows of Tristan's car shielded them from the hot sun outside. Claire looked her skin over and decided that she would need another coat of sunscreen, which would be a good job for Tristan. Unlike Tristan, who had tanned skin, she was fair-complexioned and would be red as a beet without her sunscreen.

"If you want to see where we will be snorkeling, look out over the water when we go over this bridge," Tristan said as she drove. Claire looked at the blue-green water. The entire area was alive with activity. She could see the divers' flags floating on the surface. The beach area itself was peppered with bodies basking in the sun.

Once Tristan had found a spot to park in the crowded lot, they unloaded the gear from the back of the car. Tristan threw a netted bag over her shoulder that contained masks and snorkels. For good measure, she tossed a couple of bottles of water inside, knowing they would get thirsty quickly.

Tristan led Claire down a sandy path to the water's edge. "This is where a lot of dive companies conduct their classes; the water is very clear here. Let's go around the point to the jetties. The waves wash up shells that get caught along the rocks. That's where I find the most interesting stuff," Tristan said as she led Claire along.

When they came to the spot Tristan thought was best, Tristan set the gear bag down and applied the defogger to the masks. Once the task was completed, she and Claire waded into the water about waist deep.

"Dip down into the water and slick your hair back. That way, the mask won't get hung up in your hair." Claire did as Tristan suggested. When she stood, Tristan helped her with the mask. She adjusted the snorkel until it was in a comfortable position for Claire to use.

"Snorkeling is very simple. You float on the surface of the water; the air in your lungs will keep you buoyant. When you see something you want to collect, you tuck your body and kick with your legs to the bottom. You can clear you snorkel by turning your head down and blowing the air out of your lungs before you break the surface. This will clear the water out of the snorkel without having to lift your face out of the water.

"While you're snorkeling, water will invariably find its way into your mask. To keep from pulling it on and off your face, the easiest way to clear it is to press on the top of it, breaking the seal a little and blowing with your nose. The pressure will force the water out of your mask."

When she finished speaking, Tristan noticed the puzzled look on Claire's face. "You really expect me to remember all that? I'll be lucky if I don't get choked the first minute I put my face in the water," Claire said as she kicked at the little fish that swam around her legs.

"Umm, okay, just remember this: Don't swim too close to the jetties or the waves may push you into them; they are covered with sharp barnacles. Also, don't stick your hands in any holes in the rocks. Whatever is living in there may not take too kindly to the invasion of its home," Tristan said with a smile.

After a few tries, Claire caught on quickly. She swam alongside Tristan, who pointed out different things as they went by. As they approached the jetties, they began to see small groups of silver-colored fish. Claire marveled as they bravely swam right up to her mask but darted away when she tried to touch them.

Tristan studied the floor of the warm Gulf for shells. She dived down and collected a few specimens. Finding them broken, she let them fall back to the sandy bottom. Claire watched her from the surface, still not feeling very confident in her abilities.

Instead, she would tap Tristan on the leg and point to things she found interesting. She was especially wary of the jetties, which were a big pile of slimy rocks covered in barnacles, just as Tristan had described.

After about an hour, they had gathered a nice collection of shells. Tristan was careful not to take any that had a living creature inside. She and Claire were wading back to the beach when Tristan noticed that Claire's back and legs were getting red, not to mention the portion of Claire's bottom that her swimsuit did not cover. "Claire, I think we need to get out of the sun. Your entire back side is getting red."

Claire didn't argue the point as her skin began to sting. She glanced over at two men sitting in the sand enjoying the sun. One was openly appraising her as she dried off. Anxiety and fear gripped her as she allowed the thoughts that had been floating in the back of her mind to come to the surface. Were the eyes that had sought her out so many times before now upon her? She swore those eyes were near; she could sense their presence. It was as though she had a link to the person who caused her so many sleepless nights.

Her thoughts and fears slipped back into the recesses of her mind as she felt Tristan's soft lips on her shoulder. The simple gesture filled her with comfort and the reassurance that Tristan would keep her safe from the person who sought to torment her.

They gathered their things and began the long walk around the point. Neither spoke much, being a little tired from the adventure. Tristan's long legs and stride maintained a much faster pace than Claire could keep up with, so she stayed a step or two behind. She admired Tristan's backside as she walked; the two-piece swimsuit accented some of the tall brunette's attributes.

Claire mused to herself about Tristan's sense of modesty. When they were not in the water or lying on the beach, Tristan kept her wrap around her waist. However, on their trek back to the car, the heat was too intense to bother with the wrap, giving Claire and the other beachgoers something to enjoy.

Claire admired her lover's muscular and tanned back as she walked. Her eyes trailed down to Tristan's rear end and settled there for most of the walk. The sight was having an effect on her that could not be blamed on the hot weather. Her desire was kindled further by the memory of the previous night, when she had dug her nails into those firm cheeks. The memories alone were enough to make her heart race.

When they finally made it to the vehicle, each drank an entire bottle of water. Tristan took another couple of bottles out, and they took an impromptu bath to wash the saltwater from their skin. After they had dried themselves sufficiently, they climbed into the car that Tristan had wisely started to cool when they had arrived.

Claire put her hand on Tristan's when she reached for the gearshift. "Tris, don't pull out yet. Let's just sit here for a few minutes."

"What's on your mind? Is there something else you want to do? You know, you really can't go back out into the sun today. You're a lot redder than you realize."

"That's not exactly what I had in mind, Tris," Claire said with a grin as she reached over and ran her fingertips up Tristan's thigh.

Tristan's eyebrows arched in surprise. "Weren't you the one who fussed at me last night about public displays of affection?"

"Yes, but we were outside in the open. Now, we are in a vehicle with tinted windows." Claire continued to run her fingers up Tristan's thigh, locking eyes with her as she did, grinning as she felt her lover's body reacting to her touch.

"Tris, recline that seat, close your eyes, and forget that anyone else is out here but us," Claire purred as she ran her fingertips under the thin material separating her from her goal.

"This parking lot is full of people, what if we get caught?" Tristan asked nervously as she looked around.

"That's part of the thrill." Claire said in a seductive tone.

It only took Claire a second to realize that Tristan's body was not opposed to the idea. "Tris, your body is betraying your sensibilities. Relax and let me do what I will. I promise you will not be disappointed."

Tristan did as she was asked and reclined her seat. She spread her legs a little wider, giving Claire the room to move the way she wanted. Tristan looked around for anyone who might be coming near the car.

"Close your eyes and relax. If I see anyone coming near, I'll let you know. The only thing I want you to concentrate on is what you feel," Claire said as she slid two fingers on each side of the bundle of nerves that obviously craved her attention. She massaged gently and slowly, avoiding direct pressure to the sensitive spot.

"Claire, this may take a while. I can't help but be a little nervous," Tristan said breathlessly as she shuddered under Claire's attentions.

"I'm in no hurry. The longer, the better," Claire said as she continued to massage the tender area. She watched as the muscles tensed in Tristan's legs and stomach. *Magnificent*, Claire thought to herself, as her lover's body became taut as a bowstring, displaying her muscle tone.

Claire refused to give credence to the nagging voice in the back of her mind, whispering that she had seduced Tristan to free her of the troubling thoughts that haunted her. Taking Tristan like this was a pleasant diversion, and Tristan certainly didn't seem to mind as Claire dipped her fingers in the well of her passion, then glided them back to the spot that made Tristan shudder.

Tristan's breathing became erratic as she gripped the sides of her seat. Claire had completely forsaken her duty as lookout. She could not pry her eyes from Tristan as she brought her closer to ecstasy. Tristan's breath caught in her throat, and Claire watched as Tristan's body stilled a minute before she cried out her name. "You are beautiful, baby. I love you so much," Claire whispered as she watched Tristan struggle to get her breathing under control.

As a double bonus for Claire's afternoon, she was allowed to drive Tristan's car back to the condo. The activities of the day had proved to be a little too strenuous on Tristan's legs, and she was not quite up to working the clutch. Claire wore a proud smile as she drove her exhausted lover in her sports car down the strip.

CHAPTER FOURTEEN

After a nap and just as Tristan had guessed, she and Claire spent the remainder of the afternoon going from one shell shop to the other. At one in particular, they found a beautiful replica of a lighthouse and decided it would look perfect on the fireplace mantle of the home they shared together. Claire decided to have mercy on Tristan as her eyes glazed over while she was dragged from one shop to another. The two made their way back to the condo, where they were looking forward to spending the last night of a perfect weekend together.

Tristan noticed that Claire kept wincing and pulling at her shirt collar. She also turned the air conditioner down a notch in the car. "Claire, how about we just pick up something and take it back to the condo? I don't know if I'm up to going anywhere else tonight." Claire readily agreed, confirming Tristan's suspicions that she was uncomfortably sunburned.

Tristan pulled into a convenience store. "I'm going to get something to drink and something for that sunburn of yours." She closed the car door before Claire could utter a word. When Tristan got back in, she laughed at the way Claire squirmed in her seat.

Claire tugged at her collar again. "How did you know I was burned?"

Tristan giggled. "Because you have spent the evening looking like you were at war with your clothes. I suspect you have a little fever, too, which, of course, accompanies a good sunburn. I spend a lot of time in the yard, so my skin gets a gradual tan, but the part of my ass that was peeking out of my swimsuit today is now on fire."

Claire sighed. "I wanted a replay of last night, but my skin will not allow it. I wasn't even going to tell you about it, hoping to tough it out."

As they passed through the door of the condo, Claire shed her clothes. Tristan went to the kitchen and placed the cheeseburgers and fries they had picked up on the way onto plates. She had all the food and drinks on the coffee table in front of the television when Claire joined her. Tristan was pleasantly surprised that Claire had decided to dress in her birthday suit for dinner.

"Where are your clothes?" Tristan asked with a gleam in her eye.

Claire grimaced and whined. "I tried to put on something that wouldn't rub my skin, but I didn't have any luck. Everything hurts my skin, even your robe. I tried it, too."

"After we eat, you will take something for the fever, then I will rub you down with aloe gel. If you're a really good girl, I'll let you rub my sunburned buns," Tristan said playfully as she tugged Claire down on the sofa.

After dinner, Tristan cleaned and put away the dishes. Upon returning to the living room, she found Claire holding a blanket against the parts of her body that were only mildly burned. "I know I rubbed you down with sunscreen twice. How did this happen?" Tristan asked as she took the blanket from Claire and spread it out on the floor.

"Tris, look at me. My skin is so fair, I'm nearly pink. I don't think they make a sunscreen strong enough to protect my glow-in-the-dark skin. I had no idea I was getting that much sun, either."

Claire lay on her stomach on the blanket as Tristan directed. Tristan sat on her knees next to her, afraid to straddle her because of all the red skin. She poured the gel into her hands and gently spread it across Claire's hot skin.

"Aw, look at you. You look like a lobster," Tristan chided. "Now, you'll always be my little lobster."

Claire rose up on her elbows and turned to look at Tristan. "How would you like to be on the business end of a lobster claw, missy?"

They spent their last night in Gulf Shores wrapped in a blanket on the balcony, watching the moonlight flicker off the water. Tristan made sure that Claire had plenty of wine to help her relax.

She drifted off in Tristan's arms, leaving Tristan to admire the moon alone.

Tristan held Claire close as she thought about what they would have to face together. The thing with Mike was an interesting turn of events. She gritted her teeth just thinking about him and the way he looked at Claire. She hated the feelings of jealously that Mike elicited.

The next day around noon, Tristan and Claire finished loading the car and started for home. Claire felt a little melancholy about leaving a place that she found such solace. She comforted herself with the knowledge that she would return one day with Tristan by her side.

Four hours later, they breathed a sigh of relief when they pulled into the driveway of their home. They were met at the door by an excited orange tabby cat. Lying on the counter was a water gun; next to it was Lucy's note that everything went fine while they were gone. When Tristan picked up the gun to look at it, the orange ball of fur shot off like a lightning bolt. Obviously, Lucy had been keeping Ralph in line.

Later when Tristan was cooking dinner, Claire did the laundry. She liked that they compromised on the household chores. She was really beginning to feel at home. Once she had more of her stuff there, she would feel more like it was her place, as well as Tristan's.

Before they retired for the evening, Tristan presented Claire with a small box. "What's this?" Claire asked as she sat up in bed

Tristan grinned from ear to ear. "It's just a little keepsake to always remind you of our first trip to the beach together."

Claire opened the box slowly and peered inside. She giggled as she pulled two sterling silver necklaces from the box, each with a lobster pendant attached. She looked up at Tristan, waiting for an explanation.

"Remember last night when I was rubbing you down with the sunburn gel? I told you that you were my little lobster. Now, we will always have something to remind us both," Tristan said with a lopsided grin.

"Oh, Tristan, that is so cute! Put it on me," Claire said as she turned so Tristan could fasten the necklace around her neck.

After Claire put Tristan's on for her, Tristan ran her fingers softly across the necklace lying on Claire's chest. "Never take it off, okay?" Tristan said as she looked into Claire's eyes.

"I will never take it off, I promise, and you must never take yours off."

With the deal made, the two tired lovers drifted peacefully to sleep in each other's arms. The orange tabby cat lay at the end of the bed looking on in disgust. His pet had just put a collar on what he figured now would be his pet, too.

CHAPTER 15

Monday came all too soon for Tristan and Claire. Neither was looking forward to going back to work. They would begin crew change this week, and that meant they would be busy making travel arrangements for all the boats in the fleet. Tristan went in a little earlier than Claire so she could meet with the crew coordinators.

Claire arrived an hour behind Tristan and stopped in the galley for coffee before going up to the third floor. Linda, who worked in accounting, greeted her. Claire had only chatted with her once before, but she had always felt uncomfortable around the woman and couldn't quite put her finger on why.

"Wow, you're as red as a beet, Claire!" Linda exclaimed as Claire joined her at the coffeepot.

"It was wonderful. Tristan and I went to Gulf Shores and had such a great time that I didn't want to come back."

Linda moved closer to Claire and lowered her voice. "I would watch her if I were you, Claire. You do know she's a lesbian, don't you?"

Claire felt her hackles rise. "What does that have to do with anything, Linda?"

"Look, don't get angry with me. I'm just trying to help you. If you keep hanging around with her, people will start to talk, and you will have the same sick reputation as she does."

"Sick? You think someone is sick because they don't have the same sexual orientation as you?" Claire was becoming angrier by the second and refused to keep her voice down.

"It's a perversion, Claire. God hates homosexuals, and if you spend time around them, you might just end up suffering His wrath with them."

Murky Waters

"What makes you think I'm not one of them?" Claire replied, watching as a look of disgust made its way across Linda's face.

Before Linda could respond, their conversation was interrupted by a silver-headed woman sitting in the corner of the kitchen eating her breakfast unnoticed. Her soft features were full of warmth, but when she spoke, her eyes bore holes into Linda.

"Excuse me, Linda, but I'm very familiar with the Bible, and I'm curious to know where it says that God hates homosexuals."

"It says it in the story about Sodom and Gomorrah," Linda replied smugly.

"I'm familiar with Sodom and Gomorrah, but I have not found anything that said God hates people. It does say that he hates sin, and the people in those cities were committing all sorts of sins. However, I am still curious as to where you have found it to say that God hates homosexuals." The older woman continued in a polite, soft-spoken manner. "Since you are quoting what you say is in the Bible, can you tell me what Christ himself said about sin?"

When Linda failed to answer, the woman began again. "The Bible says all have sinned and fallen short of the glory of God. Translated, it means we've all goofed up. Not one of us is without blemish, including you, Linda. I would suggest you study the Bible a little more intently before you preach any more sermons. If you continue to twist His words to suit your liking, you may find yourself suffering His wrath."

Linda's face had turned beet red, and she turned and stamped out of the galley. The older woman smiled at Claire, then went back to her breakfast.

"Thank you for stepping in. I was probably about to say some things I shouldn't have."

"God does not hate anyone. Don't ever let anyone make you believe that. He loves each one of us, and we all have a purpose for being here. Give Him a chance, and He will show you what yours is. Sometimes, He puts you in the path of just one person, and you and that person are changed forever.

"I was changed forever when my nephew committed suicide. He was gay. According to the note he left, he had struggled with it for years alone. When he finally decided to confide in his brother, the secret spread through the family like wildfire. My sister became enraged."

The older woman paused for a moment to gather her emotions. "I was never really sure why my sister reacted the way she did. If she were worried about his eternal soul, I would have thought she would have handled things differently. Deep down inside, I admitted to myself that she was simply embarrassed."

The woman sighed. "Bless his poor heart. His last words were scribbled on a scrap of paper. He said if God hated him, what hope did he have? He blew his brains out and put an end to his twenty-three-year life. Had someone stepped in and told him the truth, he might still be with us today."

Claire was at a loss for words as tears glistened in her eyes. "Thank you for sharing that with me. I'll never forget it."

"I'm glad you allowed me to share it." The older woman patted Claire on the shoulder and left the room. Claire was so intent on listening to what the woman had to say that she neglected to get her name, but she was glad the woman spoke up when she did or Linda may have found herself suffering Claire's wrath.

When Claire made it to the third-floor office, the phones were ringing off the hook. The crew coordinators were answering calls and sending their requests for travel arrangements by email to Claire's department. Her meeting in the galley had caused her to run a little late. She went into her office and quickly got set up to help her agents.

Claire glanced into Tristan's office through the glass wall that separated them. Tristan was busy on the phone and was typing on her computer. As Claire waited for her own computer to boot up, she continued to watch Tristan answer one phone line after the other. She was catching the overflow from the crew coordinators. Claire appreciated that Tristan worked with her people and shared their load when they were busy. Ellen was right when she said Tristan was an excellent boss.

Just before lunch, Cam dropped in and invited Tristan and Claire's staff to a crawfish boil at the fleet. Claire was thrilled at the prospect of finally getting real Louisiana mudbugs. When the lunch hour arrived, the entire department made a beeline for the fleet.

Tristan sat next to Claire and showed her how to peel the meat away from the small crustaceans. "Only eat the ones with curled tails. If their tails are straight, throw them in the trash. When the tail is straight, it means it was dead before it went into the boil and is not any good."

Claire did as she was instructed, carefully peeling each tail and watching Tristan as she skillfully peeled and ate twice as many. Claire glanced across the table at Mike and was disgusted by his technique. After he ate each tail, he would suck the head of the creature before throwing it into the trash.

When he caught Claire watching him with a look of revulsion, he smiled and asked, "What's wrong, Claire? You don't suck heads?"

Tristan's head snapped up, and she glared at Mike. He smiled maliciously as he stuffed another crawfish head in his mouth and sucked the juice from it. "Obviously, Tristan doesn't know what's good."

"I have no desire to learn to suck heads, Mike. I'll leave that up to you since you seem to be quite skilled at it yourself. Since you're not a Louisiana native, I can only assume that someone spent some time training you how to do it," Claire shot back, knowing she was walking a fine line and dangerously close to stooping to Mike's level.

A huge grin made its way across Tristan's face as the rest of the table laughed and chided Mike. Claire had beaten him at his own game. Mike ate the rest of his lunch in silence, occasionally glancing at Tristan with a scowl.

"So, Claire, how do you like living in Cajun country?" Allen, one of the fleet dispatchers, asked.

"I like it. It's not much different from Houston. The climate is the same, and the food is just as spicy. I'm really enjoying learning all about Louisiana and its culture, and Tristan has been kind enough to take me under her wing and show me around."

"Oh, Tris, you should take her out on one of those swamp tours and let her see some of the sights," Allen said.

"I've always wanted to do that, Claire. Why don't you and I go sometime?" Mike asked, breaking into the conversation while looking at Tristan.

Sensing the tension between Mike and Tristan, Allen tried to keep the situation from escalating. "Mike, how about we go sometime? Matter of fact, I have my own boat. We can do our own tour and maybe get to fish a little."

Mike stared at a smirking Tristan for a moment before directing his attention to Allen. "That sounds great, man. Give me a call at the office, and we'll make plans. I'll even buy the beer."

Tristan continued to smirk, but what she really wanted to do was stomp a mud hole in Mike's ass. She was livid that Mike would actually put Claire on the spot like that in front of a group of people. He was much too pushy, and Tristan decided then that she would have a chat with Mike alone.

Several of the boats were tied off at the landing barge, and Tristan took Claire down to meet some of the crews. Mike and Lauren accompanied them since neither had ever been on any of the vessels. As Claire talked with one of the captains, Tristan watched Mike out of the corner of her eye. He studied Claire from head to toe, barely able to take his eyes off her. When he glanced over at Tristan, Mike realized that he had been caught staring. Their eyes locked, silently challenging one another until Tristan's cell phone rang.

She stepped onto the stern of the boat to finish her call and lit up a cigarette as she listened to the caller drone on about a medical release for one of the deckhands. A few minutes later, she snapped the phone closed and turned to go back into the galley. It was then that she came face-to-face with Mike.

"You don't like me much, do you, Tristan?" Mike questioned, looking her in the eye.

"No, Mike, I don't care for your kind at all," she answered without flinching.

"Now, why is that? Do I threaten you in some way?" he asked smugly.

"There's nothing about you I find threatening, but your repeated attempts to get Claire to go out with you, even though she has made it plain she is not interested, are wearing on my nerves. You do know what harassment is, don't you?"

"Tristan, are you threatening me?"

"If you were one of my employees, you'd be unemployed right now. You work for Suarez and therefore are Claire's problem, but if you continue behaving as you have, I'm ready to step in and resolve the issue. If you want to consider that a threat, go right ahead."

Murky Waters

Mike pulled out a cigarette and lit it up. He exhaled the smoke in Tristan's direction. "I've heard that these boats are very dangerous. It's been said if someone goes overboard, they could very likely be pushed under the boat by the current and drown if they are not caught up in the prop first." He stared at Tristan with a cold intensity.

"You're exactly right, Mike. Should someone fall over the side, all the people here watching would be helpless if the current were just right." Tristan could feel the hair rise on her neck as she stared back at Mike. The looks between them conveyed so much more than what had been verbalized.

Mike glanced around at the people on the landing barge and levee. "Well then, I guess I better be very careful, shouldn't I?" he said before flipping his cigarette into the water and walking away.

His thinly veiled threat did not go unnoticed. Tristan had been threatened before by much more menacing characters. Mike didn't bother her in the least, but Claire, on the other hand, she worried for. Tristan watched as Mike made his way down the gangway back to the landing barge. "Yes, Mike, you should be very careful," she muttered under her breath as she went to find Claire.

Tristan knew Claire would not appreciate that she had discussed her with Mike, so she decided to keep the conversation to herself. She rode back to the office, mentally plotting how she would rid the company of Mike as Claire and Lauren chatted about the boats. It was time for Mike to move on, and she would make sure it happened.

Busy with crew change, Claire's days passed quickly that week. By Friday, she and Tristan were looking forward to a quiet weekend at home. Tristan escorted Claire to her Jeep in case there were any unexpected surprises. To Claire's relief, there was no ominous envelope waiting on her. Tristan theorized that if it were Mike or Lauren, they had been too busy this week to do anything but work. Claire listened to her reasoning, and her suspicion of her co-workers deepened.

CHAPTER SIXTEEN

The following months yielded no envelopes for Claire. She and Tristan breathed a sigh of relief. For the most part, Claire wanted to believe that whoever had been tormenting her had simply moved on.

Detective Salmetti had been in constant contact with Claire, giving her updates on how the investigation was progressing. She had talked to Mike, as well, and he feigned shock and surprise that she had implied that Mike was a suspect. Until the next envelope arrived, all they could do was wait.

Tristan tried her best to convince Claire to fire Mike herself or file a formal complaint to her superiors. He had been smart and laid low. He was polite and cordial when he spoke, but his eyes conveyed what he really felt.

Tristan had been sent to one of the boats and was not expected home until later that night. Claire walked into the deserted parking lot after leaving work a little later than she had planned. She was in no hurry to go home to an empty house. When she arrived at her Jeep, she found Mike leaning against the driver's side door, preventing her from getting into her vehicle. Claire felt her chest tighten and glanced around, hoping to see if anyone else was nearby.

Claire cleared her throat and tried to sound casual as she spoke. "Mike, what are you still doing here?"

He glared at her for a moment before answering. "Is it true, Claire?"

"Is what true?"

"Is it true that you are the new conquest of the bitch we work for?" Mike spat.

Murky Waters

"Frankly, it is none of your business who I see, and I will thank you not to refer to her in that manner," Claire said as she shakily stood her ground.

"Claire, you could do so much better than that. She has a reputation for screwing anything that moves. I cannot believe you would lower yourself by having anything to do with her. By the way, is that her way of marking you as her own?" he asked, pointing to the necklace hanging around Claire's neck. "I noticed that she wears one just like it."

"I'm not going to stand here and justify anything for you, Mike. My private life does not concern you in the least. You need to keep your nose out of the rumor mill and more on your job. Now, if you don't mind, I would like to go home," Claire said, hoping that he would step aside.

Mike's feet were firmly rooted to the spot. He stared at Claire with anger flashing in his eyes. "You let me send you flowers and spend countless hours fawning over you, and you give it up to that sorry-ass bitch."

Claire was acutely aware that the situation was spiraling out of control. She looked around again to see if anyone was nearby, and the panic rose within her when she saw they were alone. "Mike, I've been patient with you, even though you continued to ask me out after we discussed that it was not a good idea. You're not leaving me a whole lot of choices here; please don't push me to file a complaint against you."

"File a complaint?" He laughed in her face. "Do you honestly think Suarez will do anything to me? The policies regarding sexual harassment are simply something they have put on paper to make everyone believe they take the issue seriously. I've already dealt with that before. Don't you remember Charlotte? She was foolish enough to complain about me, and Suarez turned her inside out. By the time they finished with her, they had her convinced that she was the bad guy. It's still a man's world, and we will always have the upper hand.

"Oh! And don't think for a minute you are going to tag me with any stalker charges. It was a big mistake sending that detective to talk to me, Claire. I told her just how you are, and you no doubt led some poor bastard on just like you did me. Your kind always flirts and calls it being friendly, but when a man shows you any attention, you run screaming foul. Frankly, I think you like the attention."

Regardless of being alone with Mike, Claire felt every fiber of her being grow hot with anger. "You're the one with the problem, Mike. You prey on women who are polite and friendly to you. Deep inside, you know you're not worthy of a decent woman, so you turn polite gestures into something vile in that deranged mind of yours. You know what the problem really is? You're a weak and pathetic excuse for a man, and you know it! Now, get your pudgy ass out of my way!"

"Fine, Claire!" Mike hissed through clenched teeth. "You're a lot smarter than I gave you credit for. Screwing the boss is a good way to secure your position with the company. Too bad it didn't work for me!"

He stepped away and watched Claire fumble nervously with her keys. Once inside, she locked the doors and looked back at Mike, who still stood next to her Jeep staring daggers at her.

Claire sped out of the parking lot with Mike looking on. Her hands were shaking so much she could barely hold the steering wheel. She drove toward Tristan's house in a state of confusion. She picked up her cell phone and called Tristan, taking a deep breath to calm herself as Tristan answered. "Hey, Tris, do you know what time you will be home?" Her voice trembled as she spoke.

"I'm almost there. Is something wrong? You sound upset." Tristan felt her heart pound.

"Tris, I don't know what to do," Claire said as she started to cry. "Mike was waiting for me when I got to my car this afternoon. He said some things that were really upsetting."

"Okay, just calm down," Tristan said, trying to remain calm herself. "Where are you?"

"I'm on the interstate not far from the turnoff to your house," Claire whimpered as tears rolled down her face.

"I'm a mile away from the house. I'll stay on the phone with you until you get there. Did he hurt you, Claire?"

"No, but, Tris, I'm so scared. He was so angry with me. Apparently, he knows now that I am seeing you, and he was pissed. He thinks I led him on," Claire cried into the phone.

"Baby, did he threaten you?" Tristan asked, trying to keep her anger from her voice.

"No. He was angry that I was seeing you and accused me of securing my position with Valor by sleeping with my boss."

"Just come home to me, Claire. We will call the police, and tonight, we are calling someone at Suarez. I want someone in our office Monday. He will no longer be on our account, and if I have my way, he will be in the unemployment line."

As Tristan drove down her driveway, she could see the headlights of Claire's Jeep coming up behind her and breathed a sigh of relief. She jumped out of her truck and pulled Claire into her arms, feeling her tremble uncontrollably. Gently, she took Claire's hand and led her to the house. Once inside, Tristan had Claire sit down at the kitchen table while she poured her a glass of wine.

Claire was hesitant to repeat what Mike had said about Tristan, but she knew she could not leave out any details. Remembering the conversation nearly word for word, Claire told Tristan everything that was said. She watched nervously as Tristan's neck and face flushed with anger.

"Tristan, I don't want to upset you further, but I don't think we have anything to take to the police. He didn't threaten me. He simply confronted me about my relationship with you. We have no proof it is him sending me those pictures other than his behavior."

"Don't protect him, Claire!" Tristan said harshly. "Regardless of whether he is the one who has been stalking you, what he did tonight was wrong and inexcusable. I have sat back and done my best to let you handle him, but I can't do it any longer. If you don't want to go to the police with this, that is your decision, but Mike will not work at Valor if I can help it."

Tristan had gotten up from the table and was pacing around the kitchen as she spoke. Claire knew better than to argue the point with her. Tristan was right after all; something had to be done, and quickly.

"Okay, I'll file a formal complaint with my manager Monday and see where it goes from there," Claire said, hating that she was at the center of the controversy. She had failed in handling Mike and dreaded having to admit defeat.

"No, Claire, we are not going to wait and see what they decide to do. We will force their hand in this. I don't want him working on this account. On Monday, he will be removed and should be terminated." Tristan softened her tone when she saw the look of despair on Claire's face. "I know this is difficult for you, but I love you, Claire, and I can't sit by anymore and watch this. If I do, it will be as though I'm condoning it."

"You're right. You've been right all along. This was my first position as a full-fledged manager. I just wanted everything to go smoothly."

Tristan knelt in front of Claire's chair. "You're an excellent manager. Even if I weren't in love with you, I would have to admit that you've done a wonderful job on our account. I respect that you wanted everything to go well, and aside from the problems with Mike, you have accomplished your goal."

"What are you planning to do?" Claire asked as she wiped her face.

"I need to talk to Cam about this. He deserves to know," Tristan said as she continued to kneel in front of Claire, holding her hand in her own.

"How much are you going to tell him? I don't want him or Lucy to know anything about the photos, Tristan. This whole thing is way too humiliating. What if word of this gets out to the rest of the company?"

"If you don't want me to say anything about the pictures, I won't, but I do have an obligation to tell Cam about the incident that took place today. He needs to be in on the meeting with Suarez on Monday," Tristan said, trying to be reassuring.

"I agree he needs to be involved, but I am not ready to tell them anything about our suspicions regarding Mike. This whole situation is embarrassing enough. I'll make a report with Detective Salmetti. I want her to handle that part of it."

Tristan sighed. "Fine, we will only tell Cam about what happened tonight. Should you receive any more packages, we'll have to seriously reconsider. I'm sure Mike's going to be very angry with us after Monday, and I don't want any repercussions as a result."

Claire listened as Tristan spoke with Cam. Tristan had to remind him repeatedly that Claire was indeed all right and that Mike never laid a hand on her. After Tristan finished speaking with Cam, she encouraged Claire to try to eat. It was a few hours later before Tristan could get her to relax and nibble a sandwich.

That night as Tristan slept, Claire curled up close to her. Feeling Tristan's warmth and closeness made Claire feel secure. Even with Tristan near, the house alarm set, and the patrol cat lying at their feet, Claire stared into the darkness for hours before sleep claimed her.

When Tristan awoke the following morning, she lay next to Claire, looking at the tense lines across her face. She knew that Claire had not slept much. She was keenly aware that Claire had been restless for most of the night. She slipped out of bed, leaving Claire to sleep as long as she could.

Tristan padded sleepily into the kitchen followed by a very hungry orange feline. After she got the coffee going, she filled Ralph's bowl and watched as he ate. When the coffee brewed, she poured herself a cup and went into the sunroom with Ralph close on her heels.

She sat quietly on one of the wicker chairs and sipped her coffee while smoking a cigarette. She watched as the smoke rose and thought that when things calmed down, she and Claire would really have to consider giving up the habit. Now was not the time, though. It calmed her nerves as she stared out the windows surrounding the room. She wondered how much more the love of her life could take before she simply cracked under the pressure.

With all that had been going on lately, Tristan had been too busy to struggle with her inner turmoil. She was learning to cope with her feelings of apprehension and fear. Some mornings, she would lie in bed watching Claire as she slept, silently regarding the woman who lay next to her. Tears of regret would fill her eyes when she thought about what she had put Claire through. She wondered how Claire would react to knowing the depths that she had sunk to in her past. Even with all of Claire's love and compassion, she wondered if she was deserving of someone so special.

Ralph stirred and let out a soft meow when Claire walked into the room clutching her own cup of coffee. She sat in the chair opposite Tristan and smiled weakly as she lit a cigarette. The dark circles beneath her eyes were a testament to her lack of rest.

"Baby, why are you up so early? It's obvious you barely slept last night," Tristan asked gently.

"I don't know, really. I just couldn't sleep after you got up. Besides, I didn't want to sleep the whole day away. My alone time with you is pretty limited, and I'm determined to take advantage of it when I can," Claire said as she smiled at Tristan.

"I have been sitting here thinking about what we could do today," Tristan said before taking a sip of her coffee. "I think I have come up with the perfect idea. We'll shower and dress, then go out for breakfast. Then, we'll spend the day indulging in your favorite hobby."

Claire smirked. "What exactly are you thinking is my favorite hobby?"

"Shopping," Tristan replied, and Claire laughed. "We can go out to the outlet mall and see if there's anything there you can't live without. Then, I thought we could go to the mall and maybe pick out a new comforter for our bed. You know, something that represents both our tastes. I'm thinking that might make you feel a little more at home here."

Claire reached over and placed her hand on top of Tristan's. "My love, you couldn't make me feel any more at home than you already have. It's your presence that makes this place feel like my home."

Ralph decided to include himself in the conversation by coughing up a hairball next to Claire's feet. Claire swore he did it because their sweet conversation sickened him. He watched as his pet cleaned up the mess and listened to her grumbling.

After they successfully drained the coffeepot and shared a shower that left them content and happy, they set out for the outlet mall. Claire felt like doing the driving, so they took her Jeep. She watched Tristan out of the corner of her eye as Tristan squirmed to get comfortable in the passenger seat. "You don't like being chauffeured, do you, dear?" Claire asked with a grin.

"I suppose it's a control issue. I like to be the one in the driver's seat, but don't worry about me over here." Tristan squirmed a little more as she slid the seat back to make more room for her long legs.

Claire merged onto the interstate and shot off like a rocket, driving like she was in the Indy 500. When she came up behind a slower car in the left lane, she began to grumble. "It's the long slender peddle to the right. Step on it, chucklehead!" When the car did finally move over into the right lane, Claire pulled alongside and glared at the driver. "I just wanted to catch a glimpse of a total moron," she growled. "Claire, honey? You doing all right over there? You seem a little tense today," Tristan said as she hung on for dear life.

"Nope, I'm fine. I always drive like this. When you drive in Houston traffic, it tends to make you a little aggressive," Claire said with her eyes glued to the road.

Tristan reached over and took Claire's hand into her own. "What's really on your mind? You know you can tell me anything."

Claire glanced over at her and said, "It's nothing, love. I'm okay, really." After a moment, Claire sighed. "I dread having to face him Monday morning."

Tristan lifted Claire's hand to her mouth and kissed it gently. "You will only have to face him for a little while. He will not be coming back to work at Valor, and after our meeting, he will be escorted off the premises."

Claire's tension seemed to ease as the day went on. She was especially excited about the new comforter they bought for their bed. Of course, the change called for new drapes and a few other items to coordinate the look. She was glad that they brought her Jeep because it was stuffed full from their shopping adventure.

She laughed to herself remembering Tristan's excitement when they left for the regular mall. Tristan made a beeline for the small pretzel stand near the food court. Claire watched in amusement as Tristan nearly inhaled a soft pretzel. Her eyes fluttered shut as she took the last bite. Claire figured she would need a cigarette and a nap after the way she enjoyed the snack.

They decided to have dinner at one of the many seafood restaurants that peppered Louisiana. Claire marveled at Tristan's appetite as she consumed nearly an entire seafood platter by herself. Claire thoroughly enjoyed her platter of fried catfish and fries, as well as the hushpuppies that were continually brought to the table. For dessert, they dined on cheesecake and coffee until they both felt like they would explode.

After arriving home, they were too miserable to simply sit in front of the TV, so they laundered the new linens and decorated the bedroom with their purchases. Tristan presented Ralph with a new cat bed in hopes that he would take to sleeping in it instead of hogging their bed.

He circled it, giving it a few sniffs. Claire thought he looked like he was scowling. In fact, he was. If his pet thought for one minute he would sleep in that monstrosity instead of her bed, she was dead wrong, though it might prove useful for storing his belongings. He still mourned the loss of his beloved catnip toy that had mysteriously disappeared.

"Tristan, why did you buy him that? He doesn't look too pleased with it," Claire said with a laugh.

"I was hoping he would sleep in it instead of on the new comforter. He nearly ruined my last one making his biscuits."

Claire looked at Tristan curiously. "Making biscuits?"

"Yeah, you know ... when he flexes his claws back and forth, it looks like he is kneading dough, so I call it making biscuits."

Claire laughed and kissed Tristan as she went to get the new linens from the dryer. Tristan looked down at Ralph, who was staring back up at her with an indignant scowl on his orange face. "Come on, try it at least once, you little fuzzy bastard," Tristan said as she tried to stuff him into the bed. Ralph squirmed from her grasp and went off to contemplate his revenge.

Claire and Tristan made the bed together and stood back to admire how it changed the appearance of the entire room. "I think we should christen the new sheets," Claire said with a wink. "I feel the need to mark my new territory."

Tristan cast her a sideways glance. "Mark your territory, huh? If you plan on peeing a circle around this bed, Claire Murray, you'll have to sleep in Ralph's bed."

Tristan chased her into the bathroom, where they decided to share another shower. Just as Claire had desired, they christened the new sheets by making love until the early hours of the morning. Claire lay with her head on Tristan's shoulder after they were both sated, enjoying the feel of the crisp linens and the warm body next to hers.

Murky Waters

Sunday morning bright and early, Cam and Lucy arrived for their long-standing breakfast date. They were pleasantly surprised to see that they would be eating in that rainy morning. Claire and Tristan had risen early, and due to the weather, decided to cook breakfast instead of going out.

Cam hated to bring up the issue with Mike during their time together, but he felt it necessary to get the unpleasant things out of the way first. "Claire, I have been thinking a lot about this thing with Mike. I agree totally with Tristan. Because of his conduct and his unwillingness to alter his behavior, it would be best if he moved along. Tomorrow morning, I want you and Tristan to come to my office before going upstairs. I think it's best we meet with the Suarez division manager in my office first."

With this agreed upon, they spent the rest of the morning enjoying each other's company. Claire had been lovingly accepted into their inner circle, and she felt as though she was part of a family again. She watched the love of her life intently as she spoke with Cam and Lucy. Claire was amazed at all the wonderful things this woman had brought into her life.

CHAPTER SEVENTEEN

Monday morning came much sooner than Claire had desired. She held Tristan's hand and fidgeted nervously as they rode to work together. She never liked being the center of controversy and felt like her presence alone had caused all the problems they were facing. Tristan seemed to sense what Claire was thinking and reassured her that Mike had brought this on himself.

Entering Cam's office, Tristan and Claire were greeted by a man who didn't appear to be much older than they were. In his business casual attire of khaki pants and a polo shirt, he smiled and held out his hand to Tristan, introducing himself while barely acknowledging Claire's presence. That did not go unnoticed by Tristan. By way of greeting, she simply nodded her head and did not accept the handshake.

Claire had only met Eugene Morris once before and wondered why Suarez had allowed an inexperienced member of the management team to handle this situation. He had only been promoted to the position of human resources manager six months before she received her promotion.

He quickly got down to business and asked Claire to recount the events between her and Mike. After Claire explained everything in detail, she sat quietly as Eugene made notes. After a few more minutes of silence, which seemed like an eternity to Claire and Tristan, Eugene spoke.

"I agree his behavior was totally inappropriate, but I think with a transfer and a letter of reprimand, he will understand the seriousness of his actions." Avoiding looking at Tristan and Claire, Eugene addressed Cameron casually.

Tristan could not hide her anger. "So, what you're saying is, you plan to slap him on the hand and make him someone else's problem?"

"Miss Delacroix, with all due respect, I don't believe we should end this man's career for his lack of judgment on this matter."

Tristan was about to retort when she was interrupted by Cam. "Mr. Morris, from what I have heard here today, I believe Mike has some problems. I cannot force you to fire him, but I do not expect to ever see him anywhere near here after today. Furthermore, he is not to have any contact with Miss Murray at all. No emails, phone calls, or any sort of correspondence whatsoever."

Eugene was about to say something when Cam cut him off. "Mr. Morris, I've run this company for a long time. Let me say first that I don't like your attitude toward Miss Murray. The first thing you should have done was apologize for the behavior of one of your employees. You have downplayed this situation by simply giving him a transfer.

"With that in mind, I have decided to hire Miss Murray as our travel manager. Her first assignment will be to acquire a new travel agency to attend our needs. Please inform your superiors that we will no longer require the services of Suarez Travel."

Eugene paled at the thought of losing such a lucrative contract. "I assure you, Mr. Hughes, we will make sure that Mike has no contact with Claire or anyone associated with Valor. We appreciate your business, and we will do whatever we can within reason to make sure you are satisfied."

It was Tristan who interrupted then. "If you are finished with the ass kissing, I would like that piece of crap taking up my office space removed now."

Ever the professional, Cam shot Tristan a look and tried hard not to laugh at the incredulous glare Eugene was giving Tristan. She stared back into his eyes until he had to look away.

Cam addressed Eugene again. "Mr. Morris, we can consider this meeting adjourned. I'll have security escort you upstairs to inform your employees of the changes that are being made. You can make whatever arrangements you need to clear your equipment out of the building, and I would like that done today."

Cam opened his door and allowed two security guards to enter his office. "These gentlemen will escort you upstairs, and you and your staff will leave without incident, or I will have the police here in a matter of minutes. Do I make myself clear?"

Eugene Morris nodded mutely as he gathered his things and followed the security staff out of the office.

"Claire, I'm sorry that I didn't give you more warning on what I had planned to do. I was hoping that he would have been a little more aggressive in handling this issue. He made it apparent when you walked in the room with whom he had chosen to side.

"I've seen it many times before. The one who files the complaint is often treated worse than the offending party. I hope you're okay with the decision I made for you. I will assure you that you will have much better benefits with the Valor family, and we will treat you with dignity and respect."

Shocked by the change of events, Claire had not realized fully that Cameron had submitted her resignation and hired her in a matter of minutes. "Thank you," she replied, still dumbstruck by all that transpired.

Tristan was equally stupefied. "Cam, don't get me wrong when I say this, but couldn't you have at least given us a heads up on what you were planning?"

"I'm sorry, Tris, but I just didn't like what I heard. Claire has become important to Lucy and me both, and there was no way I was going to leave all this up to that little prick to handle," Cam replied apologetically.

Claire stood and hugged Cam, surprising him and Tristan. "Thank you for taking care of me, Cam. I'll never forget it."

"I'll always stand up for my girls," he said as he winked at Tristan. He made it clear that Claire was more than just a member of the Valor family, she had been welcomed into his family, as well.

"Now if you two will excuse me, I want to make sure my orders are being followed, then I have to call my attorney. Suarez may be foolish enough to give me grief over the broken contract."

Tristan reached over and took Claire's hand into hers. "Are you okay with all this?"

"Of course I'm okay. I just lost one job and got another all in one day."

Murky Waters

Tristan couldn't help but chuckle. "I think I'm still in shock. Let's go over to human resources and make this official. You have a lot of paperwork to fill out."

"I have to do one thing first. I need to tell Ellen about this. She will kill me if she finds out from someone else," Claire said as she pulled Tristan into her arms and kissed her.

Claire had moved most of her belongings into Tristan's house, and very little of her furniture remained in her apartment. Their house began to feel like a home for both of them. Even though they shared the master bedroom, Tristan set aside one room just for Claire to do with what she wanted.

One Saturday afternoon, Tristan went out to the yard to clean the flowerbeds of the plants that died due to an early October frost. Claire spent time in her room setting up her home computer and sorting out her belongings. She came across the box that contained all her copies of the pictures sent to her by the stalker. She debated throwing them away but thought better of it.

She wanted to store them in a safe place and remembered how Tristan kept her storage room under lock and key. She reasoned that the locked room would be the perfect place to keep such items. She walked into the kitchen and got Tristan's key ring off the hook where she always kept it. Claire would just slip them inside the door without invading the sacred space that held Tristan's memories of her father.

Walking back through the house, Claire caught a glimpse of her lover working in the yard. Tristan was absorbed in her work, down on her hands and knees. She pruned shrubs and pulled the dead plants out of the beds and was applying a new layer of mulch.

Claire smiled as she watched Tristan doing one of the things she truly loved. Ralph ran around the yard, pouncing on insects dislodged from their homes as Tristan worked. Claire sighed with contentment, feeling so happy and peaceful in her surroundings.

With her box at her feet, Claire fumbled with the keys until she found the right one. When she stepped into the room, the mustiness of it assaulted her sinuses. She made a mental note to air it out. Along the far wall were plastic storage bins full of all sorts of equipment she recognized from her tour of one of the towboats. She figured they were the belongings of Tristan's dad.

Claire noticed something out of place in the dusty room. In the corner sat a workstation, complete with a computer, printer, and scanner. Claire took her box over to the desk and sat down. She felt a strange foreboding as she stared at the equipment. Slowly, she opened one of the hutch doors. Her eyes widened as she looked at the contents inside.

She picked up a camera no larger than an ink pen and studied it. Dumbstruck by all the digital camera equipment, she pulled out each piece. Claire wondered if perhaps Tristan had been storing the equipment for her mother. She remembered Tristan saying at the Myrtles that she didn't even own a camera. *Why would she lie?* Claire wondered.

Sitting on the corner of the table was one of Tristan's purses. It struck Claire as odd that Tristan would leave a purse in this room. She picked it up and noticed something strange on the strap. Close inspection revealed something that nearly made Claire's heart stop. A small digital camera no bigger than a pager was clipped to the strap.

Claire's heart pounded when she remembered that the purse she held in her hands was the one Tristan carried on their first date to the Mexican restaurant. She dug frantically through the contents on the table. Her hands shook when she found a clear plastic storage box. When she opened the lid, tears of anguish slipped down her cheeks. There inside were the same pictures she had been receiving over the past year. Now, she knew for sure why Tristan kept this room locked.

She nearly fainted when she rounded the corner and came face-to-face with Tristan. The look on Tristan's face confirmed her worst fears. Claire backed up a step from her stalker

"Claire? What were you doing in that room?"

"All this time, I've been living a nightmare, and it was you." Claire's voice was barely a whisper. She watched myriad expressions cross Tristan's face as she stood in front of her.

"You know what's really sad? I pushed so hard to make you believe it was Mike that I started to believe it myself." Tristan could not make herself look Claire in the eyes. "You're afraid of me. I can feel it."

Murky Waters

Fear turned to anger for Claire. She lunged at Tristan, beating her in the chest, sending her backwards down the hallway and into the living room. Claire was hysterically screaming as she backed Tristan nearly into the sunroom.

"Make me understand, Tristan! Make me understand how you could do something like this to someone you profess to love! How the hell could you do this to me?"

Tristan's voice was low and calm. "Claire, calm down, and just hear me out."

Anger surged through Claire's veins, and she shoved Tristan hard into the door facing off the sunroom. Tristan reacted out of shock and pain. She slapped Claire hard enough across the face that the impact of the hit slung Claire's face to the side. When Claire faced her again, Tristan could see a thin trickle of blood coming from her lip.

Tristan brought shaking hands to her face. "Oh, my God, Claire! I'm so sorry." Tristan took a step back in horror. She sat down on one of the wicker chairs in the sunroom and buried her face in her hands.

Claire stood in the doorway, her facial features obscured by her hair clinging to the blood and tears on her face. "Why, Tristan? Tell me why," she demanded as she ripped the lobster necklace from around her neck. Tears spilled down Tristan's cheeks in earnest as she watched the necklace drop to the floor.

"A year ago, Valor sent me to Houston to assist in the renegotiation of our travel contract. Since I would be working so closely with the travel department, I accompanied Ellen to the meetings with Suarez. It was obvious to me when you got here that you didn't remember me, but I remembered you.

"During our stay at the Suarez home office, I noticed you. From the minute I laid eyes on you, I was consumed. I was too afraid to approach you, so I took every chance I could to just catch a glimpse. When I returned home, I couldn't get you off my mind. The following weekend, I returned to Houston. I sat outside your office until you left for the day, and I followed you home.

"I would drive to Houston on my weekends and take pictures. I could look at them when I got home, and I didn't feel so separated from you. I honestly thought the pictures would be the only things

I would ever have of you. I never dreamed that someone so beautiful would want to be involved with someone like me."

Claire was spellbound as Tristan made her confession. It was like a bad dream that she was sure she would wake up from at any moment. She was so overwhelmed that she was afraid she would become sick or pass out.

Tristan continued; her voice was monotone. "I know it seems strange, but I started to send the pictures to you because it made me feel as though I had a connection to you in some way.

"I was so happy when I learned that you lived alone. I felt a glimmer of hope. Then, I saw you go out with that girl and kiss her good night. I was so heartbroken, so jealous. That's why I sent you the note. I was hoping you wouldn't see her again.

"During the negotiations at Suarez, I developed a rapport with your superiors. All it took was one call, and they honored my request to have you come to Valor. I tried to force Rhonda out to make a spot for you. As it happened, things worked out perfectly with her getting pregnant.

"We got off to such a rocky start. I felt like I had alienated you, so I continued to take your picture. In some strange way, I felt it bound us together. After our first date went so well, I stopped. I was so afraid you would find out somehow, so I tried to divert suspicion to the travel agents. When Mike started his shit, it all fell into place. I swore to myself I would never do that to you again, but when Mike continued to pursue you, I felt threatened, so I sent you the pictures of us.

"I think the reason I kept all that equipment and the pictures is that subconsciously I wanted you to find them. I wanted to be caught. I wanted an excuse to come clean with you. I was just too afraid to admit what I had done."

Tristan stood up and walked slowly toward Claire. "I know you're upset with me, but please believe I didn't mean to hurt you."

She reached out to Claire, hoping she would accept her apology. Something in Claire snapped. Fear and anger boiled up within her. In a rage, she slammed her hands into Tristan's chest. The unexpected blow sent Tristan tumbling backwards into the French doors that gave way in a shower of glass.

Murky Waters

Claire felt numb from head to toe. She walked to the doorway and looked at Tristan's unconscious form sprawled out across the deck. Tristan's breath rose up in little puffs of steam above her in the cold air, confirming that she was still alive. Her arm lay at an odd angle; Claire knew it was broken.

Claire stood over Tristan for what seemed like an eternity. Thoughts ran through her mind like a tape recorder, replaying the conversations from the past year. She remembered what Cam and Lucy had told her about Tristan's childhood. She remembered the conversation with the silver-headed woman in the kitchen one morning. *Sometimes, God puts you in the path of just one person, and you and that person are changed forever.*

Claire looked at the woman lying before her and made the decision that would forever change her life. She picked up the phone and dialed 911. Then, she went through the house and made a few adjustments. She went back to sit at Tristan's side and waited.

As Tristan awoke, she felt a dull aching pain in her head. She felt nauseated when she tried to turn toward the sounds in the room. Her right arm felt heavy, and it ached even more so than her head. As her vision came into focus, she noticed Claire standing next to the bed, then realized she was in a hospital room.

Claire looked down at her and spoke quickly. "When they realize you're awake, the police will want to question you, so listen very carefully to me, Tristan. If you do not agree to what I have to say, I will tell them the truth, and you will go to jail. Are you with me so far?"

Tristan tried to nod her head, but a sharp pain prevented her from doing so. She tried to speak, but her throat was too dry to utter a word. Claire gave her a sip of water.

"I understand, Claire," she croaked.

"You probably don't remember, but I shoved you through the French doors of the sunroom. You suffered a broken arm, a mild concussion, and several deep cuts that required suturing. To avoid you being arrested, I lied to the police. Before they arrived, I punched out one of the windowpanes in the back door to make it look as though someone broke in. I told the officers that a man was in the house when we got home. We both fought with him, and he knocked you through the doors before escaping. You will need to corroborate this story."

Tristan lay in silence, listening as Claire spoke.

"Now, here is the part I want you to pay special attention to. I love you, Tristan. I kind of understand why you did what you did, but you need some help. I want you to see a therapist, and I will stand beside you and help anyway I can. Should you fail to honor this, I will go to the police for your sake and mine. So, what I need to know now is, will you agree to this?"

Tears streamed down Tristan's face. "I will do anything you ask of me, Claire. I swear it." Tristan's body trembled with her sobs.

Claire stood close by while Detective Salmetti questioned Tristan. She was surprised that Tristan was able to remember the description she had given her of their attacker so their stories would be the same. Claire was sure to include that the assailant's description and build did not resemble Mike's. He had been guilty of many things, but she would not allow him to take the blame for this.

After the detective left, Tristan drifted off to sleep with the aid of pain medication. Claire called Cam and Lucy, and just as she figured, they were adamant about coming to the hospital. Claire met them at the door to Tristan's room.

"Like I explained on the phone, she is not seriously hurt. They are keeping her for observation because of the concussion, and she will be released first thing in the morning. She's sleeping right now. Both of you are welcome to go in and see her, but afterward, I would like to speak to you alone."

Cam and Lucy exchanged glances for a moment, then went into the room. Standing on opposite sides of the bed, they both felt Tristan's skin, just to assure themselves that she was indeed all right. Claire gave them a rundown of Tristan's injuries and relayed what the doctor had said. Cam and Lucy visibly relaxed. Once Lucy was confident that Tristan would fully recover, she asked Claire to tell them what happened.

Claire glanced at Cam. "Would you mind staying with Tristan while Lucy accompanies me downstairs to smoke? My nerves are at the breaking point, and I just need to relax a minute before I rehash the events of the evening."

Murky Waters

Lucy wrapped her arm around Claire and led her out the door. Claire was comforted by the motherly touch. She wondered how Lucy would feel after she told her that she had been the one who inflicted her adopted daughter with such injuries. They rode in silence down the elevator to the ground floor. Lucy guided Claire over to a bench just outside the emergency room door.

They sat quietly for a few minutes as Claire smoked her cigarette and gathered her thoughts. She could not stop the flow of tears that rained from her eyes. Lucy pulled her close and stroked her back in an attempt to comfort her.

"Lucy, I'm sorry, but I've lied to you and Cam. There was no break-in. I shoved Tristan through the French doors. I lied to the police to cover up what really happened."

Lucy recoiled at the things she heard. "Then what the hell happened?"

Claire looked at her through tear-filled eyes. "Lucy, there is so much to explain. I don't know where to start."

"Start from the beginning," Lucy replied as calmly as she could.

Claire took a deep breath. "When I lived in Houston, I received pictures taken of me by an anonymous photographer. Sometimes, a typed note would accompany them, accusing me of being a slut. When I was offered the Valor job, I jumped at the chance to leave Houston, hoping that would resolve the problem.

"Not long after I arrived here, the photos started coming again. I confided in Tristan, and we began to suspect Mike and Lauren, the travel agents. When Mike started behaving the way he did, I was convinced it was him. I even reported my suspicions to the police.

"Yesterday, I decided to store those pictures in the room that Tristan keeps under lock and key. I got her key ring and let myself in. I found a lot of very expensive digital camera equipment in there, and among those cameras, I found copies of the exact pictures I had been receiving."

Lucy shook her head as though she did not comprehend. "What are you saying? That Tristan is a stalker? Claire, that just does not make sense! How can you be saying these things?"

"Because Tristan admitted to it, Lucy! She told me in great detail how she did it. She even photographed us on our first date using a lapel camera. She has some major problems upstairs!"

Lucy sat in stunned silence. "Oh, my God." As the truth sank in, she began to cry.

Claire tentatively reached over and patted Lucy on the shoulder. "Lucy, Tristan needs some help. I told her I would not tell the police anything if she would agree to see a therapist. I'll stand by her and help her anyway I can. Not having her in my life is something I cannot even fathom. Believe it or not, I truly do love her.

"When she started toward me, I just freaked out, and I shoved her back. I didn't mean to hurt her. You have to believe I would never do anything like that intentionally. I was just so overwhelmed and shocked."

Lucy pointed to the pack of cigarettes. "You mind if I have one of those? I need something to calm my nerves before I tell all this to Cam."

Claire handed her a cigarette and lit it for her. Lucy inhaled the smoke and exhaled slowly with a little cough. She looked at Claire. "So, what are we going to do?"

Claire shrugged. "I think we need a little time apart. I may stay at my apartment for a while until we get things sorted out, the lease is not up yet. I love her so much, but on the same hand, I'm little fearful. There's a side to her I know nothing about. All those months, a faceless monster terrified me. To suddenly find out that it was the woman I love and have committed myself to is more than shocking. I don't even know how to cope with all this."

"Claire, I'm not making excuses for her behavior because I know she knows the difference between wrong and right. I'm just trying to understand why she would do something like this. What was going on in that head of hers?" Lucy's hand trembled as she brought the cigarette to her lips.

"I suppose it has something to do with the way her mother treated her. She said some things tonight that have made me wonder about that. She made the comment that she thought I would never be interested in someone like her. I had no idea her self-esteem was that low."

Lucy swiped another cigarette and lit it, coughing again as she drew the smoke into her lungs. "Claire, you do realize that you are the first real relationship she has had? She has dated a few girls, but nothing has ever developed beyond a few dates. Frankly, I think it was just sex. The girls would call for her, but she would avoid them. She never got attached to anyone for any length of time before you."

"She's admitted that. I have no idea how I'll deal with this, but I can tell you that I will not turn away from her. I just need some time to work through it, then I can focus on Tristan."

After a few more cigarettes, the women made their way back upstairs to Tristan's room. When they walked through the door, they could hear Tristan's sobs before they got fully into the room. Cam held her gently in his arms, her face buried in his chest. When he looked up at Lucy and Claire, his eyes were filled with tears, as well.

Due to Tristan's injuries, Cam and Lucy insisted that she stay with them for a while. Claire returned to Tristan's house and oversaw the repairs made to the doors and windows. Claire called to check on Tristan each day, but Lucy explained that Tristan was so ashamed of her behavior that she was barely speaking to anyone.

Tristan did honor her word and had Lucy help her find a therapist. The only time she left the sanctuary of Cam and Lucy's was to go to her appointments. Claire did her best to stay out of the way and let Tristan heal physically and emotionally. She could not help but wonder if things would be normal between them again.

When she could stand it no longer, Claire found herself on the Hughes' doorstep one afternoon. Lucy greeted her warmly and invited her in. "Is there any chance that Tristan will see me?" Claire asked, the emotion obvious in her voice.

"Sweetie, she really hasn't had too much to say to Cam and me. She won't eat unless I take her meals into her room, and even then, she merely picks at the food. I've been very concerned for her. To be honest, I don't know if it would be a good idea for you to see her right now." Lucy patted Claire on the hand, trying to comfort the emotionally distraught woman.

"I miss her so much," Claire sobbed. "She's shutting me out, and I can't take it. I know she is ashamed of her actions, but I have already forgiven her. I made a commitment to her, and I'll keep it." Claire wiped the tears that ran down her cheeks. "She's become my whole world."

Lucy wrapped Claire in her arms. "Claire, honey, give her a little time. She's in a very fragile state right now. I believe, given a little time, Tristan will come to terms with what she has done. Give the therapist a little time to work with her; she may very well need you to attend some of the appointments with her."

Claire sniffed and wiped her face again. "Oh, Lucy, I miss her so much. You don't know how hard it is to resist the temptation to run into her room and take her into my arms. You're right, though. I suppose I do need to give her some time."

"Off the subject, how are you and that little orange menace Ralph getting along?"

Claire chuckled halfheartedly. "Well, he still refuses to sleep in the cat bed that Tristan got him. The high side is that he is storing in there all the stuff he steals. I have found two socks and a bra in there, although neither vaguely resembles what it originally was. I know he misses Tris, too; he seems a little confused by her absence."

Later, Claire returned to their empty-feeling home. She fed Ralph and actually enjoyed playing with him and his mouse on a string. The only good thing about her separation from Tristan was that she and Ralph had begun to get along a little better.

After dinner, she settled down on the sofa to watch TV. Shortly after, Ralph joined her and curled up into a ball in her lap. He seemed to sense her pain and loneliness. He allowed her to pet him, and before long, he was purring contentedly.

Claire stared off into space as she absently stroked his fur. It was then that she noticed something shiny on the floor near the sunroom. She stood, laying Ralph back on the sofa, and walked over to see what the object was. With trembling hands, she picked up the lobster necklace and remembered the significance of it. She remembered the look on Tristan's face when she ripped it from her neck. That one action had hurt Tristan more than the physical blow she was dealt.

Murky Waters

Claire knew it when the defeat had registered so clearly in Tristan's brown eyes. Tears streamed down her face as she clutched it to her chest and rejoined Ralph on the sofa.

Lucy opened the door to Tristan's room after knocking. Receiving no response, she couldn't simply walk away. She was more worried about Tristan than she would admit. Deep in her heart, she knew that Tristan would not harm herself, but she wasn't taking any chances with her at this point.

As she entered the darkened room, Lucy could make out Tristan's long form lying across the bed. "I'm fine, Lucy." Tristan's voice startled her. "Can I skip dinner tonight? I'm really not hungry," Tristan said without turning to face her.

"My love, you're not passing up any more meals," Lucy said as she sat on the bed and stroked Tristan's hair lovingly. "You had a visitor today. Claire came by, but I told her that you weren't quite up to seeing anyone yet. She misses you very much and wants you to come home soon."

"Why on earth would she want to see me? I don't deserve her," Tristan said with no emotion in her voice.

"Tristan, you have to quit beating yourself up over this. She has forgiven you and wants you to come home. I know it's hard for you to believe, but she truly misses you. Her love for you has not dwindled one bit."

"I'm too ashamed to face her. Lucy, I was there! I saw what I did to her, and I don't think I can ever forgive myself. I've put her through so much this past year. I have lied and deceived her while she has been nothing but good to me. How will she ever be able to trust me again?" Tristan said as tears formed in her eyes.

"Tris, she wants to work this out, and in time, she'll trust you again if you let her. Baby, the way Mallory raised you, it's no wonder you could think that Claire could simply walk away. Claire is committed to you and loves you very much. She's willing to give you a chance, won't you give her one?"

Tristan lay silent for a while before she spoke again. "I miss her, too. I just don't know if I'm ready to face her yet."

"Well, you are going to face my meatloaf in the kitchen," Lucy said as she tugged Tristan's hand. "Tonight, you will come down and have dinner with me and Cam. I have made your beloved chocolate cheesecake for dessert. Then, we can sit out on the patio and talk until the cows come home."

Cam was surprised and relieved as Lucy and Tristan walked into the kitchen with tear-stained faces. Cam tried to appear as though everything was normal, but his heart secretly broke for Tristan; he had never seen her look so broken. As they ate dinner, he brought her up to date on all the happenings at the office, watching Tristan's face intently as he spoke. Uncharacteristically, Tristan did not seem remotely interested.

After dessert, Cam sent his two favorite women out to the patio while he cleaned the kitchen. Occasionally, he would glance outside and watch them as they talked. Tristan's eyes were downcast the entire time. He wanted so badly to run out there and take her into his arms. At least she was out of her room.

"Well, it's about time you called me. Since you and Tristan have gotten together, I rarely hear from you anymore," Ellen playfully teased when Claire called her out of the blue.

"Remember when you adopted me as a little sister?" Claire asked, fighting the urge to cry. "Well, I need my big sister right now."

It seemed to Claire that she had no sooner hung up the phone than Ellen arrived. She opened the door to her friend, whose arms were heavy laden with baked goods. "I figured some homemade goodies would help Tristan mend quicker. I have no business having this stuff in my house anyway," Ellen chattered excitedly as she laid the boxes on the kitchen table.

The second Ellen's arms were free, Claire launched herself into them and gave into the tears she had been holding back. "Claire, honey, what's the matter?" Ellen asked as she held her friend tightly in her arms.

Claire took full advantage of Ellen's warm embrace and cried until Ellen's curiosity and concern could stand it no longer. She guided Claire to the kitchen table where they sat down. "What has you so upset, and where is Tristan?"

"There's a lot I need to explain, Ellen. I just don't know where to start." Claire wiped her eyes and lit up a cigarette. "Tristan is staying with Cam and Lucy right now, and I'm here with the cat from Hell." She laughed mirthlessly. "This may take a while. How about some coffee?"

Claire set two cups of freshly brewed coffee on the table and took her seat as Ellen looked at her with eyes filled with concern. "This can go no farther than this room, Ellen. Cam and Lucy would be very disappointed if this were to get out."

"Whatever you say will go to the grave with me, I promise, but if you don't spill it soon, I'm going to go insane," Ellen said as she lit her own cigarette, preparing herself for what she was sure was not going to be good.

Claire relayed the whole story of the mysterious stalker, and Ellen listened in rapt attention, having to remind herself that it wasn't a plot line of a movie. "So, do you think it was Mike who broke in here?" Ellen asked, feeling afraid for Claire and Tristan.

Claire looked at the pile of cigarettes in the ashtray and realized she had smoked a lot just to relay half the story. She was beginning to think she'd need a Valium to finish. Nevertheless, she lit another and took a deep breath before going on. "I know for certain that Mike is not the stalker."

"Then, who? And how are you so certain it's not Mike?"

"Ellen, it was Tristan all along. I found the pictures and the camera equipment in this house." Claire paused, giving Ellen a second to absorb what she had just said. Ellen sat speechless in front of her.

Ellen shook her head emphatically. "No, Claire, I'll never believe that."

"She admitted it to me herself when I found the stuff," Claire said as the tears began anew.

Ellen stammered, unsure how to react or what to say. "How ... I mean ... is she in jail?"

"I told the police there was an intruder in the house when we got home. I protected her." Claire's hands shook as she picked up her coffee cup. "When she realized that I knew it was her, she explained why she did it. I was so shocked and upset, and when she tried to touch me, I went crazy and shoved her through the French doors. When she was released from the hospital, Cam and Lucy took her home with them, so I could sort things out."

Ellen held her hands up, trying to grasp what she assumed Claire was trying to say. "So, you didn't tell the police, you just let Cam and Lucy take care of it all? And why the hell are you still in this house? I'd have packed up my things and found a new place far away from here by now."

"I'm not leaving her, Ellen. I love her, and she's getting help like she promised."

"Do you realize you sound just like one of those battered wives who ends up hacked to bits because she thought she could change her mate? She's got some serious problems, Claire!" Ellen said exasperated with Claire's naïveté.

"She won't hurt me. I know it. Lucy has been taking her to therapy, and I'm hoping that she will come home soon."

Ellen got up from the table and began to pace. "Do you honestly think a few therapy sessions are going to make the difference? She needs some serious inpatient care and, hell, maybe even some good drugs! One thing's for sure, you can't stay here with that nut case!"

Claire jumped up from her chair and came face-to-face with Ellen. "Don't you ever refer to her like that, Ellen! She's had a rough life, and if stalking me was the worst thing she's ever done as a result, then she's turned out pretty damn good!"

Shocked by the way Claire vehemently defended Tristan, Ellen tried her best not to upset her further. Lowering her voice, she asked, "Is that the worst thing she's ever done? You've just admitted that she's had a rough life. Could there be something else that you don't know about?" Ellen stared into Claire's eyes, watching her mull over her words.

"When you married your husband, did you know all there was to know about him? How does anyone know what goes on in the mind of another person?" Irritation was apparent in Claire's voice as she spoke.

Ellen gently placed her hand on Claire's shoulder. "I care a lot about you, that's why I'm so upset. I put a lot of faith in Cam and Lucy, and they love her, too, but neither of them knew what she was doing. Am I right?" Ellen asked gently.

"I know you care for me, Ellen, and I'm sorry I blew up, but I know Tristan would never physically hurt me. I love her, and I'm going to stand by her. She needs someone. She needs me."

Murky Waters

Ellen sighed. "Okay, do you have anything stronger than coffee? I need something to calm my nerves, and I think you do, too. We can talk this out some more, and I promise not to lose my temper again, kiddo."

Claire grinned and hugged Ellen. "We have some rum, but we're out of Coke. Will Pepsi do?"

"Hmm, rum and Pepsi, that might just work," Ellen said as she headed for the refrigerator.

Claire returned to work after being gone nearly three weeks. She hated that Lauren had been transferred when Suarez lost its account. Ellen worked closely with her on finding a new travel contract and spent most of her evenings with Claire, talking and being there for her adopted little sister.

Everything in Claire's life had completely changed. Nothing familiar remained for her to cling to but Ellen. Suarez was gone, and she was adapting to a new position. Tristan had still not returned to work, and the office almost seemed foreign without her.

Claire immersed herself in her work, trying to fill the void created by Tristan's absence. She would often glance over at the empty office next to hers and wish Tristan were still sitting there waiting impatiently to take her to lunch. A part of her wished that she had never found out about what Tristan had done, but there was no undoing what had taken place

. Sometimes, she questioned her sanity, choosing to stay with Tristan after all the pain she had caused her. Other times, she felt she could hardly stand another moment without her. As the days passed with no word from Tristan, Claire became more desperate. She had not given up on Tristan. Would Tristan give up on her?

"I'm not ready, Lucy!" Tristan exploded as Lucy drove her home from the therapist's office. "To be honest, I don't know if I can ever face her again. I don't deserve her."

"Then, would you at least talk to her? You owe her that. That poor child has called the house every day, and I think she is beginning to think you don't want her anymore," Lucy said as she gripped the wheel trying to remain calm

. "Would you want to be with Cam if he made your life a living hell?" Tristan asked as she looked out the window.

"You're making her life a living hell now, Tris. She misses you and feels lost without you. You may think that you are punishing yourself by staying cooped up in that room and barely eating, but it's not just you suffering. The people who love you are suffering, too."

Tristan slumped in the seat, her mind a jumble of thoughts. It would be so much easier to just disappear and let everyone go on with his or her life. She cursed herself for lacking the courage to just take off in the middle of the night.

"I know what you're thinking, Tris," Lucy said, tearing Tristan from her thoughts of self-loathing. She pulled the car into a parking lot and turned off the ignition to give Tristan her full attention. "You're thinking life would be better for all of us without you, aren't you?"

Tristan failed to hide her surprise at Lucy's words. "Are you now a mind reader?" she asked sarcastically.

"No, but I consider you my child, and I know you well. I know how you think, Tristan. Now, let me set some things straight for you. No, it would not make things better by running away. Cam and I would be distraught, and not one day would go by without wondering where you were and if you were alive or dead.

"It would be equally hard for Claire. There is something you have not taken into consideration about her. She lost her family when she was still a teen. I'm sure you can relate because of the loss of your own father, but to lose her whole family in a split second must have been a tremendous blow. You've become family to her now, Tris, and once again, that is being taken away from her."

Tristan's eyes filled with tears. Up until that moment, she had felt nothing but numb. Now, she was filled with a new hurt for Claire.

"She told me the night we went to the hospital that she loved you and would stand beside you come what may. She has not wavered on that stance this entire time. Tristan, that is the definition of love. She is making a conscious decision to remain with you even when things are tough. Do you love her enough to be that committed?"

Tristan fell silent, pondering what Lucy told her. Lucy started the car and headed for home, hoping that what she said would break through the guilt and shame Tristan was attempting to drown herself in.

CHAPTER EIGHTEEN

Claire woke up on yet another Saturday morning alone, feeling stiff from sleeping on the couch, where she had taken up residence since Tristan had been away. Ralph looked at her expectantly until she realized that he wanted breakfast. She followed him into the kitchen and filled his bowl, then put the coffee on to brew. Running a hand through her disheveled blonde locks, she wondered aloud, "What will I do with my Saturday, aside from sitting around feeling sorry for myself?"

With coffee and cigarettes in hand, she went into the sunroom, stretched out on the wicker love seat, and lit a cigarette while sipping her coffee. Ralph came in and made himself comfortable in her lap as was his new custom. It was then that she noticed that Tristan had left one of her old sweatshirts lying on a chair.

Claire pressed the shirt to her face, reveling in the scent, and cried for the woman who turned her world upside down, making her feel a loneliness she had not felt for a long time.

When she couldn't cry any longer, Claire got up and took a shower. She spent a long time just letting the water beat into her stiff shoulders and neck. Feeling a little better after bathing, she slipped into her favorite pair of old jeans and one of Tristan's sweatshirts. Returning to the kitchen for more coffee, she met Ralph, who seemed to really be enjoying himself with a stick with a white cap on it.

As she poured her coffee, she tried to remember where she had seen one of those stakes before. When the memory hit her, she nearly dropped the coffeepot. "Oh, my God, Ralph, spit that out!" She ran to the startled cat and snatched the stick from his mouth. With her other hand, she grabbed the orange tabby and ran to the phone.

Murky Waters

"Lucy, we have a problem. I found Ralph chewing on one of those ant poison stakes. Who is his veterinarian?" Claire blurted out frantically.

Claire raced to the vet's office while Ralph pawed at the latch of his cat carrier. He growled a low growl, not enjoying being in the car. Claire assumed that the ant poison had upset his stomach because a mile from their destination, he passed gas, and Claire nearly ran off the road trying to get the windows down. Only then did he seem to relax and enjoy the ride.

Claire paced up and down the tiny waiting room at the vet's office, while the doctor examined the angry orange tabby. Minutes later, she was surprised to see Cam, Lucy, and Tristan walk into the building. Claire could not take her eyes off Tristan. She was shocked to see how pale Tristan was and couldn't help but notice that Tristan had lost quite a bit of weight.

Even so, Claire's heart pounded in her stomach, and her insides fluttered.

Tristan's eyes never met Claire's. Instead, Tristan's head hung down as Claire explained how she found the cat playing and gnawing on the poisonous stake. "The doctor wants to take a look at him and maybe run some tests. That's all I really know for now," Claire said as she wrung her hands nervously.

Tristan kept her eyes cast down as she informed everyone that she was going to wait outside so she could smoke. She asked someone to let her know when the doctor came out. Lucy assured her that she would get her as soon as the vet made an appearance. Claire watched as she left, then looked to Lucy with pleading eyes.

Lucy sighed. "Go to her, sweetie, but I have to tell you I have no idea how she is going to act. She's been beating herself up pretty badly."

Claire stepped outside and hesitated a moment, wondering how she should best approach Tristan. She took a deep breath and hoped her gamble would work. She approached cautiously, lighting a cigarette of her own, needing something to calm her nerves.

"So, I guess we're even now," Claire said with cockiness.

Tristan turned slightly at the sound of her voice. "Even?"

"I poisoned your cat. I figured it would be the only way I could get you to face me. I didn't want to kill him; I just wanted to make him a little sick. I was sure you would come running as soon as you heard."

Tristan slowly turned to face Claire, looking into her eyes for the first time since the night Claire learned the truth. The last time Tristan saw those eyes, they were filled with hurt, betrayal, and fear. Now, there was something else — hope. Claire did her best to remain calm under the scrutiny and not fidget as Tristan studied her with an intense gaze.

"I don't believe you, Claire," Tristan said calmly.

"It's true. I had to see you, and I would have done almost anything to make that happen," Claire said defiantly.

Tristan laughed for the first time in weeks. "You're such a poor liar. I can see it in your eyes."

"You come home to me, Tristan, or I swear I will shave that cat and dye his ass blue," Claire demanded as tears rolled down her face.

"Do you still consider my place your home?" Tristan asked softly.

"It's not a home without you in it. I haven't slept in our bed since you've been gone." Claire sniffed and smiled. "You owe me one hell of a back rub."

Tristan's eyes filled with tears of her own. "I'll rub your back for the rest of my life if you'll only forgive me."

"I forgave you that night in the hospital, and I meant it," Claire said as she timidly approached Tristan and wrapped her in her arms. Claire marveled at how good it felt to hold her again. She could barely let her go when Lucy poked her head out the door and called for them to come in.

Claire pulled away and looked at Tristan a little shyly when she held out her hand. Tristan took it and allowed Claire to lead her inside. The vet explained that it would be the same routine as all the other times. He would keep the cat overnight just to monitor him. Judging from the condition of the stick, he didn't think Ralph got too much of the poison in his system.

Claire look confused. "Same routine?"

Tristan grinned. "This is the third time he's pulled this stunt. I thought I had managed to get all the stakes, but he still finds one every now and then."

Claire's face turned red, and she looked at Tristan sheepishly. "So, I take it you're not buying the story I told you in the parking lot?"

Tristan smiled back. "Like I said, you're a poor liar."

"Miss Delacroix," the vet interrupted, "I have another emergency case. I'll call you at home and let you know when you can pick him up." He turned abruptly and went to tend his patient.

Tristan looked at Claire. "I suppose if he is going to call me at home, I should be there to take the call." She watched as relief flooded Claire's face. Cam and Lucy exchanged happy glances.

Tristan was relatively quiet on the ride home, which in turn made Claire very nervous. She chattered away about how well the repairs to their home went. Claire anxiously played with her necklace, which she had repaired and hanging around her neck. Tristan glanced over at her, and her eyes dropped to the lobster pendant.

Claire noticed Tristan staring at the necklace. "Tristan, I ..." She choked on her words as she tried to speak. "You must have thought I had given up on you that night when I tore this off. I never have, Tristan, nor will I ever give up on you. I will not make the mistake of taking it off again, my love."

Tristan's jaw trembled as tears flowed freely down her face. "I'm so sorry, Claire." Her voice was barely a whisper.

Tristan walked into her house as though she was seeing it for the first time. She seemed almost timid as if she were a guest and waiting to be asked to sit down. "Have you eaten?" Claire asked, sensing the awkwardness.

"No, but I'm not that hungry," Tristan replied as she settled into one of the chairs.

"I'm going to brew some coffee. Would you like some?" Claire asked, starting to feel uneasy, as well.

"Yeah, that would be nice," Tristan said as she looked through the windows at her garden.

Claire set the coffee to brew and joined Tristan at the table. "You don't seem very at ease; do you want to talk about it?"

"I guess I'm just getting used to being back home. The last time I was here ... well ... things didn't go so well, and being here now is making me relive it all over again," Tristan said, avoiding Claire's eyes.

"In the past, when Ralph got his paws on one of those sticks, what was the outcome?" Claire asked as she got up to pour the coffee.

"The vet usually keeps him overnight, then sends him home. He never chews them long enough to get anything significant," Tristan answered, bewildered by the sudden change of topic.

Claire returned to the table with two hot cups of coffee. "I know the weather is cold right now, but I was thinking we could go back to Gulf Shores. It would be just you and me with no interruptions, and we could kind of get to know each other again."

"I'm sure Cam and Lucy will be thrilled to have their house back to themselves, so I imagine they'll let me have the keys to the condo," Tristan said with a slight grin.

"Let's take Ralph with us if he's okay. I'm sure you've been missing him. I do have some bad news to tell you, though."

Tristan raised a curious brow. "And what might that be?"

"Well, you know that midnight blue bra that you're so fond of? It died a grisly death and is buried in his new cat bed," Claire said with a sheepish grin.

Lucy answered her phone on the first ring, knowing in her gut it was Tristan. "Hi, baby, are you glad to be home?" she asked when she heard the familiar voice on the line.

"I'm getting acquainted with it again. Ralph has been doing some redecorating with my undergarments, but other than that, everything seems to be in order."

"That's not what I meant, sweetie. How are you and Claire?" Lucy asked as Cam perked his ears, hoping to hear good news.

"That's why I'm calling. Claire and I would like to go back to Gulf Shores for a few days, and I was wondering if we could use the condo. Also, I wanted to know how soon Cam expects me back in the office."

"Well, why don't I let you ask him? Hold on a minute, love," Lucy said with a satisfied grin.

Cam took the phone with a questioning look at Lucy, who grinned from ear to ear. "Hi, darling, I miss you already."

Tristan smiled at the endearment. "Can I have the keys to the condo, dad?" Tristan said, sounding more like her old self.

"Of course, and I'm assuming you're taking Claire with you," he said in the same playful tone.

"Yes, and that brings me to some new questions. Can she have a few days off, and how soon are you expecting me back?"

"Tell Claire she can take as much time as she likes. I'm sure Ellen won't mind subbing for her. As for you, love, you come back when you're ready, but I'll be honest, your presence has been sorely missed, and they'll be happy to have you back."

"Thank you, Cam ... I can't tell you how much I appreciate all you've already done for me. I love you both, and I'm so sorry that I put y'all through this," Tristan said as her voice cracked.

Cam cleared his throat before he could continue. "We love you, too, baby."

The next morning, Ralph was checked out of the clinic with a clean bill of health and was on his way to Gulf Shores. Missing his beloved pet, he rode contentedly on her lap in the passenger seat, sniffing at the cast that still covered Tristan's forearm. Claire watched them both with an amused smile as they blinked repeatedly, fighting the sleepiness that was quickly overcoming them.

Claire sighed happily, reminiscing about the night before and how it felt to sleep in a real bed again curled up next to her lover. She had missed the smell of Tristan's skin and hair and spent a long time luxuriating in the scent. She awoke feeling refreshed and feeling like she was starting over with Tristan.

Each time she looked at her dark-eyed companion, Claire felt the same butterflies in her stomach that she did when they first met. She wondered what it would be like to make love with Tristan as though they had never been intimate. She even experienced feelings of anxiety at just the thought of it and wondered if Tristan felt the same.

Pretending to be asleep, Tristan closed her eyes and allowed her mind to wander. There was so much she wanted to say to Claire, but she didn't know how to begin. Playing opossum, she could avoid having to say anything until she could get her thoughts together. Claire had been patient with her the night before, allowing her time to get used to being back home before getting into any serious conversation. She appreciated the kind gesture since she could see that Claire was dying to get everything out in the open.

Tristan did not realize that she had fallen asleep until she heard the sound of the chime when Claire opened her door. She opened her eyes to the gray overcast day and noticed that they were already parked in front of the condo. Claire was scratching Ralph behind the ears as he looked out at the foreign terrain.

"Time to get up, sleepyhead," Claire said softly. "Can you manage Ralph while I get our things?"

"Just let me get him inside, and I'll come back and help you," Tristan responded sleepily.

After the car was emptied and everything was put away, they went for a walk on the beach while Ralph explored his new surroundings in the condo. They walked in silence along the water's edge where the sand was packed the tightest.

"I have so much to say to you, Claire, but I can't seem to put it into words," Tristan said eventually, breaking the awkward silence.

"I understand," Claire said softly. "I feel the same way. Can I ask you some questions?"

"Yeah, that might make things easier," Tristan answered, feeling her insides tense.

"Are you in love with me?"

"Yes, very much so, though my behavior has been anything but indicative of that," Tristan replied, sneaking a nervous glance at her companion.

"Do you want me to move out of your house for a while until you can sort things out for yourself?" Claire asked, praying the answer would not be yes.

"I consider that house ours, and no, I don't want you to move out ... unless that's what you want."

Claire sighed audibly with relief. "No, I don't want to move out. Frankly, I think the best way for us to move past this is to stick together and deal with it."

Both were silent for a moment, equally pleased with the answers so far. "Tris, why did you continue to send the photos and letters after you got to know me?"

Tristan swallowed hard, fighting back the emotions that threatened her ability to speak. "When we first met, I was so intimidated by you. You were so open and friendly, even though I was an ass. I wanted you to dislike me because I already felt guilty for what I had done. I'm not sure why, but I felt like I had control over you when I made you afraid. Then, when I got to know you better, I stopped for a while.

"When Mike came into the picture, he made me jealous, and I felt like I had to compete for you, even though I knew deep inside you didn't care for him. When you didn't shut him down like I thought you should have, it made me angry, and I just reverted back to what made me feel in control."

"Do you believe that I'm in love with you?" Claire asked, stopping to look into Tristan's eyes.

"I know you love me, but sometimes, I don't understand why. The therapist says that's due to my low self-image. Even though you prove your feelings in all you say and do, I still have a hard time accepting it," Tristan replied honestly.

"That's something we'll have to work on together. You will find that I'm very patient, and I feel the reward is worth the effort." Claire smiled when Tristan reached over and took her hand, and they continued their stroll.

"Tris, is there anything else you need to tell me? I promise I won't run away screaming or judge you. I just want everything out in the open."

Tristan followed as Claire led her up to a pavilion where she sat on a picnic table and Tristan stood in front of her wrapped in her arms. "Actually, Claire, there is something I need to get off my chest," Tristan said as she burrowed her head into the crook of Claire's neck.

"Go ahead, baby, you can tell me anything," Claire said as she tightened her hold.

"Remember a while back when you cooked spinach? Well, I hid it in my napkin; please don't cook that slimy shit again."

Claire threw back her head and truly laughed, more so than she had in a month. "I love you, Tristan Delacroix, you smart-assed little shit!"

EPILOGUE

Tristan wiggled her fingers and stretched her arm as she commented on how strange it felt to have her arm free of the cast. Claire glanced over at her as she drove her home from the orthopedist. The woman sitting next to her had changed so much in the last few months.

Claire had witnessed her breakdown in the sessions with the therapist while she relayed the events of her childhood. She marveled at how Tristan was able to function on a daily basis growing up in such an abusive atmosphere.

She had grown to love Tristan even more during those meetings, and to Tristan's surprise, Claire gained a new respect for her. Each time they met with the doctor, it confirmed Claire's decision to stand by Tristan.

They had good days and bad, but with each problem they encountered, the couple grew stronger as a result. In time, the scars that both women bore would heal, cementing their relationship forever.

The End

Murky Waters

ABOUT THE AUTHOR

Born in 1965, Robin Alexander grew up in Baton Rouge, Louisiana, where she still resides. An avid reader of lesbian fiction, Robin decided to take the leap and try her hand at writing, which is now more than her favorite hobby. Other favorites are camping, snorkeling, and anything to do with the outdoors or the water. Robin approaches everything with a sense of humor, which is evident in her style of writing. To learn more about Robin and read some of her short stories, visit http://www.robinfic.com.

Other Titles Available from Intaglio Publications

Code Blue
KatLyn
1-933113-09-X
$18.50

Gloria's Inn
Robin Alexander
1-933113-01-4
$17.50

I Already Know The Silence Of
The Storms
N. M. Hill
1-933113-07-3
$17.50

Infinite Pleasures
Stacia Seaman & Nann Dunne
(Editors)
1-933113-00-6
$18.99

Storm Surge
KatLyn
1-933113-06-5
$18.50

The Cost Of Commitment
Lynn Ames
1-933113-02-2
$18.99

The Price Of Fame
Lynn Ames
1-933113-04-9
$17.99

The Gift
Verda Foster
1-933113-03-0
$17.50

Crystal's Heart
B. L. Miller & Verda Foster
1-933113-24-3
$18.50

Graceful Waters
B. L. Miller & Verda Foster
1-933113-08-1
$18.50

Incommunicado
N. M. Hill & J. P. Mercer
1-933113-10-3
$17.50

Southern Hearts
Katie P Moore
1-933113-28-6
$16.95

These Dreams
Verda Foster
1-933113-12-X
$17.50

The Last Train Home
Blayne Cooper
1-933113-26-X
$17.99

The War Between The Hearts
Nann Dunne
1-933113-27-8
$17.95

Forthcoming Titles Available from
Intaglio Publications

The Chosen
Verda Foster

The Illusionist
Fran Heckrotte

Accidental Love
B L Miller

Assignment Sunrise
I Christie

**Lilith: Book Two in the
Illusionist Series**
Fran Heckrotte

Misplaced People
C G Devize

Counterfeit World
Judith K. Parker

The Western Chronicles
B L Miller & Vada Foster

With Every Breath
Alex L. Alexander

**Bloodlust: Book Three in the
Illusionist Series**
Fran Heckrotte